STATIONFALL™

Other Avon Books in the
INFOCOM™ Series

STATIONFALL™

Arthur Byron Cover

A Byron Preiss Book

AN **INFOCOM**™ BOOK

AVON BOOKS  NEW YORK

STATIONFALL: THE NOVEL is an original publication of Avon Books.
This work has never before appeared in book form. This work is a
novel. Any similarity to actual persons or events is purely coincidental.

Special thanks to Mike Dornbrook, Steve Meretzky, John Douglas,
Michael Kazan, Richard Curtis, Lydia Marano and Mary Higgins.

AVON BOOKS
A division of
The Hearst Corporation
105 Madison Avenue
New York, New York 10016

Copyright © 1989 by Byron Preiss Visual Publications, Inc.
Cover painting copyright © 1987 by Infocom, Inc.
Published by arrangement with Byron Preiss Visual Publications, Inc.
STATIONFALL software copyright © 1987 by Infocom, Inc.
STATIONFALL and the INFOCOM logo are trademarks of Infocom, Inc.
Library of Congress Catalog Card Number: 89-91348
ISBN: 0-380-75387-1

Cover and book design by Alex Jay/Studio J.
Edited by David M. Harris

First Avon Books Printing: December 1989

Chapter One
The Space-Time Savants

IT TAKES A SPECIAL
*kind of idiot to ride the convolutions of space-time
geometry in this void,* observed Admiral Boink nervously, tiptoeing lightly between the splayed legs of
the savants whose heads were bolted to the computer
terminals. *I just hope this new batch is jake with the
cosmos.*

Boink had a right to be nervous. There was always the one-in-a-hundred-thousand chance this new
batch would botch the coordinates. Then, according
to Stellar Patrol lore, *Our Lady's Hornblower* would
spin out of its planned trajectory and emerge in the
unknown space of another galaxy. Never again would
the crew and passengers stand beneath skies they
knew.

Normally the most cautious of admirals, Boink
had ordered the old batch jettisoned once he'd learned
they were passing a common cold back and forth like
the plague, and had them replaced with new savants
from the cryogenolabs. That way, if things went wrong,
Boink could at least count on both sides of the ship
arriving in the same place at roughly the same time.
Some strange things had happened, they said, to

ships and crews whose savants had come down with the space chillies.

He took some small comfort that so far, at least, nothing about them appeared amiss. The skin of male and female alike was smooth and deathly white, free of the sores and bruises so typical of diseased or older idiots. Drops of the cryogenic iodine isotope they had until recently been immersed in still rolled down their bodies and formed red pools at their buttocks. Intravenous feeding tubes and catheters were inserted in their bodies. Occasionally their eyes fluttered and their muscles twitched, the result of electronically induced REM states. Their pupils did not even quiver as Boink passed them by. For they saw nothing, knew nothing, and were incapable of learning anything. Their minds were filled only with complex computations involving numbers of googolplexian proportions and geometrical figures with permutations of staggering subtleties.

The similar expressions of their similar faces disturbed him. The eyes were so uncomprehending. Their stares were so blank. To think that a safe arrival at port depended on the capacities of so many mindless beings to achieve a level of pinpoint accuracy beyond the ability of the greatest cognizant minds to attain! It was difficult to imagine them as being human, and of course they were human only in a manner of speaking. They were clones—grown from the tissue of some poor bozo whose name had been long lost to history, whose mind had possessed unparalleled mathematical abilities and no special capacity for anything else.

He quickly turned his attention toward the unpleasant subject of the ship's potentially disastrous position in the cosmos. The holographic map of the galaxy was suspended above the circular hub of the navigational terminals. The ship itself was represented by a single pinpoint of light amidst a field of bright purple lines roughly parallel to the coordinates of the Milky Way Galaxy in real space. The lines were curved to reflect the distortions of space by star clusters and black holes. Boink searched for a second tiny pinpoint of moving light in the field, one which would indicate that the shuttle commanded by Lieutenant Colonel Second Class Coryban had at last entered the void, on a trajectory that would intersect with that of the mother ship. *Damn that woman!* thought Boink as he searched in vain.

Boink calmed himself with an effort. He missed that woman, and felt extremely insecure without her steady, albeit insolent, presence at his side. It was Colonel Coryban who had first divined that what had merely appeared to be an inconvenience—the theft of the Ho-Ho-Kusian ambassador's luggage at the spaceport—was in actuality the harbinger of diplomatic disaster. For contained in that luggage was the sole means available for controlling the ambassador's frenzied, frustrated mating cycle.

Most intelligent creatures now affiliated with the Third Union controlled their reproductive urges with only a modicum of difficulty, regardless of condition, but that was only because most intelligent creatures affiliated with the Third Union weren't plants. Normally the average Ho-Ho-Kusian in heat, who wasn't stuck as the only one of his kind on a starfaring vessel, would dig a hole in the ground and cajole a partner into sacrificing himself by being the fertilizer for the next generation. (In exchange, the partner's personality and memory would be absorbed into the group mind of the other, thus achieving a kind of immortality.) Past experience with unsedated Ho-Ho-Kusians indicated that the consequences of the missing luggage would be dire indeed. And, as Coryban had so unerringly predicted, when the ambassador did go into an uncontrollable frenzy of plantlust, he gravitated toward the individual aboard with the greatest amount of status, whose nitrogen compounds would confer the grandest heritage upon the seeds in the pods; that is to say, toward Admiral Boink himself. Indeed, the ambassador had already attempted to insert his myriad roots into Boink in the commissary, before every man, mutant, and alien at lunch. Boink depended on Coryban's retrieval of Hunter to prevent a replay of the embarrassment.

For just as Coryban had presented Boink with the problem, so had she presented him with a solution. Music, as it turned out, had a salutary effect on the Ho-Ho-Kusian's savage urge. But only music played on a soprano saxophone, which only a human, as it turned out, could play satisfactorily. The musical vibrations would match those of a singing flytrap known for its tranquilizing effect on the plant creatures' dispositions. Coryban had determined that a Lieutenant Homer B. Hunter was the only man aboard possessing both the means and the talent to undo the ambassador's loss. Unfortunately, by that time Hunter, along with his robot assistant, had accidentally ejected themselves offship, and so Coryban had been forced to improvise.

The nature of the first improvisation had mysteriously slipped from the admiral's mind, but it had resulted in a smashed soprano saxophone, leaving Boink with no choice but to send Coryban, assisted by an annoying officer named Blather, after Hunter. In the meantime the admiral had been forced to trust a certain ambassador who, he had to admit, pursued a professional career that turned his stomach.

Boink crossed his arms and stared at the hologram, desperately hoping the tiny pinpoint of light representing the shuttle would suddenly materialize. Then, of course, Colonel Coryban's major problem would be navigating the unpredictable currents of non-Euclidean hyperspace in such a way that the shuttle would overtake *Our Lady's Hornblower*. Those permutations had precluded the mother ship's return to the world of Ho-Ho-Kus, at least if the passengers were to arrive at their destination in time for the galactic diplomatic conference. The exact subject of the conference was top secret, but rumor had it the conference would affect the history of the Third Empire for untold eons to come. Even the slightest tardiness, under these circumstances, could have dire consequences. Boink figured that if *Our Lady's Hornblower* was in fact late, becoming fertilizer would be the most attractive of his probable destinies.

Suddenly the door to the bridge dilated. Remembering his orders that he was not to be disturbed, Boink took the sensible option and whirled to face the door with his blaster drawn and pointed. He hadn't forgotten what had happened the last time he had been taken by surprise.

Boink took a deep breath and waited.

No one came through.

Boink suspected a trap. Someone was trying to draw him out. And hadn't been aware he'd tripped an electronic eye a little further up the corridor, automatically opening the doors.

But in a few moments, the Ho-Ho-Kusian ambassador rolled in, the wheels of the skates attached to his taproot smoking as they screeched to a stop a centimeter or two before a savant sprawled out on the floor. The dense green foliage of the seven-foot frame quivered in what might have been lustful anticipation. A bass voice crackled through the static of his translator speaker grille, saying, "So there you are, Admiral! You certainly know how to make yourself scarce! Hasn't anyone told you I've an urgent matter to discuss with you?"

The admiral took careful aim at the ambassador's massive taproot. He didn't know where the typical plant creature's brains were located, so he would have to be satisfied with damaging another important organ, if the need arose. He hoped it would, even as he said, "Just stay on the other side of those savants, if you value your planthood."

The ambassador waved some of his branches about. The foliage on top of his trunk ruffled indignantly. "I resent that! I'm on official business!"

"I've been on the receiving end of your official business before, thank you very much."

"But you don't understand! This has nothing to do with our relationship."

"We have no relationship, you plague of dry rot!"

The ambassador evidently chose to ignore the insult. He folded several of his branches across one another as if to indicate he was above that sort of lowbrow verbal sparring. "I have come to advise you of a situation that may have some bearing on security. One of the ambassadors has undergone a mysterious, wholly inexplicable alteration in personality. I suspect some sort of foul play is responsible."

Boink waved his blaster. "Roll one more centimeter forward and the only thing your atoms will be good for is recycling!"

The ambassador ruffled his foliage again and then gently, almost absently, ran his many roots, dirt pads and all along the body of the navigational savant before him. "Hmmm. What a beautiful body. I'd say it was a pity it had to be wasted on such a savant if there weren't so many others just like her. Say, if I ran this sucker over, would she feel any pain? In the traditional sense of the word, that is?"

"Whose tradition? Yours or mine? No, I don't want to know."

"Would she bleed?"

"Most assuredly," replied the admiral, a little suspicious of the ambassador's sudden predilection for wickedness. "But enough of this frivolity. You say one of the ambassadors is going a little weird on us? Who is he—and how can you tell?"

"His patterns of behavior are well known," replied the ambassador in a conspiratorial tone. Leaves brushed lightly against the female's breasts, a dirt pad rubbed her crotch, and the ambassador's foliage shook with delight. "He belongs to an intelligent species that's more plant than animal. He's well known among diplomatic circles for his smug, aristocratic attitude and for his disdain of mores that do not match those of his own society. But lately, thanks to what for him has become an unfortunate encounter with his primal passions, he has become strangely sociable, and the object of his desires has shifted unexpectedly."

Boink pretended not to notice what the ambassador was doing to the female. Sexual relations with the navigational idiots were not unheard of, and trysts between willing humans and aliens were not exactly unheard of either. But Boink, who regarded himself as an intellectual, sexual libertarian if not a practicing one, had never before encountered an alien who got off fondling a navigational savant in the presence of an officer. So naturally he made doubly sure of his blaster's aim before proceeding with the conversation. "All right, I'll play your silly game. Are you saying the ambassador has been looking for a new love?"

"No, I'm saying he has found it."

"Is he the resolute type?"

"He can't take no for an answer, if that's what you mean."

"I think it is. Is the, ah, ambassador in question a virtual stranger to physical pleasure?"

"Oh yes!" exclaimed the ambassador as his leaves suddenly shook so vigorously that several broke from their twigs and glided to the floor. The female savant groaned softly, and her eyelids fluttered. For a moment, as she arched her back, she seemed to be enjoying herself.

Boink wondered how the dreams of a mindless person might be affected by an orgasm. "And you also say this ambassador now has little objection to associating with those he once dismissed as common rabble?"

"Yes, yes, oh yes!" said the ambassador, his entire trunk quivering in a frenzy. His taproot swished uncontrollably about, and several times his skates almost spun out from under him.

"So why should I care?" asked the admiral with a shrug. "Lots of ambassadors grow and change as a result of their association with aliens. I fail to see what this has to do with security."

"This ambassador is growing and changing when there was no indication that any of his kind had ever grown and changed before. I tell you, Admiral, something is quirky on the decks of *Our Lady's Hornblower*, and it's not me!"

They both ignored the female's loud, eerie moan. "And tell me, Ambassador," said the admiral, "is this entity accustomed to referring to himself in the third person?"

"Maybe. His species really isn't comfortable with any mode of spoken language. It's possible, I suppose, that passion has twisted him inside and out."

"Hmm-hmm." Boink gestured with the blaster. "Get over there. Against that terminal. Right now."

"What did I do?" exclaimed the ambassador, moving away from the row of savants. "Damn! My dirt pad broke!" He held up the root he had been caressing the female with before his speaker grille as if it also functioned as a camera. "Let me retrieve that dirt. I don't have many atoms to spare."

"Soyashit!" said the admiral. "There's plenty more dirt where that came from."

"Admiral, why are you doing this to me?" pleaded the ambassador. "I need that dirt if I'm going to keep myself together! Don't you believe me?"

"I believe you've finally realized the direct approach doesn't always work with us humans, and now you've decided to win me over with sympathy. Well, I'm wise to that old ploy. Not only am I too clever, but I'll be damned if I'll let it work for you, especially since it's never worked for me either."

"What are you talking about?" said the ambassador, gesticulating madly with his branches.

"Keep those damn leaves to yourself. What kind of fool do you take me for? Don't answer that! Just stay where you are!"

"Admiral, I'm trying to tell you some sort of conspiracy is afoot. Something heinous, insidious, beyond the scope of our imaginations."

"If it's beyond the scope of your imagination, then how come you know what it is? Wait! Be quiet!" Purely by chance, Boink had noticed from the corner of his eye a tiny light where before there had been none. It was positioned approximately where they had lost Homer Hunter. Coryban was returning! She and Blather had found their man! Boink repressed a surge of delight. He could almost hear the verbal report right now, coming in on the hyperwave: *Lieutenant Colonel Second Class Coryban reporting as ordered, sir. I'm glad to say the mission has been successfully accomplished, sir, with the loss of only one man. Lieutenant Hunter's with me now, while I regret to report that Ensign Blather was gobbled up by a giant centipede. It was a horrible death, sir. I daresay not even Blather deserved it . . .*

"Admiral Boink, aren't you listening to me?" shouted the Ho-Ho-Kusian ambassador with a great squawk of static. "I'm trying to tell you, I'm not the Ho-Ho-Kusian ambassador!"

"Right, and I suppose next you'll be telling me that this isn't reality, that we're just a couple of characters in a story!"

"If we were, we'd probably be two maids dusting the furniture before the main players come onto the stage," said the ambassador. "And in a way, that's just the point. I strongly suspect that even as we speak, there are things happening completely beyond our control, as if our most private, innermost thoughts have become naught but putty in the grip of some omnipotent, sociopathic being. Why, this being is so heartless, so merciless, that he might even manipulate you into falling madly, hopelessly in love with a creature whom you right now regard as the most despicable in existence."

Only his innate sense of discipline prevented Boink from frying the ambassador on the spot. "Aha! You see, we at last arrive at the crux of the matter. You're just trying to get me to acquiesce to being the fertilizer of your insane reproductive hungers."

"No! That's not what I meant at all! Don't you believe me when I say I'm not the Ho-Ho-Kusian ambassador?"

"No."

"You decide that quickly? How do you know I'm not another Ho-Ho-Kusian?"

"Because according to the register, there's only one aboard. Besides, you see one tree, you've seen them all."

"Ha! I suppose I should resent that!" the ambassador said in tones that could almost be called a snarl. "But I'll show you there are more things in the cosmos than are dreamt of in your puny philosophy."

Suddenly the ambassador disappeared, engulfed in a momentary flash of blinding light, and reappeared metamorphosed into a mass of white protoplasm. The protoplasm rested on top of an electronic skateboard. A special translator and speaker hung over his coned top. The translator resembed a small, old-fashioned wooden radio.

Boink holstered his laser. At last he remembered how Coryban had requested that a certain ambassador, with the ability to alter his appearance at will, deflect the Ho-Ho-Kusian ambassador's amorous attentions by changing himself into a tree of accommodating morals. "You're Dr. Proty! Why didn't you say so?"

The mass of white protoplasm quivered pathetically. "I was afraid I'd lost my touch, and . . . and . . . I wanted to see if you found me attractive."

"Why? I never found a Ho-Ho-Kusian attractive before. Why should your being one make any difference?"

"Didn't you at least want to urinate on me?"

"Ah, I think you've got me confused with another Terran species."

"Yes, you're right. A natural mistake."

"Would you please tell me what's going on? I'm trying to keep on top of another hopeless situation."

"Well, it's the Ho-Ho-Kusian ambassador."

"Thank you, Dr. Proty! What about him?"

"He's stopped paying attention to me."

"Terrific. Who's he paying attention to now?"

A glob of protoplasm drooped over the translator, as if Dr. Proty was abjectly hanging his head. As a result, his next words were a trifle indistinct. "I, too, wonder who he's accosting now. He hasn't seen fit to confide in me. Admiral, I'm sorry to be bothering you with this, but I'm afraid that in Coryban's absence I have no one else to turn to."

Boink crossed the room and gently patted the top of Dr. Proty. Though he really wasn't the sympathetic type—the only broken heart he'd ever cared about was his own, and even then it wasn't exactly the heart—his diplomatic training obligated him at least to pretend. "There, there, that's all right. Why don't you tell me all about it?" he added, dreading every word.

"Well, I normally don't spill my guts out to bipeds . . ."

"You don't have to . . ."

". . . but if you insist. As you know, Admiral, I am a gritologist who specializes in the graphic details and the emotional complications of sexual relations between members of separate and distinct species."

Boink blinked. "I know that."

"The greater the differences between the partners in question, the better, so far as my colleagues and I are concerned."

"I know that, too."

"But to understand the underlying psychological reasons why an entity might wish to defy the social taboos against cross-genus fornication, you must also thoroughly grok the range of sexual appetites normally available to the participants in question. And you must admit, the opportunities to observe a Ho-Ho-Kusian pitch woo have been extremely limited in the past."

"And I think I know why, too."

"I tell you this so you'll understand I only took the job to distract the ambassador from his unruly lust because it dovetailed so neatly with my own academic studies. It certainly wasn't because I found him interesting."

"Of course not," said the admiral, gritting his teeth from boredom.

"Like you, I found him rude, arrogant, egotistical, stubborn, illogical, temperamental, childish, hu-morless, bigoted and close-minded in virtually every respect imaginable, and generally devoid of redeem-ing social values. For me it was all just a game. I figured I would lead the ambassador on in Ho-Ho-Kusian guise, and then, at the proper time, would confront him with the knowledge that he had been just a plaything to be used, abused, and jettisoned the moment I became interested in another. All in the name of science, of course."

"Of course."

"How was I to know that his romantic eagerness, his utter simplicity of thought, word, and deed, and his somehow preternatural ability to anticipate my every desire would eventually win me over? How was I?"

"I agree. Who would have thunk it?"

"My point exactly. It was last night, theoretical real space time, as the ambassador slithered his roots about my trunk and gently, oh so gently, slipped the root hairs between the cracks of my bark, telepathing sweet nothings to my essence, that I finally realized how helpless I was in the relentless wake of his persistent woo. Suddenly my efforts at scientific ob-jectivity became futile, and my spirit soared into hyperdimensions of ecstasy I'd previously believed were experienced only by naive school bipeds. I be-longed to the ambassador heart and soul, and if there had been enough dirt available on the spot, I'd have . . ."

"All right, all right, we don't have to go into the sordid details of your fantasy life. Then what happened?"

"Well, without warning, the ambassador disen-gaged himself and said he had to go fix a busted dirtpad. He promised to be right back. But his dirtpads as he skated away were all intact. I waited and waited for him, but he never returned. Finally I went to his quarters to confront him, but he was nowhere to be found."

"Hmmm. I take it you searched the ship for him?"

"For chrons and chrons. You bipeds have got to find another timekeeping system, by the way—I can't make head or tail of it."

"It keeps the enlisted men busy. Go on, please."

"Well, long after I'd given up, I saw the ambassador skating down the corridors, pingponging back and forth against the walls, muttering incoherently, singing gaily but tunelessly."

"What did he say?"

"It was difficult to tell. There was so much static from his speaker. But some of the words bore a distinct resemblance to 'How terrific a bag of dirt, me, thee, and thou' and 'Ah, budding mystery of sprouts.' "

"Yes, that sounds reasonably incoherent. What did you do then?"

"Well, I called out to him. But if he heard, he paid me no mind. I considered going after him, but I still had my pride. I figured he would come to me when he was ready."

"And in the meantime you could come to me," said Boink.

"I don't care what you think of me, but please don't speak harshly of him. I couldn't bear it. You must try to understand the extreme conditions under which he was raised: sprouting out of the soil with all those tiny subidentities already telling him how he should deal with every single experience, each one constantly insisting he take each byte of conflicting data as gospel. The poor dear's lucky to still be cognitive."

"I'll refrain from comment. You say he ignored you?"

"Completely," said Dr. Proty, with a burst of static like unto a sob.

"And no one else was with him?"

"Not that I could see, and I'm sensitive to the entire light spectrum."

"Then what you're trying to tell me is . . ."

"Yes, that's right. Somehow the ambassador has learned I was an imposter, and despite the pure bliss of our encounters, he has decided to hold the truth against me. You must help me find him, Admiral Boink! You must convince him to give me a second chance! I know he can learn to love me even though I'm not really a plant! Don't you think so, Admiral? Don't you? Don't you?"

Repelled by Proty's unabashed desperation, Boink turned away and attempted to think fast. For a moment he was afraid all this could only mean the ambassador's search for the fodder with the greatest status was still on. Boink's bowel muscles tightened. His heart beat furiously and his temples throbbed. Nervously he brushed flecks of dust from the array of medals studding his jacket. He habitually wore all his medals, and had recently obtained so many he had been forced to pin some to his sleeves. He wondered why he bothered worrying about them so. They couldn't possibly comfort him in this life-or-death situation. They couldn't even be effective as a shield. Thank Seldon he had his blaster. He actually anticipated the ambassador's next move. *That plant's charcoal*, he thought, visualizing the scene. He took some comfort in the observation that there was no problem an intelligent, clever, quick-thinking human couldn't solve, especially with good aim. Boink had good aim.

Suddenly the door dilated open. Another tree with dirtpads skated through, and this time there could be no doubt who it was.

"My little berry sniffer!" exclaimed Dr. Proty. "You've returned to me at last!"

Boink would have disintegrated the Ho-Ho-Kusian ambassador on the spot had he not been distracted by the blinding flash of light that came from Proty's direction. When his eyesight cleared, two Ho-Ho-Kusians stood tall among the navigational savants, and for the life of him—literally—Boink could not tell which was which. Both moved their twigs and branches in complex, enigmatic patterns, and their speakers squawked madly. Exactly what they were communicating, Boink had no idea, and he was reasonably certain he did not want to find out. It was all he could do to refrain from blasting them both on the spot, just to be on the safe side.

"All right, out with it, you oversexed ragweeds," he demanded. "Which one of you is Dr. Proty?"

Boink's answer came with the third blinding flash of the evening, but when his vision cleared up this time, it was apparent his question had had nothing to do with it.

Holding forth two protoplasmic appendages imploringly, Proty wept milky tears in a line around his cone. "I can't bear to lie to you any longer! I admit it! Your impertinent suspicions were dead on! I am a pleasure-mongering imposter, a mere bureaucrat of lust! But don't you understand that what happened between us superseded the limitations of our physical bodies? For a time our souls touched and were as one! Our desire to be together was nobler, more profound than mere passion. Suddenly, for the first time in both our lives, we had found someone who meant more to us than our own selfish needs and desires. Never before had I possessed such an overwhelming reason for living. What I'm trying to tell you, my little berry sniffer, is that I love you!"

The Ho-Ho-Kusian ambassador didn't miss a beat. "And what I am trying to tell you, my little berry eater, is that an object of desire I no longer desire to be. I have found another."

Hallelujah! thought Boink. *Well, maybe!*

"Who?" demanded Dr. Proty, drawing himself up to a height of ten meters, dwarfing the others. The top of his head flattened against the ceiling as he gathered vast portions of his mass into a makeshift chest and thrust it outward belligerently. "It's not another Ho-Ho-Kusian, is it?"

"Certainly not. If another of my kind had been aboard, I wouldn't have been desperate enough to fall for your shallow gag," replied the ambassador with a remarkable lack of arrogance and disdain. Apparently he was doing his best just to state the facts.

"Just show me the varmint," said Dr. Proty, "and I'll expose it for an amoral social climber who's only interested in taking advantage of your diplomatic privileges. You'll learn soon enough that it's not easy for a sumbitch as prickly as you to overwhelm the average entity."

Boink leaned back against a terminal, holstered his blaster, crossed his arms, and watched eagerly as the ambassador said, "If you insist," and held out a dirt pad on the end of a primary root toward Dr. Proty.

The pad quickly became infused with a pink light radiating from within. The strings binding it unfurled as if manipulated by invisible fingers. Then, as the strings fell on top of a savant's stomach, the pad opened to reveal, not dirt, but a tiny winged creature releasing her grip at the root's end. She was the source of the light, and the light's source was inside her. More or less humanoid, she had three legs and a tail, all covered with thick white hair, while the complexion of her bare arms and torso was ebony, both shades unaffected by her pink glow. Her translucent wings sparkled like diamonds. Boink noted her pointed ears and the streak of white hair in the middle of her bald dome, but it was only through gut instinct that he conceived of her as feminine.

"At last you can die fulfilled," proclaimed the ambassador, "because now you have seen love incarnate!"

Proty shrank to his true height and formed two eyes on pseudopods, which he extended to facilitate his inspection. "Get serious," he squawked. "She's just a bug! If she was any smaller, you'd have to use a microscope to see her wazoo—an organ I hasten to point out, my dear stamen sucker, is of no value to you regardless of its size. And she's hardly big enough to fertilize an Arcturan dandelion! How can you possibly hope to consummate your love with this . . . this glorified insect?"

"She is not bug or animal," replied the ambassador haughtily. His branches trembled in umbrage. "Nor is she machine or plant or any combination of the above. She is a classification unto herself, and possesses within her the embodiment of pure spirit. My love for her transcends the base physical desire so commonly expressed among you pitiful, unenlightened beings."

Convinced that if an embodiment of pure spirit had signed the register, he would have heard about it before now, Boink moved along the line of consoles in an effort to get a better look at the creature's face. "Tell me, Mr. Ambassador, just how did you two lovebirds happen to intertwine?" he asked.

The ambassador just stood there, unspeaking and, for all practical purposes, probably unthinking as well.

"Go on, scoop it out!" said Proty, his patience exhausted. "The only time we were separated during our brief yet historic affair was when you retired to soak your dirtpads. Again, my apologies for not realizing what a private act such a soaking must be. My protest at our separation must have been another one of my awful gaffes that's resulted in your low opinion of me. In any case, was that when you met this so-called love incarnate? Those precious few moments when you were alone? Was it? Answer me, you petrified two-timer!" One of the eyeball pseudopods transformed into a sledgehammer, stretched past the winged creature, and smashed the ambassador on the lower trunk. "Scumbag!" said Proty, adding insult to injury.

"Inducing vast quantities of agony will get you nowhere," replied the ambassador stiffly. "I have transcended the barrier between body and spirit, and so it matters no longer what happens to my physical self now." Then he bowed his crown of foliage and turned away, as a near-inaudible groan wafted from his speaker.

The winged creature remained stationary, hovering between the antagonists. Boink could see her face plainly now—an oval, smooth plane, devoid of mouth, nose, and eyes. The sole features were those pointed ears. If she had had a reaction to Proty's violent gesture, or even to the ambassador's pain, she did not show it. Indeed, she seemed oblivious to everything, and remained in place even as the ambassador accidentally rolled his skates over an idiot's leg.

The savant groaned in pain but did not react to the flow of blood from her leg. Nor did anyone else.

"Who are you?" Boink asked of the creature. "Where did you come from?"

"What a stupid question!" exclaimed the Ho-Ho-Kusian ambassador. "She's been with us since the beginning of our journey!"

"Oh? Then what kind of creature is she? Where's her homeworld?" demanded Boink. His confidence that the questions were beyond the ambassador's ability to answer faded almost as quickly as he had formed them. He had the distinct feeling that the answers were coalescing in his own subconscious even as he spoke, and that they would emerge, fully conceptualized and an integral part of Third Union history, at the proper time: A time he was convinced was only a few minutes away. Already his desperate curiosity concerning her origins was fading, and he doubted he would ever remember that her appearance had caused such surprise and consternation.

Dr. Proty, sped to the dilating door and shouted, "You'll regret this, you mental dry rot case!"

After the door closed, Boink and the ambassador stared silently at one another. At least Boink thought the ambassador was staring. Since the ambassador perceived the surface of things with his keen radar, it was always difficult to guess exactly where he was directing his concentration at any given moment. The winged creature, meanwhile, hovered between them, and moved only to grasp the tip of the root that reached out beside her.

Finally the ambassador spoke. "That life-form who just left, some vague recollection of him is receding in my myriad minds. Do I know him?"

"I have the impression you did," said Boink, "and very well too."

"Intimately?"

"Yes, according to him."

"Strange. I don't seem to recall him at all, though I suspect I should."

"Intimate relationships are his life's work."

"Are they? How droll. I wondered if he's studied the blissful effects of love incarnate. I'll have to ask him sometime."

"I see." Boink too was gripped by a funny feeling. Here in the navigational room, everything was exactly as he remembered it having been a few chrons before. Yet he could not suppress the notion that once he went outside, he would encounter subtle differences between the way things had been and the way they were now, and that he would be hard-pressed to articulate those changes. "Tell me, just out of idle curiosity, how long have you and this entity been an item?" he asked.

"That is a mystery to me. It seems like forever, though the relationship is still fresh and new. It must resemble what you bipeds call true love, though at this particular point in time every racial identity in my head is screaming that it's more profound than that."

"Uh, I don't want to burst any bubbles, but it's impossible for you to have met her before boarding *Our Lady's Hornblower*."

"It would certainly seem that way, but that hardly seems to matter now. I'm in love, you understand."

"Naturally," said Boink. Fearing this was all a ruse, that the ambassador would suddenly spring into action with his carnal intentions plain, the admiral moved away as if to inspect a detail on the map. "What's her name?" he asked, almost casually.

"She has none. She needs none."

Finding it awkward to have a full view of the map and keep an eye on the ambassador at the same time, Boink shifted his line of sight to the wound of the savant on the floor. The poor clone's twitching in her REM state appeared more violent than usual, but otherwise she gave no indication the pain had adversely affected her higher functions. "What world does this love-incarnate friend of yours hail from?"

"She has never seen fit to communicate that information, and I have never seen fit to ask."

"Aren't you curious?"

"Why should I be? She has already told me everything of conceivable importance about her, and once I have done with my business here, we will seek out some privacy and she will fill me in on the petty details. In any case, having evidently come here with nothing particular to say, I would like to conclude my errand and take my leave."

Boink nodded his assent with an audible sigh of relief. Even so, his fingers grazed the handle of his blaster as the ambassador and the winged creature took their exit. He would have difficulty getting the winged one out of his mind. Already he recalled distinct facial features, hinting at incomprehensible beauty, even though he could not be sure he had actually seen them.

Shrugging, he turned to the map. By now the funny feeling had evolved into foreboding disquiet. He remembered it was important that Coryban and Blather return with this Hunter character as quickly as possible, for Hunter was needed to perform music on the soprano saxophone for the express purpose of pleasing a diplomat. Yet the identity of the diplomat had become a complete mystery, while the need for none other than Hunter to play the music had become an inexplicable absurdity. Boink felt as though a veil had enshrouded his brain. His every instinct— indeed, each succeeding rush of adrenaline in his system—screamed *panic! panic!*, but he could not for the life of him figure out what he should be panicking over. Even now, some details of his conversation with Proty and the ambassador had become frighteningly vague, and he was certain he wouldn't have a prayer of filling in the gaps until Coryban returned.

Where's that shuttle now? he asked himself, pooring deep into the field of lights.

Boink couldn't believe his senses. The tinier pinpoint was there, all right, but it was going in the wrong direction! His panic exploded in a mindless rage, and he jerked the nearest savant off the console terminal and, heedless of the savant's torn scalp and arterial blood spurting high in the air, began choking the helpless clone with all his might. "You're making a mistake! You're making a mistake!" he shouted, red-faced, punctuating his sentences with the most colorful expletives he had picked up during his tenure in the Patrol. "They're not going anywhere else! They can't be! It's impossible!"

But it was still happening. Navigational savants, even malfunctioning ones, didn't make mistakes like that. As the echoes of his last words died out against the metal walls, Boink finally realized the senseless insanity of what he was doing and let the idiot fall to the floor. By now the savant had ceased spurting blood; its heart had evidently stopped beating, but not before the admiral, the nearby terminals, the floor, and the savant himself glistened with the bright stuff.

Boink stared at his stained sleeves. On the verge of hyperventilating, he tapped the fingers of his right hand on his kneecap. Now he would have to call someone in here to take away this body. He wouldn't have to explain why he had choked the savant to death—he didn't think he could make such an explanation plausible in any case—but the situation would be embarrassing nonetheless. He would have to change his uniform and clean all his medals too. *What a lousy day this has been*, he thought. His only consolation was the hope that Coryban knew what she was doing. It wasn't much of a consolation, but it was the only one he had.

Gradually, he calmed down and found himself distracted by the groans of a nearby female. She twitched and stretched enticingly as a result of her dream state. The fluttering of her eyelids and her flushed complexion cast a mesmerizing spell on his soul. He couldn't help but speculate on what sort of dreams she, who had no life experiences to draw upon, might be having. He wondered if her dreams were being affected by what he had done to the savant beside her, if she had somehow sensed the pain the dead savant had been incapable of recognizing as such. The temptation to discover if she was capable of recognizing pleasure was overwhelming.

But he resisted, contenting himself with a mere kiss before exiting through the dilating door. The corridors beyond were only superficially familiar.

Chapter Two
Islands in the Sky

A BIRD SOARS HIGH above a lake of clear blue water. The bird spots the tiniest flicker of motion deep beneath the sun-flecked surface and, acting with the unerring skill of instinct honed by the process of trial and error, takes a spectacular nosedive and slips into the cool water with barely a splash. The bird first feels its feathers warmed by the hot sun, then its wings pinned by the pressure of its dive, and finally the water eradicating all warmth in an instant.

Now imagine how an innocent, unsuspecting parasite attached to the bird's neck must feel, and you have some idea how a harried rocket jockey feels when his shuttle makes the drop from the ultraspectrum of hyperspace back into the real galaxy. Only in this case, the parasite has the responsibility of driving. One slow reaction on the parasite's part can cause the shuttle to emerge in a solar system nobody's bothered to map yet.

So when the holomap above the dashboard indicated I'd hit my target, I chalked it up to the accuracy of Oliver's computations rather than to my piloting skills. I'd had too many things on my mind during the trip to take the credit, and besides, this rocket jockey had come down from the heavens on an all-time low.

"Pretty good flying for a guy whose career should be passing before his eyes," sneered Ensign Blather behind me. "Of course, it's been a short career, so you haven't had much to think about."

"I've managed not to let the repetition bore me," I replied with a forced smile, but I couldn't repress my smug satisfaction at seeing Blather strapped in his safety harness, with his feet tied to the legs of the chair and his hands bound in his lap.

"Boss, the implications of your theoretically casual remark interest me," said Oliver. The cables protruding from his barrel-shaped body were connected to the computer terminal before the copilot seat. "Are you implying the phantasm of your career playing across your mind resembles a Möbius strip, with no definite beginning or end?"

"You'd better detach yourself from the board, old buddy," I said. "Your chips weren't designed to take the stress of rampant speculation." Which was another way of saying I didn't think his personality program was holding up against the additional influx of artifical intelligence from the terminal. "I can take it on full manual from here."

"Yeah, and if we're lucky, we won't crash into an asteroid," snarled Blather.

"You know, I can always ask Oliver to gag you, Blather," I said reasonably, "though unfortunately the chances are you have another orifice that will activate itself to take up the verbal slack."

"Huh? What do you mean by that?" Blather snapped.

"Disengaged, Boss," said Oliver, stretching his arms as if winding down from a long exercise bout, "but I do wish you'd answer my question about the Möbius strip."

"I have some questions I'd like to ask too, Lieutenant Hunter," said Lieutenant Colonel Second Class Coryban, tied up in the chair to Blather's right. Coryban had been mostly silent ever since I had hijacked the shuttle and tied her up beside Blather and our other passenger. Though she was second in command only to Admiral Boink, I'd never seen or dealt with her until she had rescued me from my planetfall, but already she had lived up in every way to her formidable reputation—she was aloof, efficient, maddeningly precise, and often devastatingly sarcastic. She was also beautiful beyond words, a tall, big-boned, redhaired amazon of the bureaucratic set. "For instance, while it speaks well for you as a biped that you would willingly risk everything to rescue your robot friend from this existence beyond death, as you call it, I can't see how the survival of one artifically intelligent entity rates an importance equal to the successful conclusion of a galactic conference."

"Suppose you tell me, Colonel, just why my presence is so essential?"

"Because the Ho-Ho-Kusian ambassador has been on ... on ... on a ..." She turned to look at Blather.

Who had turned to look at her. His confused expression reminded me of a Geckian Amphibo whose lily pad had just been stolen out from under him. "He needs to hear the music of a soprano saxophone played by a human," Blather said haltingly, "for some reason of vital importance to his mental health and to the social stability of the ship, but I'll be hornswoggled if I can remember exactly what it is."

Coryban again faced me, her green eyes as penetrating and enigmatic as jade jewels. "You were the only person on board with a registered musical instrument matching its description. Unfortunately, by the time we'd discovered that fact, you had already fallen out of the void."

"Through no fault of my own, I might add," I said. "Didn't it ever occur to you that my abilities with the soprano saxophone might be a little inadequate? I mean, I played it some during my youth, but I'm woefully out of practice. In fact, that's why I brought it along. I was expecting to have a lot of free time on this mission."

"You c-can't p-play the so-soprano sax-saxophone!" Blather stammered. "Then why in the na-name of Seldon did we rescue your ass?"

"Obviously because you screwed up," said Oliver. "But with you, Ensign Blather, that's generally a foregone conclusion!" He twisted an eye toward me. "My stint as the Holy Spectre gave me some new perspectives on bipedal behavior, Boss!"

"I can see that," I replied, adding to myself, *Plus enabled you to rise above the limitations of your personality programming. What's happening to you, Oliver? No normal robot of your make and year would have the maturity to talk back so openly to a Stellar Patrol officer.*

Then again, maybe he and a whole lot of other robots from roughly the same line did have it. Oliver's intelligence had been growing in a lot of inexplicable leaps and bounds lately, and I didn't think a stint as the Holy Spectre and a period connected to a copilot's terminal could claim full responsibility.

That partially explained why we'd come to the Avidya System. The rest had to do with the apparitions of my first faithful robot companion, Floyd, that had kept appearing to me on the unnamed world where I'd made planetfall. Needless to say, I was surprised to see him, even as a relatively coherent roboghost. The poor robot had gone insane before he'd managed to get it together enough to sacrifice his life for me on the Space Station Gamma Delta. In his latest appearances on this mortal coil, however, Floyd claimed that while his body was probably still dead, his mind was very much resurrected and in the company of other minds in a place that resembled traditional descriptions of limbo. It was up to me to get him out of there, and of course he had no idea, really, where he wanted me to look first.

Complicating matters was the possibility that the strange developments occurring to my current faithful robot companion, Oliver, were connected, in some subtle way I was as yet unable to fathom, to Floyd's predicament. Though both Floyd and Oliver had been manufactured at different locales, their designs had been developed on the Avidya world of Nippon, and their first experimental models had been manufactured on one of the factory stations in orbit above the planet. Presumably the models all met galactic standards, and perhaps that was precisely the problem. If it was, then chances were I was the first to become aware of it. Communication between Nipponese and Union citizens is always kept to an official minimum. The Nipponese are so secretive about their planet and society that not even the other residents of the solar system are permitted to set foot there. The Nipponese maintain control of the Avidya System through feudal means, with a complex, loosely-knit organization of space station lords and barons, each buttressed by his own private police force. They deal with off-worlders only for purposes of trade and commerce. Because their brain trust is one of the best in the galaxy, no one in the Union can afford *not* to deal with them.

Naturally the Nipponese don't care to burden their intellects with the details of extradition treaties, either. Consequently, the Avidya System is one of the great gutters of the galaxy, a haven for every sort of outcast, honest or otherwise, who hasn't found what he's looking for in any mainstream of proper Union society. Apparently the Nipponese feel quite comfortable knowing their baron henchmen have surrounded themselves with criminals and cultists, hedonists and heathens, fortune hunters and thrill seekers, not to mention every conceivable stripe of freethinking existentialist. It's no wonder the Avidya System was declared off-limits several generations ago.

Then again, if there was ever a heaven in real space time for disgraced saints and fallen heroes, as Floyd had indicated, then the Avidya System was it. I had to admit, I did feel an unusual excitement at the prospect of nosing around the factories there. Despite considerable trepidation about my future in the Stellar Patrol, I felt that I was at last arriving at the home I had never known.

Maybe my all-time low was finally bottoming out.

"Lieutenant Hunter, I am afraid you've committed an error of grievous proportions," said Coryban, not unkindly. "If you've indeed discovered compelling reasons why a mission should be mounted to . . . to . . ." She craned her neck for a better look at the holomap above the dashboard. And gulped. ". . . the Avidya System, then you should have gone through proper channels. You could have performed your duties while Admiral Boink secured clearance, and since you're the one this Floyd robot has been making contact with, you might even have been selected as a member of the team."

"Pardon me, ma'am, but I can see several flaws in your reasoning almost immediately. First, you can't remember why my presence on ship is needed, except to play an instrument I'm not even sure I can play well anymore."

"That is my problem, soldier, not yours," said Coryban sternly.

"And second, do you really expect Admiral Boink to realistically assess any situation and then actually make an intelligent decision?"

Her face turned red. "Hunter! That is insubordination!"

"Answer me honestly now."

"Honestly?" I had her there. She deflated in a matter of moments. "Boink never makes a realistic decision. I make them for him." She appeared to be studying me in a new light. "Couldn't you trust me?"

"It's too late for that, but even if it wasn't, I still couldn't be sure of your decision."

"You're a man of convictions, Hunter, I'll give you that."

"I'll tell you what he's a man of," snarled Blather.

"Here comes that bleeding orifice again," said Oliver.

"Blather! Be quiet! I'll handle this," hissed Coryban.

"You're doing such a great job so far!" he said.

"How does a count of gross insubordination sound, mister?"

"Excellent," he said with a smile. "But I think you should add desertion, dereliction of duty, and," he nodded toward Oliver, "tampering with Patrol property too."

"I was talking about you," Coryban replied testily.

"Oh," said Blather, suddenly crestfallen. For some reason he reminded me of an overbearing rooster who had just discovered new competition in the barnyard. "Can't you at least get him to untie us? If I don't pee soon, my eyes are going to turn yellow."

"Still a class act," commented Oliver to no one in particular.

"I'm working on it!" hissed Coryban between her

31

teeth. She turned back to me, her face suddenly softening with a sweet smile. She arched her back stiffly and tugged down her fatigues, displaying her contours in a new light. "Hello, soldier. New in this solar system?"

"Save your dignity, Colonel. No offense, but as a man-trapping sexpot, you're a total loser."

She turned red and demanded, "What's the matter with me?"

"Nothing at all," I bustered, realizing I hadn't said exactly what I'd meant. "It's just . . . just that I could tell you were acting, that's all. You weren't sexy because you weren't being yourself."

"It would have worked if some floozie had come on to you this way."

"That's my point exactly." Then, more wistfully than I'd intended, I sighed and added, "Besides, floozies generally don't come on to me because my credit's so lousy."

"We kinda figured as much," sneered Blather.

Coryban sneered back, "One more word out of you without my permission, and I'll have you cleaning the grotch cages."

Blather blushed and managed a hapless grin. "Yes, ma'am."

"With your tongue!" Coryban added.

I turned away and tried not to feel sick.

"Whew! That'd be a nasty job," said Oliver. "He'd be up to it though."

"It's all right, Colonel, I said. "I'm used to Blather's nonsense by now."

"What does he have against you, Lieutenant?"

Blather opened his mouth to answer before me, but Coryban deterred him with another stern stare.

"Damned if I know, ma'am. He's always treated me mean—since I was a green-faced grunt. He even tried to punish me once for keeping a diary."

Blather opened his mouth yet again, but Oliver stretched out his arm and put his cold, metal hand over it. Blather made an angry noise—half bark, half groan.

"Calm down, Blather, before you have a conniption," said Coryban. Then to me: "He's really quite reasonable most of the time, and occasionally he even strikes me as being a good soldier. It's only where you're concerned that he gets totally out of line."

I shrugged.

"Listen, Homer—can I call you Homer?"

"Sure."

"Homer, I doubt much harm has been done to the mission—especially since neither Blather nor I can quite remember why we needed you and your soprano saxophone in the first place. I'm sure I can testify that being in close quarters with Blather drove you temporarily insane. I might even be able to prevent a court martial, but if not, I've enough pull to make things easier on you. What do you say, Homer? It's still not too late to turn back."

Coryban and I ignored the reactions from the peanut gallery.

"Sorry, ma'am, but you don't impress me as the rule-bending type. If we turned back, you'd do your duty, no more, no less. You might go easy on me, true, but you wouldn't lie for me. And you know I'm no more insane than you are."

She pursed her lips thoughtfully, raised her eyebrows, and nodded. "You're right, Homer, I wouldn't lie for you."

"See? You have your own criteria of integrity too."

"Come on, Hunter, confide in me. What harm can it do to trust me now? I trust you."

"Well, *that* can do a lot of harm!" said my third unwilling passenger, the young lady tied in a chair on the other side of Blather. She yawned, then added, "I trusted Hunter once, and in exchange he gratefully turned my whole life upside down."

"That's because I didn't know what I was doing," I said.

"He is the consistent sort," said Oliver. "Nice of you to finally join us, Reina."

Reina yawned again. "I did not mean to sleep. How long was I out?"

"Almost from the very moment we went into hyperdrive," said Coryban smoothly, with deliberate kindness, which was probably not a bad idea, considering that the majority of the girl's homeworld population, including perhaps her own tribe, had been wiped out in a senseless war between giant robot cities several chrons before takeoff. "Don't be concerned, though," Coryban continued. "It happens to a lot of people the first time."

"It's a lot like sex," sneered Blather. "Or didn't Hunter tell you?"

"No, he didn't," said Reina, pulling as far away from him as possible, "and furthermore, it is a matter I doubt you've ever had the opportunity to understand. Surely only outcasts would bed someone with your manners, and then purely as a business transaction. Even then they'd boot you from their tents the moment you spilled your seed. Though in your case, perhaps I should say, 'dripped your seed.' "

"Remind me not to alienate that woman," said Oliver.

"Blather, there's a reason why I ordered you to keep your mouth shut," said Coryban.

Blather glared at Coryban, but obeyed.

Coryban then said to Reina, "If I recall Hunter's psych profiles correctly, it's unlikely he deliberately harmed you. It must have been inadvertent."

"Trying to get on my good side, Colonel?" I asked slyly.

"Maybe. But maybe I meant it," Coryban replied with a scowl. "Now you'll never know." Then she asked Reina, "How, if I may inquire, did Lieutenant Hunter violate your trust?"

"I met him on the day before my wedding. I took an interest in him because I'd never before seen a man with brown skin and white streaks in his hair. And because he seemed so much more interesting than any man of my world could ever hope to be, I confided my name to him. I knew that was a reckless deed. It is the custom of my tribe, the Heechie-Heechie, that a woman's name is secret to all but her family and the man who takes her as a life partner. The next day, my husband and I happened to pass by this man, and he, evidently in some state of delirium, stated my name aloud for all to hear. My indiscretion was revealed. Thanks to him, I was disgraced. My husband had nothing more to do with me and I remain a virgin to this day."

"We'll soon fix that," said Blather.

Coryban ground her teeth as if imagining Blather's throat between them. "One more word, mister, and you'll be a falsetto for life! Do we understand each other?"

"Boss! Boss! Do you want me to untie the colonel now?" asked Oliver eagerly.

"No, let's keep him in suspense."

"I'm sorry," said Coryban to Reina, "but you're free now to do as you please, to marry or not to marry, or even to make love to whom you wish without fear of prolonged social entanglement."

"I know. Perhaps the most fortunate side effect of my self-imposed exile is that now I can tell whomever I please, without any fear of disgrace, that my soul name is Reina. So many customs of my tribe now seem so arbitrary to me. And there is still the matter of virginity to contend with. I was raised to believe a girl's deflowering should be an occasion, achieved only with a partner worthy of the honor. And because marriage seems out of the question for the moment, I haven't yet decided what qualifications are most suitable to help me fulfill this end."

"Do you like officers?" Blather asked.

Reina sighed and ignored him. "I was thinking that perhaps I should yield myself first to a warrior who has conquered me in battle. Or perhaps to the first holy man I meet in a city of sinners, or to a lusty, brawling womanizer." She shrugged. "Maybe I'll settle for something as mundane as true love. I just don't know. I confess, though, I didn't leave my planet because of any desire to . . . to . . . you know, find a suitable partner. I left because I want to join the Stellar Patrol."

"And you'll have the opportunity to decide if that's really what you want, my dear," said Coryban. "In the meantime, consider yourself a free agent until you make your decision."

Reina bowed politely. "My name means *White Hawk* in my own tongue."

"Is that your totem?" Coryban asked.

"The creature mirrors my soul, if that's what you mean."

"Only males of her tribe are supposed to be intimate with their totems," I explained. "But Reina took it upon herself to learn all the male secrets of her tribe. She only consented to marriage out of a reluctance for her family to be disgraced."

"She's a genuine jungle girl," put in Oliver.

"Yes, I sense she is an extraordinary individual," said Coryban.

"You sense it?" I asked. "Forgive me, Colonel, but I thought you were too logical to rely on intuition."

"There are a lot of things about me I fear you'll never know, Hunter," Coryban replied coldly, almost enigmatically.

I raised my eyebrows by way of response, but spoke to Reina. "Are you enjoying your first space flight?"

"I did not think it would be so confining," she said. "These walls are so close. They seem so thick and bulky."

"They are, strictly as a matter of necessity," I said. "But there are ways to give you an illusion of where we are, a clearer illusion than you can get by studying the holomap, anyway."

"How?" Reina asked. "Does your Stellar Patrol have a ceremonial substance that transforms the workings of the mind and elevates it to a higher state of consciousness?"

"In a manner of speaking," I replied, pushing buttons. "It's called technology."

The shuttle walls became screens and faded away. Reina gasped. To her untrained eyes, it must have seemed the walls had evaporated, leaving the shuttle's interior—not to mention the passengers—directly exposed to the harsh vacuum of space. She laughed weakly, half-embarrassed, half-amazed, as she realized the view was only a computer-generated illusion of compressed distances, an interpretation of reality in accordance with a program. Meaning that when we traveled through a body's orbit, the program presented us with a clear, sunlit view of it, regardless of its actual place in the solar field.

"One world of Nippon, dead ahead," I said, as the wall to my left was filled with the picture of a frozen world with three tiny moons. The outermost satellite was crisscrossed with intersecting buildings a kilometer wide and several kilometers long; due to the moon's glassy white surface, the buildings made it resemble a great floating cracked egg. As the planet receded behind our seats, a comet shot past us on the right so fast that Oliver practically jumped in my lap.

"Sorry, Boss, I forgot that when the pictorializer's on, you have to trust the holomap more than your own senses."

"That's all right," I said.

"What a mouthful of soyashit," mumbled Blather.

Oliver turned to him and said, "Would you like me to turn on the water faucet, so we can see if you've got a man's bladder?"

Blather paled and shook his head no.

"Drip, drip, drip," Oliver said. "Sheesh. What a maroon."

"Quiet, please," said Reina, staring wide-eyed at a green and gold gas giant with a glittering ring system and twenty-six visible moons. The three largest moons were concealed by thick, colorful cloud covers. "Is all the universe this beautiful?"

"Not if you're actually stuck in some of these places you're only looking at now," I said. "Then you tend to view things from a different perspective."

"Don't let the beauty completely color your view," said Coryban. "The universe isn't cruel, but it's not benign either. It's indifferent, coldly indifferent."

Reina scowled at her. I don't think Coryban realized yet that Reina must not only have witnessed the indifference of nature but have been an occasional instrument of it, as she lived off her world's great variety of animal life. I had no doubt Reina would adjust quickly to life in the Union. The essence of the two ways of life was, after all, very similiar.

Quickly we passed through the orbits of three other gas giants, each presenting progressively more evidence of the extensive industrialization Nipponese society had cultivated over the generations. Some moons were totally blanketed with buildings, roads, and atmospheres beneath clear plastic domes, and all the giants had artifical satellites as large as their natural companions. An asteroid belt was equally populous, and quite a few asteroids appeared to have been deserted after generations of mining operations. On those the man-made domes were frequently cracked, the buildings reduced to rubble after having been buffeted for decades by space stuff.

Beyond the asteroid belt were the factories—huge space islands, erected in complex patterns of interlocking cylinders closed by hemispherical endcaps and surrounded by agricultural modules, all augmented by rotating mirrors collecting the sunlight and providing the inhabitants with the illusion of a regular progression of night and day. Though the basic cylinder designs dominated, other shapes were used, including pyramids, spheres of many textures, webs of double helices, a wide variety of polyhedrons, and combinations of these designs. All were augmented by mirrors and modules, and many were evidently made for those inhabitants born and raised in space, who had no need or desire to live in an environment mimicking planetary gravity and light patterns. The pictorializer could not show us all the space islands, just as it could not show us all the asteroids in the belt, but it did give us a pretty good idea of what this system had to offer, just as it presented enough images of shuttles, ships, and freighters to give us a good idea of the intensity of the traffic flow in the navigational lanes.

"By Crom, I had no idea there were that many social deviants in the galaxy," said Blather in awestruck tones.

"I'm sure you'll be just as much at home as we," said Oliver.

"I doubt it," Blather replied, his awe smothered

by a wave of loathing. "Everybody knows this is no-where," he added a few seconds later, in a whisper.

I punched the braking mechanisms into operation as Nippon came into view on the left. "Here you are, Oliver," I said. "Your spawning grounds at last."

"So this is the cradle of A.I.," he said. "Kinda brings a leak to your oil pan, don't it?"

"Stop torturing me," said Blather, grinding his teeth.

Nippon boasted deep shades of pristine blue, and its three major land masses were a rich green. White clouds like fresh cotton wisps swirled in the atmosphere. The world radiated a sense of cleanliness and hospitality. Most worlds, at even a cursory inspection, presented evidence of the scars of life—this world of Nippon had no such scars. It might have been born only a millennium before, and quarantined from all intelligent life since then.

The space around Nippon, however, hinted at a different story. The sheer number of articial satellites and colonies, both large and small, indicated that the scars hadn't been prevented, just ruthlessly exiled to space. Vast plumes of smoke and chemical exhaust spewed from mighty exhaust pipes in swirling clouds that drifted indifferently toward the sun. The bulk of the space islands were positioned in a great ring over a hundred kilometers wide above the equator of the world, but many bigger factories and colonies were in other orbits, stretching the band of civilization by another several thousand kilometers in all directions, until they formed the outlines of metallic petals in bloom about a lovely flower. Finding the secret of Floyd's continued existence in this urban sprawl was going to be like finding a proton in a nuclear explosion.

"What now, Boss?" Oliver asked.

"Indeed," said Coryban. "I would very much like

to know what you intend to do with us on this next stage of your journey."

"Maybe I'll let you go if you give me your word to accept a truce, with me as your leader," I said.

"Don't count on it!" said Blather.

"I'm afraid I must concur with the ensign," said Coryban. "My duty will force me to bring you back at the earliest opportunity."

"I'll go with you," said Reina eagerly, her green eyes bright with anticipation of adventure. "I've no obligations."

Instead of refusing at once, which of course I would have to do sooner or later, I found myself distracted by those jade eyes of hers. I hadn't noticed before, but they bore a startling resemblance to Coryban's. I wondered, since all like atoms and molecules are identical, was it possible that Reina's and Coryban's eyes were also identical, an indication that they were, in some unfathomable way, reflections of each other?

My musings were abruptly cut short by Oliver, who pointed at the monitor and said, "Trouble, Boss!"

The majority of blips on the holomap indicating traffic flow were a muted green; but what was I to make of the two bright white blips, invisible on the pictorializer screens but growing larger by the second on the holomap?

"They want to make radio contact, Boss," said Oliver tensely. "Who are they? What do they want? I thought this was a free space zone."

"We can't take anything for granted," I said.

"I guess your posterior is fried now, Hunter," sneered Blather.

"Make contact, Oliver," I said.

"This is the Space Police," barked a voice through the speaker on the console. "Identify yourself and your mission in this solar system."

"I don't have to identify myself," I said. "I'm a free agent."

"Our scan shows that you are piloting an official Union vehicle," replied the policeman. "That makes your business our business."

"Uh-oh, Boss, they've got us in a tractor beam," said Oliver. "We're being pulled right toward them."

"Can we break away?"

"I doubt it. It's too powerful for this heap."

"Might as well surrender now," said Blather, "and make it easy on yourself. If you're lucky, you won't serve less than sixty trillion chrons at hard labor on a prison planet."

"He's only exaggerating by thirty billion chrons or so," said Coryban. "I won't have any more last chances to give you after this one, Homer."

"What are we going to do, Boss?" asked Oliver, elongating his eyestalks closer and closer to the holomap: they looked like two snakes that had been accidentally mesmerized by their victims.

"Yes, Homer-B-Hunter," said Reina, "what are you going to do? Will you take me with you? Please! Please!"

I smiled weakly at her and then turned back to the holomap. I didn't know how to tell her I had absolutely no idea what to do next. I hadn't expected to be trapped so quickly in the game. It hadn't even occurred to me that being in a Union vehicle would be tantamount to broadcasting across all bands: *Hi, I'm in the Stellar Patrol. Would you please send someone to arrest me now?*

Even more humilating than the prospect of being thrown in the brig was being captured before Coryban and Blather. For the thousandth time I regretted not leaving them on that nameless world Reina hailed from. Then, at least, I could have taken a reckless chance on firing a laser torpedo or two on these so-called Space Police, and faced the possibility of being disintegrated in the retaliatory blast with a clear conscience. I could take no chances at all while Reina and Coryban were my responsibilities.

Floyd, I've failed you, I thought, filled with anguish. It was remarkable how hollow an experience abject despair was. *If only you'd talk to me, give me some sign that at least I've come to the right place* . . .

"Boss!" shouted Oliver. "The map! Look at the map!"

"Holy Seldon!" whispered Blather, with more genuine awe than I'd thought him capable of.

"What kind of Null-A syllogism is taking root in reality here?" demanded Coryban.

I had to admit, I was a little surprised myself. I hadn't thought the computer was programmed to create that sort of image in the holomap.

"I know you!" Reina exclaimed at the image. "You're the roboghost who led us to the Transcendenticon city!"

Wanta play Hucka-Hucka-Beanstalk, folks? said the image of Floyd.

"Good to see you again, kid," I said as soon as I realized it was the real thing, or as close to the real thing as was being permitted these days. "But I'm afraid I haven't got much time to talk."

That's all right. Neither do I. Something's started keeping my mental capacity pretty preoccupied all of a sudden.

"But, Floyd, I'm about to be arrested by the Space Police, whoever they are."

Relax, they're always arresting somebody. It's nothing to be concerned about.

"Floyd, I don't want to be arrested. What can I do?"

The image of my old faithful robot companion put its hands behind its back and bobbed up and down. *The only advice I can give you is: Use the farce, Boss. Use the farce.*

"That's the stupidest advice I've ever heard!" exclaimed Oliver. "What the hell is that supposed to mean? *Use the farce!* Sheesh!"

"Maybe he wants you to throw a pie at the police," suggested Blather with mock sweetness.

"Feets—get moving!" I yelled, bolting from the chair.

"Boss, where are you going?" Oliver yelled.

"To the lifepod. While they're busy talking, we'll give them the old slipperoo by going out the back way."

"But what about us?" demanded Blather.

Oliver stretched out his hand and tickled Blather on the ribs.

"Not that!" said Blather between bouts of uncontrollable laughter. "Anything but that! Oh, you tin-headed, positronic moron—I'll get you for this!"

Oliver's metal eyebrows, crescents of tungsten steel, rose up and down licentiously. "I bet you say that to all the young dudes, big boy."

Blather repressed his peals of laughter to a few halting giggles as his complexion grew as white as chalk and he stared forlornly at his lap. He grimaced and nodded, then stared at Oliver and nodded some more. "One of these days, it's going to be just you and me, gooseberry breath."

"Just be sure to shower first," said Oliver.

I instinctively wrinkled my nose in disgust. "Sorry, old bean," I said. "A tough break."

"Don't get superior with me, Hunter," he snarled in reply. It was nice to know his spirit wasn't broken.

"Identify yourselves!" came the voice through the speaker grille. "Identify yourselves or we'll board you immediately!"

"Maintain the radio silence, folks, will you please?"

I said, leaving the folks tied as Oliver and I stepped into the pod in the shuttle rear.

And as the transparent shield doors slid closed, Reina craned her neck and said, "I'd wish you luck, Homer-B-Hunter, but I'm afraid that—"

"We'll need it as much as you," finished Coryban.

Their words and faces haunted me as the pod disconnected and sent Oliver and me on a wild tumble to the space factories of Nippon. I couldn't help but wonder if I would ever see them again.

Chapter Three
She Does the Mystery Dance

MEANWHILE, ON the doughnut-shaped Space Island I was about to arrive on, a goddess named Marie was being revered at her local temple—a water tower. Her disciples were housewives and mistresses, secretaries and school marms, plus those destined to be such, and they danced the dance known only as the mystery dance. They danced to silent music only they could hear, broadcast through the ether directly into their hearts and pelvises, bypassing completely their ears and their brains. They danced long after their breathing had become labored and their faces flushed, long after they had perspired so their clothing clung to them as if it had been stapled there. In their abnegation the women found their greatest self-realization. In their acceptance of the feminine role in the birth-rebirth cycle, they discovered their potential for defiance. In their worship of the creative essence, they nurtured their need to commit acts of destruction. By revealing their sensuality, they fulfilled the demands of their intellects, and by admitting their need to serve Man and all things masculine, they confessed their hatred of Him.

It was that hatred which inspired the men wearing hardhats on the scaffolds to remain in place despite a certain urge to get close to the women. The men watched in fascination as the women became dance, dance of the night and of the wind, up and down and back and forth, shoulder up and shoulder down and hips cocked right and hips cocked left. Their skin glistening with perspiration or cool and drying with the caress of the breeze. Each one danced the mystery dance to exhaustion, and then, still unsatisfied, danced on until she had become the essence of dance, until she felt she had satisfied Marie. The goddess drawn on the water tower had the word "love" written on the knuckles of one hand and "hate" written on the other.

Among the women was the young Yangtze Derringer, a nubile maiden with a round, broad face, bronze skin, and yellow-orange hair with day-glo blue highlights. Her supple body, with its long torso and narrow hips, was capable of doing the mystery dance with a frenzy equal to that of even most experienced, uninhibited worshipper, but thus far she had been holding back, going through the motions with only a modicum of sincerity. Perhaps she still couldn't hear the music right. Perhaps she still wasn't used to wearing naught but a strategically placed semitransparent loincloth that revealed as much as it concealed, and a huge feather headdress that hung past her buttocks. Perhaps it was the sight of so many adults she was used to seeing act so prim and proper suddenly acting so carefree, so deeply and openly in touch with impulses Yangtze herself was only beginning to comprehend.

Or perhaps it was the sight of her mother among them, someone who, until then, Yangtze had never believed capable of dancing totally naked in public, with a knife in one hand and a dildo in the other. Her

47

mother was a high priestess of the order, and though Yangtze had of course always been aware of her mother's religious activities, she had never quite connected the person who fixed her meals, made her clean up her room, and told her to say "no" to drugs (until she was old enough to handle them) with the frenzied leader of the dance. On one level, Yangtze was proud that her mother was the Gatekeeper of Ecstasy, but on another, she was completely horrified at the responsibilities which came with that title. Furthermore, she was totally mystified that women could actually take delight in licking the blood from their comrades' superficial wounds, wounds her mother had inflicted with such knowing skill, and she was both disturbed and fascinated that women could find such pleasure in having certain orifices so terribly abused. At least her mother seemed to be enjoying her work.

If only Father could see her now, she wondered, what would he think? Yangtze had been very young when her parents had separated, but she did distinctly recall her father expressing a strong disapproval of this particular cult.

But mostly Yangtze was preoccupied with the matter of her dimly comprehended impulses. So when her mother beckoned, Yangtze came. When her mother caressed her with the dildo, she came again. And when her mother cut a razor-thin slice into her skin running in a straight line from the top of her sternum down to her belly button, she dipped her fingers in her blood and tasted it, then offered herself to the other women and, in a prolonged flash of ecstasy, permitted them to tear off her loincloth and lick the shiny red liquid as it dripped down her belly and onto her thighs. Only then did Yangtze truly understand. Only then did she feel truly initiated into the mysteries. Only then did she finally begin to know what it truly meant to be a woman.

Marie understood. Yangtze could see that in the eyes of the old, peeling portrait of Marie—spray-painted a generation ago on the water tower, long before the cult had become established in the colony. The portrait reached high above and far beyond the three levels of scaffolding, and extended far out on both sides of the only ladder in the vicinity. Marie had frizzled hair like a mass of snakes bent at sharp angles. Her hexagonal bosoms were shaped like another space island frequently seen in the artifical sky. The portrait widened at the hips, and ended at the pubic hair, a flurry of lines that appeared to have been sprayed in a great hurry, without much thought; indeed, there was something childish about the craft in that part of the portrait, whereas the rest revealed an artist very much familiar with the techniques of cubism and aboriginal reptilian art.

The longer Yangtze looked at the portrait, the more convinced she became that Marie did far more than merely understand. For as the women of the cult dutifully licked the blood from her body, igniting a series of tiny explosions within, Yangtze actually saw the goddess's eyes—round and stylized—turn and look through her own heart. The hard edges of the mouth softened and smiled, and the outlines of those fingers stretched outward, as if in anticipation of catching a breath of soul.

You have awakened, my sister, said the goddess in a voice that was here, there, and everywhere.

"You can speak!" exclaimed Yangtze as someone lightly caressed her lips, making it difficult to enunciate clearly.

And you, sister, can see, said the goddess Marie with a grin.

"See . . . and hear," replied Yangtze as she shuddered involuntarily from a tiny explosion. "Have you come to reveal a mystery?"

Mysteries are not so much revealed as they are expounded upon.

"I'll be honored to answer any riddle you offer me, goddess."

Unfortunately, I have no riddles for you. My colleagues in the pantheon already have several in the offing, I'm afraid.

"That's too bad," said Yangtze, with another shudder. She would have pushed a few of the women away, or at least directed their tongues to more acceptable portions of her anatomy, but her muscles were too weak to obey, her mind focused, really, only on her vision. "I was so hoping for an opportunity to prove my worthiness."

All who are women are worthy.

"But isn't there anything you want to tell me? I mean, it's not that I'm unappreciative or anything, I'm very grateful you've chosen to speak to me. But all your advance press has led me to believe I'd get a riddle to ponder, or at least some homespun kernel of wisdom."

The goddess Marie nodded thoughtfully. **Yes, I think a homespun kernel of wisdom would be appropriate, and wouldn't violate any of the myriad destinies I sense converging around you.**

"Whose destiny? Mine? How much is a myriad?"

SILENCE! I must think! The goddess Marie blinked twice, which was a pretty good trick since the artist hadn't provided her with eyelids. **Ah! I have it! Listen closely, my dear Yangtze, because I will have time to say this only once before other events capture the greater part of my attention.**

"Shoot, O Goddess Marie." Yangtze took a deep breath and thrust out her chest, completely failing to notice that the women surrounding her had taken this proud stance as a signal to renew their own intensity.

Marie nodded in approval. **The flash of lightning arrives from a turbulent sea of mist, yet is apt to die upon solid ground.**

"Huh? What the hell kind of wisdom is that?" inquired a stunned Yangtze. A tiny explosion was arrested in mid-spasm. She shook herself free of the women, happened to glance at her mother cutting a razor-thin "X" on someone's back, and then glared at the water tower.

But the goddess had reverted to mere paint on metal.

"Come back here!" Yangtze demanded, futilely.

But then a portion of the scaffold broke. Obviously Marie's attentions were elsewhere.

The goddess looked down indifferently as the screaming men fell from the broken scaffolding. Yangtze watched in horror as the men struggled to reach solid rigging. Those who couldn't pull themselves up to safety managed to hang on until help arrived, but one man happened to be hanging from the lowest point of the scaffolding, beyond the reach of his buddies.

"Hallelujah, mothers and sisters! Marie's favored us with a sacrifice tonight!" shouted Yangtze's mother. The gray-haired woman twirled her dildo and pointed her knife at the man. "Charge!"

The women gathered under him like a swarm of locusts, and Yangtze noticed he happened to be directly beneath the goddess's hand that read Hate. Some of the women rode on the shoulders of their sturdier sisters and grabbed for his feet. He succeeded in kicking them away, but just as the men above threw down a rope tied together from shirts, the scaffold lurched downward again. The men holding the rope immediately became preoccupied with preserving their own skins. They succeeded, but two women riding piggyback grabbed the hanging man around the waist and pulled him down into the swarm.

The women cheered. "It's never enough!" they shouted, not quite in unison. "It's never enough until your heart stops beating!" The object of their affection screamed. The men on the scaffold looked away. Marie moved again, subtly, to smile at her worshippers below. And Yangtze stared in horror as her mother held her knife high—and then brought it down sharply. A rivulet of blood spurted up like a geyser and showered the women in bright red drops.

Meanwhile, other women began climbing up the scaffolding. Some men ran away; others stood their ground, holding their work tools in defensive positions. Now the goddess looked down with an approving smile, and her eyes widened in anticipation. Yangtze felt in her heart that the goddess was fueling the women's frenzied lust. Unable to bear the thought of seeing more blood, Yangtze turned and fled.

Racing between interlocking systems of pipes, Yangtze heard the screams of more men. Their dim echoes bounced off the factory buildings and the artifical sky above, but they echoed in her consciousness even more loudly.

Suddenly she tripped. She struck the ground hard, the breath knocked out of her. For a moment she lay there and tried to gather her wits. To her left was another series of interlocking pipes. To her right was a stretch of magnetic monorail tracks. She was near the section of the space island where people and aliens were at work in the factories.

And, except for her headdress, she was naked. Normally that wouldn't be such a big deal, but there were some places on the island where even a rabid hedonist wouldn't want to be caught naked.

She tried to stand but was still too weak. She couldn't help but wonder what she would say to her mother tomorrow. Surely her mother would inquire, oh so innocently, if she had had a good time at the ceremony. Surely Mother would be curious if Marie had favored her daughter with a vision. *And on the first night too!* Mother would say. *Wait till I tell the girls!* But the big question, so far as Yangtze was concerned, was how many other lives had her mother taken in the name of religion? Sacrifices were theoretically illegal on the island of Aurelian, but the truth was that here, as elsewhere in the Avidya System, the only crime was getting caught. So unless the worshippers had accidentally squashed an individual of political or financial importance, the only retribution they had to worry about was the possible revenge from any cult or block group the man belonged to. Yangtze knew better than to think her mother might feel guilty about the deed on the morrow.

She crawled under the pipes and sat up as best as she could. Not only did her rib cage throb as if it was about to be cracked open by a chest-burster, but the wound itself had began to sting. All the activity had deepened and widened it, and Yangtze knew she would have to have a heart-to-heart with her mother tomorrow, if only to set up an appointment with the cult healer so she wouldn't scar.

The wound also still bled. Yangtze wondered how much blood she could lose before passing out. She didn't want to return to the place of worship so soon, but perhaps she wouldn't have any choice. Doubtless, some sisters were being treated by salves and prayers right now.

Yangtze's resolve weakened and she might have staggered back if only the screams had died off completely, but the slaughter was still going on. Yangtze felt disgusted. Couldn't the worshippers of Marie find some volunteers from a suicide cult? Or would that take some of the joy out of their misdeeds?

But somehow, listening to the wails and cheers of thirteen apostles blazing on a rooftop in the distance, dancing the dance of bliss and death as they burned into crispy ashes for some god she had never heard of, Yangtze knew in her heart that alternatives were unlikely. It had all been *karma*. The time had come for the men to die, and that was that.

Suddenly Yangtze felt extremely dizzy. Her heart pounded furiously. She stared up at the artificial sky, wondering if she was experiencing a prelude to death. She felt like an utter fool, not for having deserted the ceremony, but for not having hidden a first-aid kit on her person. Of course, where she might have put it was another question.

If only Marie's homespun kernel of wisdom hadn't been so enigmaticaly silly! If only—!

Suddenly a bolt of lightning crashed through the sky. She thought it was a meteor coming through, a not infrequent occurrence in this part of the solar system. She felt the slightest indication of a breeze, as air escaped from the hole in the shield which hastened to repair itself. She bumped her head on a pipe, but ignored the pain . . . meteors here didn't have time to burn up in the atmosphere the way they did when they fell on planets. They just smashed through the sky and broke the ground.

This something, on the other hand, was already leaving bright red trails against the starry black. It plummeted straight down toward a residential area. Then she watched in amazement as it turned at a right angle and began flying straight toward her!

At first she was relieved for the people who would have been killed or injured in the crash. She was confident that it would fly directly overhead. But her relief turned to sheer, blood-curdling terror when she belatedly realized it was in the process of completing an impossible trajectory.

Impossible for a mere meteor, that is.

Yangtze ducked the instant it hit. The ground shook as if the space island had been ripped asunder. Half her body was warmed by intense heat as she was pressed against the pipes by the shock wave. Protecting her head with her arms, she peeked out from under them as debris showered the artificial ground with bits of scorched metal and melting plexiglas. The meteor—or whatever it was—had struck an automated chemical processing plant on the other side of the monorail tracks. No human presence was ever required in the plant, which was why Yangtze knew of it; it had recently been the target of union protests, and several block kings had ordered their medicine men to direct curses at it. At least she could be reasonably certain no entity had died as a result of the crash.

As the rain of debris diminished, Yantze walked toward the plant as if mesmerized. She watched the jagged hole in the center of the roof widen as other portions of the plexiglas and steel crashed. The tremendous outpouring of fire and smoke from the hole in the roof was fascinating, but she reminded herself she'd better be careful—many of the chemicals used there were toxic and those that weren't tended to be volatile under the best of circumstances. Yangtze was willing to bet that the sprinkler system inside was inadequate for the task at hand.

Gingerly she crossed the tracks and walked across an open space of concrete riddled with debris. A few signs posted nearby announced a new project going up there soon, but she didn't bother to read them. She was too glad that the screams in her head had been smothered by the crackling of the fire in the air, by the hissing of the water putting out some of the flames, and by the tiny crashes caused by the continued crumpling of parts of the roof and walls. Already sirens pierced the air, but Yangtze intended to be the first to learn the secret of the meteor.

Then, halfway across the open space, she got an unpleasant whiff. She yelped as something burned her skin. Her feathers were on fire!

She threw off her headdress and stomped on it. She was so sickened at the thought it had been damaged that she forgot she was barefoot. She yelled at the unexpected flash of pain, grabbed her burned foot, and fell down.

Then her eyes practically bugged out of her head.

Because at that moment she saw a black man with white streaks in his hair staggering from the processing plant. He wore tattered fatigues, blackened and smoking from the heat, and was followed by what appeared to be a rolling, chugging fire hydrant. Further details were obscured by the fact that both man and hydrant were silhouetted by near-blinding light from the flames.

"It's all right, it's only me," I said to the buck-naked, bronze-skinned girl with day-glo blue highlights in her hair. She sat on the ground and nursed her foot when she should have been nursing a wound that ran completely up her belly and between her budding breasts. What was left of her clothing burned right in front of her.

Forgetting all about my own myriad aches and pains I rushed to her, knelt, and looked down in horror at her wound. "By the seven moons of Gallium!" I said. "I'm sorry! When the fuel tank ruptured and we started to spin out, I tried to maintain enough control to steer completely clear of all inhabited areas. For some reason my instruments didn't register you in the plant. I . . . I'm really sorry! Holy organlegger! The fire must have burned every stitch of clothing off of you!"

She stared at me, her expression a mixture of awe and shock. *"The flash of lightning—,"* she said.

I hit her with Friendly Smile #4. If I was going to help her, she had to trust me. "Not hardly. I just had a more complex landing than I expected."

"Your fuel tank didn't really rupture all by itself," she said accusingly.

I felt my cheeks getting hot, and it wasn't just the proximity of the fire. I always blush when I tell a lie. "Yes, it did. My ship wrapped itself around an asteroid some megaleagues back."

"You know something, mister? You really are a bad liar," the young lady said as I helped her stand.

"The Boss sure is!" exclaimed Oliver, his eye-stalks stretching close to the girl's body, ostensibly to inspect her wound. "He could charm the last bar of steel from a star lummox, but not if he had to tell a lie!"

"The Space Police had something to do with it," I said tersely, helping her favor her injured foot. "Listen, those sirens are getting too close for comfort. I can help you if you want, but not here. Otherwise, I'm sure the authorities will be glad to assist you."

"That's all right," she said. "I didn't lose my clothing in the fire."

"You didn't? Do all the girls on this island dress like you?"

"Only for religious purposes. Come on, help me run. We can find a hiding place on the other side of the monorail."

We ducked out of sight just as the combined might of the sirens in the vicinity threatened to split my eardrums, and a horde of police, firefighters, and paramedics—accompanied by all manner of people, aliens, and robots—converged on the crash site. The girl, Oliver, and I huddled behind a metal shed next to a deserted factory in the process of being torn down, bit by bit, by a squad of droids. I figured we were safe because the droids' shape and the configurations of blinking lights on their headbands indicated they possessed only the most rudimentary senses and certainly wouldn't take any notice of humans who had strayed into the area.

"Oliver, give me the survival kit."

"Sure thing, Boss," Oliver said, opening up a compartment on his side and taking out the metal box.

"You didn't get this in a fire," I said, as I put a medicine on the wound that would first stop the bleeding, then accelerate her natural healing processes.

"Of course not. Mother did that," she said proudly.

"Some mother," said Oliver, rubbing the indentation below his mouth that served as his chin. "Does she wear black leather and tie people up a lot?"

Yangtze laughed and quickly gave us a rundown of her activities of the evening. Naturally I'd encountered some peculiar religious and social customs in my day—the most recent being those of the humans inhabiting the Transcendenticon cities—but previously I had always thought such openly savage religious practices occurred only in the most technologically underdeveloped societies. I was particularly horrified at what Yangtze's mother had done after cutting her own daughter. "Holy Soldon," I said with a whistle. "An innocent man died for no reason."

"It was just his *karma*," said Oliver sagely, with a nod and wink that weren't so sage.

"It was Marie's way of making room for you," said Yangtze.

"I like Oliver's explanation better. Besides, I don't plan on being here that long. Oliver and I have a mission of galactic importance to perform, and then we've got to be on our way. We're in dutch with the Stellar Patrol."

"Ah, I think I know the syndrome," said Yang-tze. "You're defying the express orders of your superiors in order to save the galaxy, not because you're a hero, but because your principles won't permit you an easy out. Right?"

"Right," I said.

"I'm not sure principles have a lot to do with it," said Oliver. "Desperation is more like it."

"How did you know?" I asked her.

"My old man used to be a Union secret agent. He retired here several years ago because he wanted to spend his last days drinking the illegal elixirs of youth in as pure an atmosphere of moral ambiguity and decay as the galaxy had to offer."

"So he lives here on . . . on . . ."

"Aurelian," she said.

"A bona fide retired secret agent on our side could come in handy, Boss," said Oliver.

"Yes, if we could trust him," I said, rubbing the salve on Yangtze's belly. She was a little young for me to view her as a woman, but even so, touching her disturbed me. I gave her the tube and, ignoring her look of disappointment, said, "Here, you put on the second layer. The bleeding's already stopped anyway."

"What's this fizzing? It tickles."

"That's because it's cleaning the wound too."

"Will it work on my foot?" she asked, already applying it. Obviously she was the impulsive type.

"Sure."

"Hey, it feels great!"

"Yeah, some people get addicted to it," said Oliver. "Three guys on the ship always check out the computer records to see if anyone's been requisitioning suspicious amounts."

"Interesting," she said. "We don't have narcs here."

"Why not?" I asked.

"Because everybody's interested in some high or another. What difference does it make if it comes from within you or without you?"

"I suppose this is an aspect of the moral ambiguity you referred to."

"I suppose," she said, standing and turning around, tightening her buttocks. "Am I bruised?"

"Doesn't bother me!" exclaimed Oliver. "I like you anyway!"

"Ah, it appears that way. Just apply the salve yourself."

"I'll volunteer!" said Oliver, moving forward with his hands outstretched.

I pressed my hand down hard on his head, holding him stationary as his exhaust pipe puffed out little curls of white smoke. "Steady, big fella! What the hell's on your mind, anyway?"

"What do you think?" he said, exasperated.

"You're a robot!"

"True, but my mind's been playing pubescent tricks on me lately!"

"I can see that, Mr. Holy Spectre, and we'll investigate these matters as soon as we have the chance. But for the moment I think you'd better restrain yourself."

"Anything you say, Rose, but I must warn you, I feel a surge of independence coming on."

"So what else is new?"

Having finished repairing the damage done to her backside, Yangtze stood on her toes and looked over her shoulder at me, her eyelids fluttering. "How do I look?"

"Pretty terrific," I said, "but I must warn you, I've got a cellulite fetish."

"Too bad," she said, blushing. "You're pretty."

"Thanks."

"Do you have something I can wear?"

"Don't do it, Boss! This is an important formative experience for me!"

I gave Yangtze my shirt. It hung down past her thighs, and with belated modesty she pulled the back between her legs and tied it to the front with a spacer's knot. "Thanks. You're a spaceman and a gentleman."

"So who's your old man?" Oliver asked, with his usual lack of diplomatic flair.

"He doesn't have a real name, or at least he doesn't use it. He goes by his old code name."

"Oh? And what's that?" I asked.

"00π," Yangtze answered nonchalantly.

"Be still, my magnithruster!" Oliver exclaimed, wobbing precariously. He barely managed to keep his balance as he added, "I thought he disappeared uncountable chrons ago!"

"He did," said Yangtze. "He just disappeared to Aurelian."

"Hmm. I think you're right for once, Oliver. 00π's assistance, if he's willing to give it, would be invaluable."

"Really?" asked Yangtze. "He's always telling me these stories about how famous he used to be out in the real galaxy, as he calls it, but something about them always seems so exaggerated, I tend not to believe him."

"I don't know what he was like personally," I said. "The Union doesn't permit its secret operatives to be interviewed by hypernews services and the like, but judging just from what leaked out about his exploits during his active tenure, he probably doesn't need to stretch the truth much."

"Did he really decimate nitrous, brain-sucking

globules from the Dark Dimension?" Oliver asked. "Huh? Huh?"

Yangtze shrugged doubtfully. "That's what he says."

"And what about those Com Symps? Did he really throw their economic system into chaos by introducing mutated green apples as a food staple? Did he really invent a weapon that made the warlike drillheads rust, and did he really—?"

"Enough, Oliver," I said. "I think we both get the picture."

"Oh wow," said Yangtze with admiration in her eyes that certainly wasn't directed toward either of us. "Pops really was a hero! I can't believe it."

"I take it he seems average enough these days?" I asked.

"He's fallen on hard times."

"Too bad," Oliver said sincerely.

"Don't get me wrong. He's still looking for solar sails to blast at, and I'm sure he's far more than a shadow of his former self," Yangtze said. "I'll take you to him."

"That would be most kind of you," I said.

"Yeah, well, Mom won't like it, but that's too bad. I've got a few soyburgers to square with her anyway."

Suddenly a bright light stabbed out of the sky. A chopper hovered overhead, the beam of its spotlight shining directly at us. The rotors scattered the dust around our feet, and the light kept us firmly in the view of the pilot and passenger as the chopper descended for a landing.

"Come on—let's go!" Oliver urged.

"Why?" I asked. "We haven't done anything wrong—and by now the authorities should have decided that whoever was piloting that pod died in the crash."

Yangtze *aargghed* in frustration. "Don't you realize who they are? They're the Brain Police!"

"Is one missing?" said Oliver.

"If so, I think I know who's got it," I replied.

Yangtze balled her hands into fists and beat the air. "You don't understand! It's not how much you've got, it's how you use it that concerns them!"

"In that case, Boss, you've got nothing to worry about."

"Remind me to be your character witness someday."

Yangtze grabbed my elbow to pull me away, but by then it was already too late. Both the pilot and the passenger got out and walked toward us into the light. They were huge men with square chins and barrel-shaped chests. Obviously steroid junkies. Their uniforms consisted of transparent plexiglas helmets with antennae and wafer-thin electronic equipment on the left side, shiny black boots and jodhpurs, and heavily starched brown shirts with padded shoulders that accentuated their ridiculous muscular development. They had huge ray guns holstered at each hip and carried metal truncheons I could have sworn were notched, an observation I was certain boded ill for the immediate future.

"Hi!" I said, with a friendly wave.

They stopped a few meters from us and glanced at one another. It was one of those looks that mean something only to the participants. When they looked back at us, they smiled woodenly. "Hi," they said in unison.

"You are Yangtze Derringer," said the pilot, holding his hand over the apparatus in his helmet, "but I fail to register the brain scans of your companions. They must not be natives of this island."

"We just dropped in for a visit," said Oliver. "Oops. Bad choice of words, huh, Boss?"

The other policeman crossed his arms and tapped

his foot. "Yes, Computer Central has received a report from the Space Police on you. Fortunately, our institution has no formal extradition treaty with that organization, and so we may pursue a variety of options at this juncture."

"Yes, we work for competing barons," said the pilot. "Otherwise we would have no choice but to incarcerate you."

"Uh, forgive me, but I'm not familiar with the social customs here," I said. "You mean you do have a choice?"

They said nothing, but their silence, as it lengthened, became very meaningful.

"Give them something!" Yangtze whispered.

"But I don't have anything!" I whispered back.

Yangtze reached out with the tube of salve. "Here, take this, it's the best we've got."

They stared at it. The pilot's eyes grew bigger, while the other maintained a strict poker face.

"Here, have the whole survival kit," said Oliver.

They stared at it too, but did not move.

"It's got a towel in it," I said. For some reason, the Union insisted towels be included in every survival kit. "Not to mention all sorts of Union equipment that should fetch a pretty credit on the black market," I added, hoping there was a black market for Union equipment.

"It's a deal," said the pilot, taking the tube as the other took the kit. Then without so much as a thank-you or a by-your-leave, they turned and walked away, examining their ill-gotten gains as if we no longer existed.

"Bye," I said, with a friendly wave.

"And get those brain scans registered at the earliest opportunity," said the pilot offhandedly as he climbed back into the chopper. "You know what to do!"

"What does he mean by that?" I asked. The light blinked out and we watched the chopper rise silently into the night.

"Anyone with the right connections can have their brain patterns illegally secreted into Computer Central," explained Yangtze. "Most block kings order it done, for a price. They can order the patterns rearranged, too. It's one of the ways they maintain their control over residents of their districts, especially the ones who don't subscribe to all the belief systems."

"Why are the Brain Police so interested in keeping a steady supply of painkillers and towels?" asked Oliver.

"You would be too, if you'd spent a lifetime drying yourself in a radiation shower. When these guys find themselves some contraband water, they're going to have a good old time."

"So who do the Brain Police work for?" I asked.

"Actually, they're officially independent, but the majority of their funding is arranged by Baron Hardehar Cohen. Different barons fund different police groups, but naturally there's a lot of co-operation between them, especially in terms of corruption."

"I take it this Hardehar Cohen's a Nipponese surrogate?" I asked.

"You could say that, though he's far more of a hedonist than any Nipponese could ever hope to be. He's not as popular as most barons, but he's so wealthy and powerful that he has to be respected. He's an enemy of disorganized religion. Says it destroys worker productivity. 'A narrow mind is a satisfied mind,' he's supposed to say, often."

"I know a few admirals who'd agree with that. Come on, let's find 00π," I said.

"Okay, but remember: *The flash of lightning ar-*

rives from a turbulent sea of mist, yet is apt to die upon solid ground." quoted Yangtze.

"We all arrived from a sea of mist," I said. "Especially when you consider the stellar mists that form stars and solar systems. So you see, Yangtze, like most sayings of that sort, your goddess's words were vague enough to be applicable to any situation you choose to apply them to."

"Maybe, but you must admit, your arrival does seem to fit the bill."

"We'll see. I have no intention of dying, either on solid ground or in a vacuum. Now where's your old man?"

"I think tonight he should be at his nightclub. We should be able to get in without having to pay a cover charge."

"Sure you're up to it? From what you've told me, you've had a long night so far."

Yangtze grinned. Her teeth were white and straight, and while that grin lent her an air of incredible purity, there was a mischievous glint in her eyes that could not be denied. "Are you serious, Homer Hunter? The night is young—indubitably, undeniably, fantastically young!"

Chapter Four
Scientific Delirium Madness

T HE MASSIVE IN-
sect stood with stooped shoulders at the corner of a
building, holding out a tin cup in one pair of pinchers
to every entity who passed by. He was probably naked, but with his kind it was hard to tell. In any case,
his body was scaled with intricate, dull red and blue
patterns, and his wings glimmered with bright waves
of maize and black. He had a single orange compound eye in the center of his head, and a single
segmented antennae rose from the top of his skull
like an open jack-in-the-box.

Oliver sped slightly ahead of Yangtze and me
and plopped down a few coins in the insect's cup,
which the creature acknowledged gratefully.

"Where did those come from?" I asked. "Have
you been holding out on me?"

"Not really," said Oliver with a shrug. "They
were just in a secret compartment that was a secret
even from me. Evidently I was programmed to know
about it only when the need arose. It arose, so I paid
up."

"Any more credits where those came from?" I
demanded.

"Plenty. Here. Have some pocket change."

I tried not to notice Yangtze smiling as I took the credits and stared at them with wide eyes. "Oliver, I've taken you apart piece by piece, but I never saw this secret compartment before."

"Well, Boss, if you could discover it just by taking me apart, then it wouldn't be much of a secret compartment, would it?"

"Do your fellow models have these compartments?" I asked.

Oliver gestured helplessly. "How am I supposed to know? You know I never associate with those types."

"Oliver," I said seriously, "how many other secrets have you been keeping from me?"

Yangtze laughed, took me by the arm, and led me down the street. "By the sacred googolplex, you don't want there to be any mysteries at all in life, do you?"

Oliver rolled past us and waved. "Besides, Boss, I promise I'll be the first to tell you about my secrets—as soon as I find out about them!" He disappeared around a corner.

"Now where is he off to?" I exclaimed.

"Relax, you big lug," said Yangtze. "I gave him the co-ordinates of our destination. He's going ahead of us to check out the security."

"You sure?"

"Hmmmm. It was his idea. He seemed eager to go once I mentioned there would be loose women and illicit substances present."

"Terrific." Once again, I was temporarily deserted by my theoretically faithful robot companion. This seemed as good a time as any to access my situation, to refresh my memory on the points that had gotten me onto this space island in search of my disembodied friend Floyd, and to attempt to plot a course of action. But all that impressed me as being incredibly boring, so I attempted to picture those I had left behind to the cold, insensitive devices of the Space Police. That is to say, I attempted to picture Reina. I couldn't help but wonder who she was infatuating now. Strangely, though, another face kept getting in the way, the face of Colonel Coryban. I had to concentrate to keep Reina's face in mental focus. One thing, though: no matter who I was seeing, the eyes remained the same.

"Wake up, big boy," said Yangtze at my side. "You're in the midst of a brave new world for moderns."

She was right about that. I believe she wanted to engage me in conversation, but at the moment I was too overwhelmed even for small talk. This section of Aurelian, half slum, half entertainment district, was a dizzying kaleidoscope of sights and smells, sounds and stimulations. Everywhere indications of the people's quasi-religious fervor were in evidence. A naked, ancient holy man wallowed in an oil slick in the middle of the street. A green-scaled alien with crimson, glazed eyes puffed a reefer that emitted a cloud of yellow smoke. A street musician played a guitar with tentacles, and sang through an immense proboscis. A round-faced man with a hairy belly button peeking from the mound beneath his shirt glanced furtively about, then led a squat creature with skinny, boneless arms and single thick eyestalk atop her headless torso into a basement bar and grill with a distinctively seedy atmosphere.

"Jeez, what kind of pervert is that?" I wondered.

"The shy kind," Yangtze replied.

A glowing skeleton man from Androgyny 5 turned cartwheels around four red-robed priests. A Brain Police person paid for a baggie of purple powder with a credit card. Wearing only a blue plastic loin covering, a street shaman shook a rattling monkey wrench at passersby, condemning them for sins even my sophisticated translator was incapable of comprehending. Another shaman, clad in a glittering jockstrap and sporting a band of yellow feathers about his liver-spotted head, threw golden dust into the air. Three young priestesses wearing gray robes with phallic red spaceships sewn on the backs sang a restrained madrigal just before they entered a casino. Three female children sprinkled metal shavings from a hoverfloat with a masthead shaped like the serene face of their god; the girls didn't seem to mind that their hands were bleeding. A scientist with cybernetic vocal chords proclaimed in ultrahigh frequencies his devotion—either to the gods or to a nearby female with tracts of land so huge you could smother in them, it was difficult to tell which. A stern, long-faced man, wearing a crooked black stovepipe hat and a somber black jacket, tap-danced to swinging inner music; the taps of his shoes sparkled with the colors of the rainbow. Their skin baked and sooty, four emaciated, naked philosophers sat on a street grille with divine ecstasy mirrored in their eyes. A man with a brain doped up by a powerpack at his hip swayed drunkenly into a streetlamp.

"I grew up on these streets," Yangtze said, her eyes misty with sentimentality, her face bathed in neon light. "Home sweet home."

Yeah, well, I felt as if I'd taken a wrong turn since entering the Nipponese system. If there was any proof to the age-old maxim that reality was something you made up from the pieces of a shattered dream that had once upon a time, maybe, made sense, then the space island of Aurelian was the star stuff old maxims were made of. No matter where I looked, no matter what I saw, I couldn't help feeling that at any moment a wind machine would switch on full blast and all the building fronts would fall over back-

wards like a row of stage flats. I was certain, too, this
was an entirely justified paranoia, derived from base
instinct and from keen insight into the layers of being
just beyond the doors of perception.

Furthermore, despite the presence of a nubile
young female with warm hands at my side, I had the
distinct impression I wasn't exactly welcome here.
People looked at me. People, aliens . . . and things.
Things like a mechanical wasp that kept buzzing by,
taking snapshots of me with a tiny camera. Things
like two white orbs peeking out from under the upraised lid of a trash receptacle, and a digital scanner
running parallel to my movements along the edges of
the rooftops. Slithering reptiles gave me a wide berth.
Canine men growled suspiciously. A cylindroid deflated to two-dimensional mode until I passed by. A
creature resembling a red basketball with feet bounced
merrily down the street until he came close to me, then
bounced high overhead in a panic. Meanwhile, human and humanoid mumbled among themselves while
glaring at me. And the Brain Police spoke tensely into
their portable radios while hastily scribbling notes.

Yangtze seemed blissfully unaware of this. I had
the impression she was only too happy to be holding
the elbow of a mature male. She yammered on and
on, touching on many subjects I'm sure would have
embarrassed me if I'd been paying close attention.
She was a romantic of the most brutally frank sort.
Someday soon she was going to make soygrits out of
some poor, lucky boy.

As for me personally, I couldn't be sure if Aurelian
was saying what it meant, or if it meant what it
said—but I had my suspicions. As I was analyzing
the situation, the beings around us suddenly pointed
in our direction, screamed, and ran away as fast as
their feet, or other suitable appendages, could take
them.

No, my fly's zipped, I observed as Yangtze looked behind us at the wall, in the general direction where the others were pointing. At the moment I preferred to take the psychic waves of fear emanating from the fleeing crowd with a shaker of saltpeter, because, frankly, I had been so lost in my philosophical ruminations that even the boldest brushstroke of reality was questionable. Which was why I grabbed hold of my zipper and pulled it up, even though I knew perfectly well that it was fastened about as securely as it could be. I looked behind me. Then I followed Yangtze's gaze upward.

Up, up, up.

To the top of the brick wall.

Where a head was forming, the nose, forehead, and two triangular ears stretched out from the level plane. The mouth, its teeth made from the white cement between the bricks, opened. **Lump have bad attitude toward you,** said a voice that perhaps originated in the wall, or perhaps originated instead from the very bowels of the space island. The voice reverberated off the artificial sky and shook the ground beneath my feet; it rumbled in my very marrow. **Lump demonstrate his bad attitude in most painfully obvious way possible.**

"Run!" exclaimed Yangtze, trying to pull me along. All she succeeded in doing, however, was tripping against the curb. She fell down and almost took me with her.

Two fists formed below the head, quickly followed by the formation of arms and shoulders. The fists reached out from the wall. Each fist opened into four thick, twitching fingers.

Toward the ground, a knee stretched out from the brick plane and became part of a leg. It was already in the process of stepping toward us when another leg appeared. The Lump looked about, looked at its hands and its legs and then at the sky. It reached toward the sky as if to grab one of the other space islands glowing there like a bauble. **Free—free at last,** it said. **Free to get down, to boogaloo, to impose my destructive will upon the universe at large.**

Even after the Lump was three-quarters distinct, it was apparent that its torso and the wall would remain connected via a wide brick umbilical cord. This would have been a positive development had it not become apparent that the cord was elastic—the bricks stretched, and when they could stretch no further, more bricks materialized somehow, from somewhere.

The Lump had been distracted by its freedom for only a few moments when it looked down and noticed us. **What? Motes run away? How gauche!**

"So sue us!" I said, helping Yangtze to stand. Then to her I said, "I think we'll just lose ourselves in the rest of the crowd." A quick glance informed me that the crowd had other ideas—it was already a safe distance away. Only the brave and the curious lingered near us. Once Yangtze could run—she had twisted her ankle, but was too considerate to lean on me overmuch—I bolted, half carrying her along.

Unfortunately, general circumstances prevented me from bolting more than a few steps.

The exact circumstances had to do with the metal pole that materialized directly in front of me, and the fact that I ran smack into it.

I made a grab for the pole as I fell. I missed. I didn't miss the ground, however. I was lucky my brains didn't splatter against the macadam.

"We're trapped!" Yangtze exclaimed.

Big deal, I thought.

I watched the curved row of metal poles waver in and out of focus. One chron they were only a few centimeters apart, and then the next they were kilometers apart. I was on the verge of passing out for a millennium or two.

Yangtze knelt beside me. She slapped my face again and again, pausing only to shake me. "Homer, wake up! Stand up and run!"

Gradually the cobwebs cleared to reveal that a tiny dwarf was carving out a homestead with a itty-bitty icepick in the back of my skull. My voice resonated between my ears, its vibrations rattling my pea-sized brain within the otherwise hollow cavity. "I'll run, but . . . do I have to stand?"

The shadow that fell over us forced me to find the strength. Getting up on my knees, I refused Yangtze's assistance as I gathered myself for the push upright. I made it. Then I promptly fell against the row of poles. I noted the row made a neat half-circle, with the side of the building the diameter. Even if I could run, there was nowhere to go.

"Hi," I said, looking up into the monstrous face of the Lump peering down at me.

So you are the creature whose presence so gravely offends my soul, said the Lump.

"Is it my breath? I mean, I know I need to wash up, but I was planning on doing that anyway."

Your frivolity is but a mask to disguise your true malevolence against the balance.

"Says who? Who sent you anyway? Why have you emerged for me?"

Lump not care. Lump only knows the fires of change must be stoked only by the hands that have forged them. Lump only knows the Union does not belong to the pattern. The Union is not order; it is disorder. The Union must not fall, but neither must it stand. Lump said this without apparent animosity toward me, but as he spoke he interlocked his hands into one gigantic fist and brought it down with all his might.

So disoriented was I that for a while it seemed the fist was taking its own sweet time coming down. I think Yangtze screamed—I couldn't be sure. My instincts took over at the last possible nanochron and I ducked—just in time.

The fist opened a huge fissure in the street. The Lump's pinkies also cracked, and it cried **Owww!** and straightened up. The Lump opened his hands to stare in amazement as the cracks spread and his pinkies started to crumble apart.

So—you will not submit easily to the inevitable, said the Lump, his cement-white eyes glowering.

"Why should I?" I said, laughing. "You're such a klutz."

"Homer, don't get it mad!" warned Yangtze.

I laughed again. "What difference would it make?"

Lump not have to tolerate this! the brick creature exclaimed, raising a foot over my head.

I rolled out of the way and dashed behind the creature, then crawled under the brick coil connecting it to the building and stood against the wall while it looked around for me. So far it had expressed little interest in Yangtze, but she was still just as trapped, and presumably she was in equal danger. I signalled her to stay far away just before I avoided a foot stomp.

Lump chastise you severely, it said, making a grab for me with a crumbling hand. I avoided that hand quite easily, but unfortunately I ran directly into the other. The fingers wrapped themselves around me and I felt my feet lift off the ground. **Lump make you suffer for breaking the pattern.**

"Homer—do something!" Yangtze called.

"Good idea! What?"

The creature leered as it held me in both hands

and brought me closer to its face. Beyond those cement-white teeth was an exquisite absence of light.

I struggled and struggled, yet all my efforts accomplished was to provide a good excuse for those crumbling fingers to tighten against me. The universe swirled around me and I realized my rib cage was about to collapse.

Ah, soon your blood shall flow freely around my fingers, and your every nerve will scream with intense, unimaginable, unforgettable, mindnumbing, torturous agony.

"Not if I pass out first," I gasped.

It will smart, too.

Suddenly the smell of burning sulphur enveloped the proceedings. The Lump's grip loosened almost imperceptibly, but it was enough for my rib cage to experience a semblance of relief and for me to suck in another tiny breath. I looked down and what should I see but a fat guy in whiteface and a clown outfit, with a big red nose and a bright orange skullcap. The outfit consisted of baggy white-with-black polka-dot pants, a chartreuse shirt with a ruffled collar and ruffled sleeves, and big flat shoes. The guy leapt over the poles one-handed, leaving his other hand free to throw some sort of white powder to the ground. Yellow smoke carrying more of that sulphurous stench resulted.

Now so far, I'd had no indication the Lump could breathe. Its chest had remained unmoving regardless of its actions. But once that yellow smoke reached the vicinity of its head, it whispered a barely-audible **Aaarrgghh!** and clutched a hand to its throat.

The Lump eased up enough on the pressure for me to wriggle from its crumbling grip. Quickly I freed my right foot entirely and used it to its fullest advantage—by kicking as many bricks as possible from the wrist.

"Careful!" screamed Yangtze, dodging a few.

If the clown had any reaction to my efforts, he managed to keep it as invisible as his other emotions. The grin beneath his greasepaint, though real, was as fixed and eerie as the grin on a man dead for a thousand chrons. Once the clown had landed on the ground within the barrier, he whipped out a metal stick from a hidden pocket, flicked it twice like a magician's wand, and lo!—out popped a wheel with pedals. He balanced the wheel on the ground, produced a leather seat from yet another hidden pocket, and put them together to create a unicycle. He hopped on and commenced to pedal madly in a circle around the writhing Lump, reaching into the depths of a leather sack slung over his shoulder to toss out more handfuls of the exploding white powder.

And with every explosion of smoke, the Lump's contortions grew more violent. It fell to its knees and almost toppled the clown by accident. But the clown was an expert unicycle rider and avoided the Lump's knees at the last possible instant.

Lump not pleased with this poison! the creature whispered. **Lump chew you cell by cell. Lump spit out your heart and shit out your brains and then stomp on them!**

The clown laughed. He wheeled the unicycle around to a spinning stop, reached into his bag of tricks one last time, and then paused long enough to wink at Yangtze who looked away haughtily. The clown brought out a huge handful of shimmering blue powder and threw it at the Lump. It arced to the ground between the creature's feet and exploded in a cloud of black smoke. Suddenly I felt like I was being blasted in the face with the heat of an atomic furnace. The fingers crumbled of their own accord and I fell, none the worse for the impact because I was already lost in the ozone.

I stared at a piece of gravel until I saw my hand, which appeared to be connected to an arm that reached a thousand kilometers away. Beyond that the brick creature knelt, the stumpy fingers of both hands clutching at its throat as if it was actually gagging on that black smoke.

The brick creature turned to look at me. Its hollow black eyes widened. Its mouth moved but it made no sound.

The Lump fell. For a moment my distorted perspective made me think it was going to fall right on top of me, but since I was too groggy to move, it was well my perspective turned out to be wrong. The brick creature crashed to the ground and began to fall apart. The cord connecting it to the building also began crumbling.

And during that brief instant, the clown on the unicycle whizzed past me. He raced up one of the Lump's arms and across his back—and then up, up, up into the air, hurtling over the metal poles like the most experienced of stunt drivers.

Clown and unicycle landed perfectly and, without looking back, disappeared around a corner at full speed.

"Who the hell was that masked man?" I gasped as Yangtze helped me stand.

"That was no masked man," said Yangtze as she helped me stand. "That was his real face, or as real a face as a shaman ever has."

"All right, so who was that shaman?"

"He's known simply as the Anti-Curly. Works for a block king who's allied with my own."

"That's nice. Is that why he helped us?"

"No. That pile of brick dust on the ground used to be a building *hoodoo*, that is, a building possessed by a demon. The Anti-Curly is sworn to fight and destroy such demons wherever and whenever they may appear."

"What a swell guy. Shall we ever see his like again?"

"I hope not. He's totally unpredictable. You never know who or what he's going to exorcise next. Come on, let's get out of here before the crowd returns and the Brain Police decide we were personally responsible for this mess."

Looking at the huge hole in the wall, I couldn't help but agree. I wondered if the Aurelians had *hoodoo* insurance, or if such incidents were simply written off as Acts of Demons.

"It sure was a lucky thing for us the Anti-Curly happened to show up when he did," I said, as Yangtze, singing *Hoodoo, who do you think you are?*, led me around the corner opposite the one the Anti-Curly had taken, and onto a street leading to a subway entrance.

"Luck had nothing to do with it," she replied. "Didn't you hear what the Lump said about your presence busting up the pattern?"

"Why, yes. It specifically mentioned my Union affiliation, little realizing that my affiliation at the moment is dicey at best."

"Don't kid yourself. Whatever's going on here, you're a Union player. One thing about Aurelian, Homer, everything's balanced here. Pleasure is balanced by pain, love by hate, passion by indifference, bravery by cowardice, and life by death."

"Yeah, I kinda noticed that."

"And good's usually balanced by evil, when you can tell the two apart, that is. The gods balance their actions as well. They can show you love or they can show you hatred. It's all the same to them, and they feel you should be grateful for the attention. Anyway, a *hoodoo* attack presents us with a definite indication that someone mightily tapped into the essence of the Aurelian worldsoul is anxious about your presence. That someone's messing with the balance of power, and he doesn't like the direction you might tip the scales."

"Yangtze, this is all mystical mumbo jumbo. I'm here to rescue the trapped mind of a dead robot."

"Hmmm. Now *that's* the pragmatic mission of a realistic individual. In the future I'll stick to mysticism, thank you."

"All right, let's assume that what you say is true. Let's say someone mucking with the balance of power on this space island wants to get rid of me. How do I find out who he is?"

"Beats me. You'll have to ask a deity. But they tend not to talk to those who don't believe. I mean, they'll kill, torture, or maim a nonbeliever, but they won't talk to one."

"Think it would help if I made a sacrifice?" I asked sarcastically.

"It might," Yangtze replied, in all seriousness.

This someone messing with the balance might know how to get at the mind of Floyd, I observed. Indeed, the mysterious someone might have already made some arrangements to prevent Floyd from contacting me. Even Floyd's single message since I entered this system—*"Use the Farce!"*—could be part of some clever ploy to misdirect me. As of yet I had no idea what the Farce might be, but I was willing to bet a certain Anti-Curly was locked into it.

Yangtze led me down an escalator. The stone walls of the subway corridor were painted with an extended tableau. According to the story on these walls, humanoid gods with the faces of aliens had once existed, along with the rest of the matter of the universe, in a single point of space. Apparently one male had expressed a profound admiration for a fe-

male already committed to another, thus precipitat-
ing a series of altercations that ultimately resulted in
the explosion known as the Big Bang. Whether or not
anyone actually believed in this particular story, I
cannot say because I never had the nerve to ask; I
was too afraid the answer might be yes.

The story did not indicate what form the gods
might have taken after the Big Bang. The next in-
stallment must have been at the next stop; but by
then my mind had already been distracted by other
matters. There I was, a passenger on a magnetic
subway car, sitting next to an idol worshipper who
was completely naked except for my shirt and who
claimed to be the daughter of one of the most famous
heroes of the Third Union, and I couldn't stop thinking about that so-called *hoodoo*. "It's impossible," I
said. "The whole episode was impossible. There's no
way that brick could have moved the way it did."

"But it did. That's the nature of *hoodoo*," said
Yangtze patiently. "When the spirit's willing, so is
matter."

"Sorry, but I need a more thorough explanation
than that. I saw those bricks materialize out of nothingness. I can't exactly describe the process, mind
you, but I know that when the Lump was fully formed,
there were more bricks on that side of the wall than
there were before, and that's supposed to be impossible!"

"I notice you said 'supposed to be.' "

"I only say that because my rib cage is in tremendous pain."

Yangtze shrugged with a sly smile. "That's what
any shaman worth his salt will tell you—even the
Anti-Curly. The *hoodoos* are real, very real. Don't get
me wrong on that. But the *hoodoos* also exist only in
the mind. It's because we believe in them that they
are able to cause us pain, and even to make more

bricks appear out of nothingness when they are needed."

"But you're making one mistake. I didn't believe in the *hoodoo*, so how could it have affected me?"

"But you believe now."

"That's only because it almost crushed me and because when it disintegrated, it left a big hole in a wall."

"And that is all the belief that's necessary."

"But . . . but . . . you're saying I helped make the *hoodoo* real before the fact of my actually believing in it. That's . . . that's a retrogressive conceptual syllogism! *Ex post facto!* I don't believe—the *hoodoo* tried to beat me into a pulp—therefore I must have believed all along!"

Yangtze shrugged again. "You'll get used to that sort of thing after you've spent enough time on Aurelian." She bent down to pick up a half-smoked reefer someone had left the floor. The green alien with the compound eyes and the tiny yellow beak in the seat across the aisle from us looked envious for a moment, then he pulled out his own reefer. Yangtze fluttered her eyes and leaned over the aisle. "Got a light?"

As he kindly lit her reefer, the alien said something to Yangtze I couldn't quite catch.

"On that beak? No way!" she replied, coughing smoke into his face. She plopped back on the chair next to me. "Some entities just have no respect for us humans! I've never actually done it with an alien, but he's at least going to have to take me out to dinner first!"

"I agree," I said. "I think it's very important for women to maintain high standards."

"You're not a liberal!" Yangtze said accusingly. "You're a prude!"

I let her remark pass, mainly because she was

half right. I settled back comfortably in my chair and let my mind wander, staring at the other passengers. A bald lady with a red-green scalp droned a chant at a scintillating gyroscope floating centimeters above her two hairy hands. An immensely fat man floated beside her, reading a newspaper. I think they were together. Beyond them a black-and-white man who emitted light in negative frequencies read a newspaper, while a creature that looked like a cross between a head of lettuce and a carrot absently shuffled a deck of Tarot cards. I didn't have the courage to look behind me, but I did hear someone talking in rattling noises and being answered, heatedly, by someone who sounded like an out-of-tune organ. My translator had difficulty mastering the meaning of their communications.

Later, after we'd gotten off the subway and had walked back up to the street, a screaming vegetable man ran past us, bleeding human blood as if he was suffering from a bad case of the stigmata blues.

"Ah, yes, the Tenderloin," said Yangtze, staring misty-eyed into the neon lights.

Chapter Five
Oddballs Out

"**H**OMER, I'D LIKE to introduce you to Scorpion Mandando, a friend of my father's."

Yangtze gestured to the space-game hunter with the shrunken head on his shoulders, sitting at a table in the back of the club sucking his meal through a straw. He wore a crimson, skin-tight space suit, big boots, heavy gloves, and ribbons of bones and fangs on his sleeves and chest. Though his head was only a fifth of what it should have been, a full-sized space helmet rested on the table next to his meal.

"I say, old bean," the man called Scorpion Mandando replied in a sqeaky voice, standing up to give me a robust handshake, "you must be Homer B. Hunter."

"Why, yes," I said. "How did you know?"

"Well, it didn't require ESP," he said conspiratorially, his beady little eyes darting back and forth. "The truth is, I've been informed, through secretive sources who prefer to remain anonymous, that your robot's been sighted on these very premises, flirting with waitresses."

"Poor women. Where's the scamp now?"

Scorpion tensed up. "That I cannot say with any degree of certainty. He seems to have disappeared. There's been a lot of curious activity in this district recently. Maybe he's gotten himself mixed up in it."

"Uh-oh. I bet Oliver's already gotten himself mixed up with my old man, who's doubtlessly in the back, arguing with the staff as usual," said Yangtze dryly. "Am I correct, Scorpion?"

The space hunter with the shrunken head attempted to squeeze a wink from the folds of skin around the right eye. "Surely it's a possibility worth investigating."

"Terrific," she said dryly, turning away.

"Hold it a second!" I said.

She stopped for the briefest instant and smiled mischievously. "Okay." Then she walked away and disappeared behind a nearby purple curtain.

Scorpion offered me a chair and said, "Forgive me if I seem unduly forward, but you're probably wondering what happened to my head."

The skin was charcoal black, and only scattered tufts of white hair remained on his skull. His lips were blood red and his ears had shriveled to practically nothing. I tried not to frown as I tried not to throw up. "Nawww. I've seen worse."

He smiled, his mouth contorting strangely because his teeth hadn't quite shrunk proportionately. "You don't have to coddle me. I appreciate frankness in all things. Those who become my friends get used to seeing my hideous mockery of a face after a while. Furthermore, the more open-minded ladies don't seem to mind."

"Uh, did you say ladies?"

"Yes, as in women." And he made an obscene gesture indicating the sort of activity he and open-minded ladies indulged in.

I arched my eyebrows.

"I can see, sir, by the cut of your fatigues, that you are a Union Man," he said testily. "Normally I would immediately appreciate that—immensely. On the other hand, should you reveal yourself to be a stiff-necked Union prude with a hyperthruster stuffed up his posterior, then, sir, I don't mind telling you that I shall be extremely disappointed. Yes, sir, extremely disappointed."

"Just keep a cool head on your shoulders. It's just that I'd assumed you'd be a two-bagger. You know, in addition to putting a bag over your head, your partner would put one over hers, in case yours broke."

A nearby crystal creature moved away with a suspicious glance at us as Scorpion threw back his tiny head and laughed heartily in high-pitched tones. "Ha-ha! That's very good! I'll remember that the next time I meet a shy one. You see, sir, while I may be in my current state a barker in the most profound sense, you must recall what they say about Aurelian. All aspects of life are balanced here. Life against death, beauty against ugliness, believers against non-believers, idealists against cynics—and size against size. Know what I mean? Nod-nod-wink-wink-say-no-more!"

"Ah, yes, but you know something, Scorpion? I'm still wondering."

"Oh, about how I got this way? A block king had a curse put on me. That's all, and that was enough. It is my personal belief that the gentleman was over-reacting. All I did was kiss a girl," he added with a shrug. I was afraid his neck was so rotten his head might fall off. "Of course, the fact that it was his daughter possibly explains his ungentlemanly reaction. I don't really mind. It hasn't adversely affected my health, and I'm tired of gallivanting around the galaxy in search of trophies. Thankfully, 00π's something of a folk hero here, and the people request his

assistance straightening out their personal conflicts;
he's kept me occupied on a few local missions—finding
the missing, the wanted, the occasional stolen item,
things of that nature. It's not the same as hunting
Banths on the snow-capped mountains of Capistrono,
or contraband Fuzzies on Zarathustra, but there's a
certain magician I'd like to have in my sights one
day, if you divine my meaning."

"Any chance that you might revert to normal?"

Another shrug. "Sir, I am an optimist, and I
always look forward to tomorrow." Another suck on
the straw. From the smell of it, the paste was soy
raspberry. "I confess, though, my experiences on
Aurelian have forced me to reconsider those axioms
of life I once held most dear. Time was when I looked
down my nose at the superstitious natives of many
worlds with their strange customs and beliefs in magic.
I'd always thought religion was like the arts, that is,
like something man and alien alike invented out of
thin air. Well, heh-heh, I can't really look down my
nose at anything anymore, you grok me?"

"Well, no."

"Come, come, sir. You've been around. Surely
you've wondered if the ether itself hasn't invented
both man and alien, and their religions with them.
Surely you've noticed every world you've ever been
on has its own inherent, unique sense of power. The
primitive entity seeks to control the elements through
a variety of measures, all designed to placate the
spirits and to care for the dead. Now whether or not
the magical means devised on a particular world cre-
ates the laws of the elements or merely adapts to a
pre-existing condition is beside the point. The fact is,
there are levels, my good man. It requires an in-
tensely creative but illogical mind to make the direct
connections between the universe that is and the
unseen universe that also is. These connections are

emotional, frequently intuitive, and are the antithesis of rationality. Surely, though, if you accept the proposition that each world in the galaxy is an organism unto itself, then its interaction with the parasites inhabiting its surface is likely to be beyond the ability of rational minds to comprehend."

"That's quite a mouthful, but I suppose I've sensed it."

"Ah, so you still hedge your bets. The wise course for the uninitiated. Take my word for it, my good Union Man, as long as you are on Aurelian, you might as well give in to the inevitable and acknowledge the existence of gods and goddesses, angels and demons, voodoo and *hoodoos,* not to mention many other things which I swear to you are only now beginning to come to light."

"Do you actually believe worlds are entities of some sort?"

"Of course I believe it. Every time I look in the mirror, I have no choice but to believe. The power is there. It did not ask my opinion if I thought it existed. It merely acted. Think on it, sir. Maybe planets have no minds of their own and are just basically evolving along until intelligent creatures come along. However, if there is any truth to my supposition, then it stands to reason that if the first gods came into existence thanks to the psychic intervention of hunters, farmers, warriors, and their women, then what sorts of gods might spacemen and scientists and factory workers create? Especially on a small world where over a million entities with their own strong minds live. You think there might be enough power on such a world to do this?" And Scorpion pointed a massive, stubby finger at his pathetically tiny head. "I think, sir, the answer is one vaulting dead weight!"

"Forgive me, but I'm certain there must be a

scientific explanation for everything unusual that's
ever happened—including *both* your size changes!"

"Then I wish you the best of luck in your search,
Mr. Hunter. However, before we terminate this part of
the discussion, I prevail upon you to consider the
matter thusly: Here we are in the very midst of
the Tenderloin, that district of the space island
where those who are expressly nonreligious come to
party in their own inimitable style. As a man well
traveled throughout the galaxy, surely the essence
of some hot, hot, hot primitive ceremony still sticks to
your memories. And now I implore you, examine the
activities of these good souls currently inhabiting this
environment and tell me one thing: What's the diff?"

The space hunter had his point. A more blatant
display of joyous decadence it had never before been
my privilege to witness. Through a multilayered haze
of smoke and a tangle of odors so thick it verged on
the visible, I saw a cast of thousands and a host of
others cavorting on a vast expanse of rectangles that
flashed in a multitude of colors. Most were dancing,
while others pushed their way through to tables or
into the throng milling about at the bar. Most were
human enough. But nearly all had their eccentrici-
ties. Some might have been genetically altered at one
time, while others might have voluntarily become
cyborgs, and still others might have had the cybernetic state volunteered upon them. Some, I suspected,
were aliens, and some of those might just have been
aliens in funny costumes. It was difficult to guess
who was deliberately beautiful and who was deliberately ugly. I was particularly impressed by a buxom
lass with blonde hair from the tip of her head to the
pads of her feet; she wore black briefs and a black
ribbon on the end of her tail. An entity with his brain
and most of his major arteries exposed danced with a
lithe neo-archaeopteryx, while nearby a pair of Sia-

mese-fem cyborgs did the frug with a muscle-bound lesbian swordswoman whose brass bra reflected light into my eyes. A Saturnian rock man did the Burmese quickstep with a Saturnian methane woman, whose body was kept in shape by a plastic starch suit. These weirdos and many like them in spirit, if not in form, mingled with the young Aurelian crowd, all punked-out and spiced-out for the duration of the proceedings, and all, to an entity, dancing to the music of a live rock-and-roll band who put down a beat that unfortunately wouldn't quit, supporting a mind-bogglingly simple melody that wouldn't stop either and, worse, threatened to stay in my head for the rest of my life.

"All right, Scorpion, your point is taken. If this isn't a pagan ritual, I don't know what is. Now, who's that band, and is that music they're playing?"

"Ah, that's Spaceside Hodgson and the Ashton Gluons. Pretty heavy stuff, wot?" It turned out he was a fan and knew all their names.

I'm a victim of Beta Decay/Everyone knows I'm here so what the hey? crooned the lead singer as the lead guitarist, who Scorpion informed me was the famous Jive Electro, mimicked the words with a piercing run of notes. Silver and red droplets of light burst into the air from the upper frets of Jive's axe. He had curly black hair topped off with a generic Space Cowboy hat. A cigarette dangled from his mouth. His faded green jumpsuit clung tightly *very* tightly, to a skinny frame bordering on the two-dimensional. Jive Electro looked normal in comparison to most of the crowd, except when you took into account his sharp-edged, metal teeth. At first I figured the women wouldn't care for it when he got too personal, but then I considered the crowd.

The beefy hands of Tiny Habibula banged all over a massive drum kit that yielded a solid back beat as well as sudden yellow and green flashes. The rest of Tiny was beefy too: he hailed from the planet of Sirloin, where the inhabitants were the descendants of genetically altered bovines who had initially been bred for their culinary attributes, but who had then developed—over the objections of the human race—digits, intelligence, and a propensity for playing the blues. Tiny had long horns, wore a ring through his nose, and in between beats gobbled quick bites of oats and hay from a feedbag strapped around his neck.

According to Scorpion, vid-bassist Mike Chane was so enamored of his instrument that he'd had it permanently grafted to his body. He was rumored to be somewhat less enthusiastic now that his social life had been severely curtailed, but you couldn't tell from the spiritual look on his freckled face as he plucked those strings. Semi-circular waves, alternating russet and purple, cascaded from his vid-bassed bod.

Sulphate Eddy, meanwhile, played a rhythm guitar while surrounded by a jagged green aura. He slid back and forth across the stage in invisible high-heeled boots. His slimy head, glistening like a giant slug's on a dew-drenched morn, was just about the most repulsive thing I'd ever seen. Sulphate Eddy often nodded with approval at the notes Yep So Wha (the best the translators could do with his real name, which was spoken on ultrasonic frequencies) coaxed with black tentacles from his array of keyboards. Scorpion confessed it was difficult even for him, a tried-and-true fan, to believe a sensitive id resided somewhere behind the mass of writhing, snakelike filaments comprising the majority of Yep So Wha's face. But in the end I couldn't deny that Yep So Wha's lush but heavy keyboard sound provided conclusive proof that you didn't have to be human to have soul.

I've been detected, I've been defected/My heart radiates love, my chest is about to explode! sang Spaceside. *You ain't never gonna give me no choice/ I'll put on a dress and call myself Joyce/And do do do do the neutrino/Do do do do the neutrino!* Spaceside didn't emanate colors. He didn't have a mike rigged up inside his larynx, the way so many rock singers did (he used an old-fashioned, Second Empire radio mike), and his face was essentially so ordinary, so totally devoid of distinguishing features, that he could doubtless hide from the Brain Police in a mob of accountants on their lunch break. But he had a voice that said it all, even though I was having a little problem figuring out what it meant. He had the unique gift of effortlessly elevating the most trivial lyric into the realms of profound, poetic observation. This in turn gave weight and meaning to the music—which I confess was beginning to grow on me, like a fungus— lending it an aura of studied simplicity that bordered on sophistication. Where the lyric indicated sadness, Spaceside wrenched anguish from his heart and spat it onto the stage. Where the lyric indicated lust, Spaceside sang with a leer in his tone that strongly implied he was on the verge of whipping it out right then and there. Where the lyric indicated existential doom, he pleaded piteously to an uncaring universe, and where the lyric indicated that he should chuck all his worries to the winds and get down to do do do do the neutrino, he sprang about the stage like a ricochetting rabbit. He swang from Tiny's massive gong, he played air guitar while walking backwards, he shook tha' thang, he twicked Yep So Wha's writhing face, and he plucked a young vixen with luminous breasts from the crowd before the stage and planted a long, passionate kiss on her mouth.

"Great show, eh, Boss?" Oliver asked, startling me. "That Spaceside's a close personal friend of mine.

He told me so himself, when I met him a little while ago. Why don't you meet another friend of mine?"

I stood up to shake the steady hand being offered to me, and looked into light brown eyes with flecks of gold, burning with youthful fervor, the only youthful aspect of the wrinkled, heavily scarred face that had seen too many battles in its day. "You must be Oliver's 'Boss', Homer B. Hunter," said the man kindly, in a soft voice with an edge that nearly cut through the smoke.

"And you must be 00π," I said, my voice breaking with awe. "So-called because . . ."

"Yes, yes, I know, because the accounts of my exploits stretch into infinity. You'll be happy to know it's only a minor exaggeration." What might have been mere bluster was imparted with an easy smile. 00π pulled out a chair for Yangtze, sat after she did, and gestured for me to sit. "One of the first things you will learn dealing with me, though, is I don't dwell overmuch on the past. It's the present that interests me."

"Not to mention the spectre of future developments," added Scorpion Mandando, lifting his soy raspberry as a toast. 00π nodded his agreement.

"Can I have a drink, Daddy?" asked Yangtze eagerly.

He stared at her. "You're a little young, aren't you?"

"Daddy, I was initiated tonight. I saw Mother make a sacrifice, and I had a vision of the goddess Marie."

"Seldon save me, she's gotten happy!" exclaimed Scorpion.

"Keep your hands to yourself," warned 00π, albeit in friendly tones. Then, more seriously, to his daughter: "You're a woman now."

"Yes," she replied, "whatever that means."

"Still a nonsmoker, I hope?"

"Dad!"

"Just being a father. You know I disapprove of metaphysically induced hallucinations. They rob the individual of even the illusion of free will, thus ridding him of the belief that he's responsible for his own fate."

"Well, I wasn't responsible for Mom and the sisters butchering that poor worker tonight."

"Then who was responsible?" asked 00π.

Yangtze shrugged. "No one. It was his time to die."

"*Karma*," I said.

"Maybe the poor bastard just happened to be in the wrong place at the wrong time," put in Oliver.

Scorpion more or less smiled as he raised his glass at the robot. "I like the way your friend thinks, Union Man. He has an admirably practical view."

"Well, Mr. Hunter, your admirably practical robot has informed me you have an admirably impractical problem on your hands," said 00π dryly, giving Yangtze a firm we'll-talk-later look.

I explained how I had twice seen Floyd in drug-induced visions, and twice as a ghost, once on another world and once upon entering the Nipponese system. "And then all he said was '*Use the Farce!*' I have no idea what he means by that, but Yangtze told me that the Anti-Curly is an adept at using the Farce. Do you think that the Anti-Curly might have some knowledge about Floyd?"

00π smiled, and the number of laugh lines around his eyes tripled. "It's unlikely. Let me tell you a story of the Farce. When I'm finished, I think you'll understand that we're not dealing with your basic existential, supernatural, quarter-rational, quasi-philosophical, convenient explanation for both mundane and extraordinary events here. The Farce is whatever it wants to be, and what it wants to be is confusing."

"Indeed," put in Scorpion. "Just last night I read an exhaustive study of the exploits of the Anti-Curly, and the scholar was at a loss to decide if the Anti-Curly used the Farce, if the Farce used him, or if it was all just some sort of PR hoax, with the Farce lying in wait high above all our heads, just waiting for the perfect moment to confusamax the issue."

00π cleared his throat and glared at Scorpion.

And Scorpion's head actually seemed to shrink down a tad deeper into his massive shoulders. "Sorry, old bean. I just can't help opening my big mouth sometimes."

Evidently 00π didn't like to have his storytelling interrupted. So Oliver and I listened fascinated, while Yangtze was bored and Scorpion had an air of bemused tolerance, as 00π told how he first came to know the Farce. 00π had thinning, bronze-colored hair. He had an unusually high forehead, a nose which appeared to have been broken so many times the robomeds had given up straightening it, and a missing half-earlobe. His blue business suit, which he wore with a white shirt and a loose, wide, red tie, hung on him like ragged sheets tossed on a bulky scarecrow. Though the weight of his shoulders had pulled them forward, making it appear as if age had bent his spirit as well as his physical self, it was easy to envision him standing straight and tall, his massive frame strong and perfectly proportioned, a man of indomitable spirit to whom doubt was a stranger, justice a faithful friend, and ambiguity a flattering foe. And indeed, such had once been the precise truth. For a time.

00π's father had been a wealthy and resourceful individual, a man of determination and vision, capable of bestowing great attention upon his son even as he used him as an experimental animal. His father trained 00π to be a hero almost from the day of his birth. From the day after, to be exact. For on the morning of 00π's second day of life, his father left him alone and naked near the edge of a towering cliff, in a forest filled with carnivorous beasts and poisonous plants, as a tremendous lightning storm raged overhead. If 00π survived, then he was worthy of his father's vision, and if not, well, then it wouldn't have mattered.

00π did survive. Later that day, his father found the baby sitting at the edge of the cliff, admiring the view. Next to him were the corpses of three strangled snakes.

00π refrained from mentioning the world of his birth. But whatever world it was, it must have been a dangerous and harrowing place for a young boy. 00π's training routine was strict, and it was performed every day, regardless of the likelihood of flash floods, erupting volcanoes, exploding geysers, or swooping birds of prey. Every day he ran from twenty to forty kilometers; every day he performed a difficult regimen of isometrics, weight lifting, *tai chi*, and dance exercises. He also took heavy doses of several drugs, all calculated to increase his muscular power and mental might. When he slept he did not dream; instead his mind absorbed information on learning tapes, and when he woke, his mind was expanded by pictures of worlds and times he had never seen, pictures that lingered like unearthed memories from past lives. His sole playmates were robots, and the games they played honed his already swift natural reflexes, challenged his already quick-witted thinking, and increased his already considerable stamina. His sole relationship with a fellow human being during those early years was the stiff, formal one he had with his old man, who was frequently aloof and withdrawn and who sometimes laughed hysterically at the skies for no apparent reason.

00π and his father lived alone on that world. 00π did not see a woman in the flesh until he rebelled against his father and ran away to join the Stellar Patrol. This was in the old days, before robots replaced the master sergeant organisms, and 00π's first master sergeant was a female of striking proportions. He impressed her with the way he handled himself during his first brawl on his first weekend leave, and evidently he impressed her later, too, because for the remainder of his tenure at boot camp, they were inseparable. When the time came for him to go on his first assignment, she got on her knees and begged him to take her with him and swore to resign from the Patrol if that's what it took. When 00π's sense of duty proved to be too unswerving for that, she begged him never to forget her, a promise 00π faithfully kept for all those years. After all, who could ever forget his first mother figure or his first mistress, especially if they happened to be the same person?

00π referred sparingly to his actual missions. His exploits simply weren't part of this story. Instead he told us of a young man filled to the brim with the sorts of ideals only youth can harbor. We learned of a youth highly motivated to rise through the hierarchy of the Stellar Patrol, thanks to his desire to see as much of the galaxy as there was to see. Dream images (he was off the learning tapes) were insufficient. The holographic pictures shipboard computers conjured up lacked the depth and weight of reality. Complicating matters was the desire his father had instilled in him to have adventures. Only when his life was in some sort of jeopardy did 00π feel truly alive. And danger, in and of itself, was also insufficient. 00π needed to experience danger for a reason, and that reason was nothing less than his desire to throw the yoke of tyranny off the galaxy and to make a humble contribution toward intelligent life's long march toward ultimate freedom and democracy.

He had a simple code in those early days; he did what his superiors told him, and then he took time off to party. When it came to pleasure, 00π was strictly a libertarian; anything that got you through the night was all right. During those rare moments when 00π wasn't on a mission or experiencing pleasure, he felt a curious kind of listlessness; he felt anxiety and boredom. He realized that one reason why he was so consumed with the desire to stay busy was, in part, to avoid self-confrontation. The identity of 00π, which had begun as a disguise to foil his enemies, had become a means to hide from himself.

Yet he wanted to be real. Every time he tried to take off the disguise, part of it stuck like an exaggeration. Whenever he thought he was on the verge of achieving a clear view of himself, circumstances (in the form of a new assignment) dictated he put the entire disguise back on. Making the galaxy safe for democracy, the act that had once given his life purpose and meaning, became but a shadow game, to be played again and again. Making his life as pleasurable as possible between assignments also became a meaningless pastime, a role played out for the purpose of satisfying those he came into contact with rather than for himself. His greatest desire was to be a simple man of honor, a knight, who strode down mean space corridors to resolve simple questions concerning simple good and evil. Yet the more questions he resolved, the more complex the game became and the more nebulous seemed the core of his inner self.

Even so, 00π was content to live the life he had been dealt, until the day he received the news that his father had died. The death affected him strongly. He was seized by convulsions of grief; he wept before the tough, stoic men he was working with at the time; and yet inside of him there remained a part as frozen as the ice of a methane moon—indifferent, and orbits away from the fire and fury that had urged him to participate in the great adventure in the first place. His conscious mind grieved. His body was racked with listlessness and pain. And meanwhile, his subconscious clung remorselessly to the supposition that nothing had changed, that life would go on as it ever had and that he was as whole as he would ever be.

00π returned to his homeworld, ostensibly to clear up matters of estate, but in reality to discover his father. He realized that he had never truly known him. His old man had taught him everything, up to a point, and what he had demanded in return was, in a sense, everything—worship, blind obedience, and excellence. But his father had never asked for love, nor friendship, nor kindness. He had seemed above all that. Upon examining his father's papers, reading his letters to friends and his entries into his journals, 00π discovered that there had been a good reason indeed for never wanting him to be a traditional son.

Love simply hadn't been part of the experiment.

00π had assumed, as his father had intended, that his mother had died as the result of an accident with the anesthetic during his birth. 00π had further assumed that his father had been so overwrought with grief that he had chosen never to speak of her, as if her memory would uncover a vein of grief too powerful to bear. The truth was far less romantic. In a manner of speaking, it wasn't even human. The ovary 00π's father had impregnated with his seed had resided in a test tube, and 00π's real mother was the specimen space savants were cloned from. Once the zygote was formed, 00π's father had eradicated the undesirable genetic traits, such as the propensity toward mindlessness, and replaced them with others of his own choosing. Even those traits inherited from his father were often revised. And after his birth, 00π's father had kept extensive notes on his son's developments—physically, intellectually, and emotionally. His father had seen to it that his son received only the minimum amount of love and nurturing required for basic survival. Anything more would be a luxury that would shift the emphasis of the experiment. What that primary emphasis was, 00π was never able to determine. Perhaps he had seen clues in the papers and had deliberately, or subconsciously, glossed over them. It was hard enough to accept that his father had never meant for him to be a son.

Indeed, it transpired that the streak of rebelliousness had been a factor his father had never anticipated. 00π's goodness, his compassion for the poor and the unfortunate, his loathing for the tyrannical and the merciless, were all aspects of his personality that his father had not only steadfastly ignored, but had at one point predicted would never come to be. 00π's father had wanted his son to be as cold and indifferent toward intelligent life in general as he himself had striven to be toward 00π personally.

00π was well aware that, with the acquisition of this knowledge, he should hate his father, that he should curse his father's name and never again think back fondly on his childhood. Yet he could not do this. The attention his father had shown him during his early training sessions was the only attention his father had ever shown him, period, and 00π recalled those moments with sadness and regret. He remained on his homeworld much longer than he had anticipated, for an entire standard year in fact, reading his father's papers, writing friends of his father's and devouring their replies for reminiscences of the man he had never known. Sometimes, just wandering through the dusty, deserted labs, including those once off-limits to him, he felt as if he could almost conjure up his father's personality from the knickknacks and other items that might have had some significance to him. Above all, he searched for an answer, not only for the purpose of the experiment, but for the deeper motivating factor that had sent his father on the quest in the first place. What had it been? Had his father formulated some seemingly outlandish theory that had damaged or destroyed outright his scientific reputation? Had his father been rejected by a lady love? Had his father gained some philosophical insight into the universe that had prodded him into viewing his own flesh and blood as objectively as one might view an amoeba on a slab of glass? Or had his father foreseen that the galaxy needed a man such as 00π?

One day 00π realized there could be no answers, and he decided it was time to return to the life he had left behind. It was time to be a hero again. It was time to face down the forces of chaos wherever they might appear, and to restore peace and freedom and order wherever it was necessary, at whatever the cost.

And, perhaps, it was time to find a new kind of love. In between the exploits for which he became justly famous, 00π embarked upon a series of self-destructive affairs, giving way to passion as he never had before, losing himself in fantasy and lust and romance, coming out of each affair empty-handed and broken-hearted every time. 00π responded to each personal disaster by throwing himself headlong into his next case. Eventually he no longer found it necessary to await orders; the cases seemed to find him. Within a few years, 00π was that rarity of rarities: a free agent of the Third Union.

He was also the most eligible bachelor in the

galaxy, and women would have gladly thrown themselves at his feet had not his disguises kept changing all the time. He had long since mastered the art of leading women to believe they had volunteered for an affair anyway. It all would have been so wonderful, he would have always felt so delightfully giddy, had he not felt so empty inside. He had thought by now he would know his inner self, yet it seemed his reason for being was merely to be.

The choices between good and evil, once so clear-cut, had become nebulous. As time went on, 00π failed to discern the difference between his tactics and those used by his opponents to bring about their nefarious schemes. One day, after he had completed a self-appointed assignment that ended with him personally pressing the button which released a flurry of bombs destroying a planet and every creature on it, 00π looked into the bathroom mirror of his personal spacecraft and saw the face of his enemy. It was his own. Now he was nothing but a disguise. As he read the hypergram congratulating him for successfully completing another mission, 00π knew it was time for him to retire. Perhaps in losing himself, he could find the part of him that was real.

He did know this: if there was an oversoul, as galactic philosophers had theorized, if there was indeed an invisible force binding together all life throughout all the worlds, then it was looking down on him and laughing. The joke was on him, and the joke was life itself.

So 00π stunned the Third Union and retired. He settled in the no-man's space of the Avidya System. He rejected the ideals that had once sustained him and lived solely for himself. At one point he even managed to settle down successfully with a woman, Yangtze's mother, but her religion came between them and they'd had no choice but to separate. Despite everything, 00π remained too much his father's son to cut himself free of the shackles of rationality. There was nothing the gods could give him that he had not already given himself.

00π became a businessman. It was one profession he had thought he would never be involved in. He lost himself in the maze of booking acts for his club, seeing to his supplies and bribing the proper authorities. He became preoccupied with numbers on ledgers and the realities of cash flow, and yet 00π found he could not renounce his former ideals entirely. Everywhere he looked there were still people in trouble, people confused and suffering, and so gradually, without realizing it but merely by following the dictates of his instincts, 00π became a knight again. In the twilight of his years, this knight was bent but not broken, and perhaps he was capable of returning the laughter of the oversoul yet. Here on Aurelian he did not try to fight for noble ideals, for races or peoples; he fought instead for the happiness of a few select individuals, and in that regard his current work was the most satisfying he had ever done. Here on Aurelian this part-time businessman, part-time father found a measure of peace in being also a part-time knight fighting for the modest goals of modest people of modest means.

"So where's the Farce?" I asked, when it was apparent 00π's story was done.

"The Farce?" 00π replied, with a mischievous smile that informed me where Yangtze derived that streak in her nature.

"Yes. When you started this story, you promised it would illustrate how the Farce has affected your life, but frankly I can't see where this Farce thing has had anything to do with it."

"Oh, but it's had *everything,* my good sir," said Scorpion.

"Everything—and nothing!" said 00π.

By now it was late in the morning. Save for us at the table and a few sanitbots cleaning things up, the club was empty. Outside, clear rays of the sun were beginning to shine through the protective dome, while inside, long streaks of light illuminated facets of the furniture and cast long shadows across the floor. "Never underestimate the pervasiveness of the Farce," said 00π, lighting up the latest in a long string of cigarettes. "Because of my knowledge of the Farce, it's no surprise to me that your faithful robot ex-companion appeared to you as a ghost, and that that was enough to put you on the right track. The primeval forces gathering power here during the last few decades have been becoming exponentially stronger. And with each surge of strength, their ability to affect reality has grown. I fear the time shall soon come when the nature of reality is no longer a subjective thing, distorted by the necessary detachment of the observer, but an objective dynamism that will sweep us headlong into rapids beyond our ability to comprehend."

"All this is terrific," I said, "but none of it is helping to find Floyd."

00π smiled condescendingly but not unkindly at me. "Your loyalty is touching. Just remember an Aurelian maxim which it took me many years to appreciate: *Sometimes the most direct route to a goal is the most indirect one.*"

"That's like saying the shortest distance between two points is a circle," replied Oliver snidely.

Scorpion and 00π looked at one another and nodded. "Good point," said Scorpion.

"And here it could be true," added 00π.

"Listen, fellas, it's been great talking to you two all night," I said, "but if you would just tell me where to start looking, then I'll start."

Scorpion leaned back in his chair and laughed. "That's like asking where the Farce begins and ends!" he said.

"Maybe I've been missing something here, so why don't you folks just pretend the Boss and I just arrived on this space island and tell us what this damn Farce is?" Oliver asked.

"It's like a punchline that's not funny if you have to explain it," answered Yangtze. "The Farce is a philosophical concept that has no meaning if you try to explain it."

"But Floyd said that to find him I had to use the Farce. I still don't get it, so how can I use it?" I asked.

"Don't worry about that," replied 00π. "You don't find the Farce: it finds you."

"I can't sit around here all week waiting for some nebulous philosophical concept to hit me on the head."

"And you won't. Nor will we," said 00π. "If I've got this figured out right, the fate of your missing robot companion is tangled up with a lot of other unusual goings-on that have been popping up lately. That *hoodoo* you tangled with, for instance."

"Yeah," said Yangtze, a realization just occurring to her. "I thought *hoodoos* were supposed to be smaller than that."

"How small?" I asked.

Instead of replying directly, Yangtze pointed at Oliver.

"So why is this unusual?" I asked. "From what you folks have been telling me, anything is possible here."

"By itself, the event would mean nothing," said 00π. "But put it in context with others, and it takes on many shades of meaning. Recently the various balances of power in the Avidya System have tipped one way, then the other, for no apparent reason."

"Traditional boundaries between block kings have

been disputed," said Scorpion. "Rancor between various religious factions has been heating up. Plus the number of involuntary sacrifices has increased greatly."

"So greatly that the various police departments have been using the technique they call the Hammer, which means they've been sweeping through districts renowned for their unsanctioned religious activity and arresting anybody suspected of taking part in an involuntary sacrifice," said 00π. "As each police force has sworn allegiance to a different baron, they sometimes come into direct conflict with one another. Then the gods take delight in a bounty of involuntary sacrifices."

"What constitutes, ah, a 'licit' religious activity?" I inquired.

"That, my young man, depends on which baron you happen to be talking to," said Scorpion.

"Great Janissaries!" I exclaimed. "There's no government here! It's anarchy—complete and totally chaotic anarchy!"

"Only to those who haven't gotten used to our somewhat complicated, yet admittedly quixotic, means of governing ourselves," said 00π. "But I confess, even that nebulous circle shows indications of being unable to hold much longer."

I cleared my throat. "So am I to surmise that when we find the entity responsible for social chaos, then we might also be able to find out where Floyd is?"

"That's my gut feeling," said 00π.

"Great," I exclaimed, rubbing my hands together in anticipation. "Where do we begin?"

"That's what I've been trying to avoid telling you," said 00π. "I have no idea where to begin."

"WHAT? Do you mean to tell me we've been sitting here chewing the soycud because you've had absolutely no idea what we should really have been doing?"

00π nodded enthusiastically. "Yes, that's it exactly. You catch on fast."

"What the hell kind of hero are you, anyway?"

He shrugged. "Basically retired, Homer, though I haven't ruled out all altruistic services."

"I'm certain 00π would be only too happy to perambulate into action," said Scorpion, "but he must know beforehand where he is supposed to be going. That's one of the problems in dealing with a space island which is power incarnate. If the solution to a problem can be discovered in one place, it's just as likely to be discovered in another."

"And is equally likely to be discoverable nowhere," said Yangtze, "except in the mind." She tapped her temple.

"That's where most of my problems begin," I said, barely able to restrain my helpless rage.

"Don't worry," said 00π. "I'm sure that *hoodoo* wouldn't have tried to stomp you if someone hadn't felt your very presence made you a worthwhile pawn in whatever game is being played here."

I simply glowered at him.

Oliver's arms suddenly stretched toward Yangtze and embraced her, pulling her from her chair. They retracted until she was held fast against him, and his eyestalks bent down so that his eyes looked directly into hers. "Good, now that business is out of the way, I've been meaning to tell you, young lady, that I'm madly, hopelessly in love you. I want to bear your children!"

I leapt from my chair and extracted the laughing Yangtze from my faithful robot companion's arms with difficulty. "Oliver, what's gotten into you?"

"Sorry, Boss," he said sheepishly, rolling back on his skates. "It's just that something came over me and I had no choice but give in. I know that if I can only convince this sweet young thing to do the same, we'll both be blessed with a consciouness-expanding experience."

"I'm sure something else will also expand," said Scorpion dryly.

"Hi, folks," said a voice new to the room. We looked up to see Spaceside Hodgson, still dressed in his ice-cream suit, walking toward us.

"Sorry, but your check hasn't been made out yet," said 00π lightly.

"That's to be expected, but it's not why I'm here," said Spaceside with a wry grin. "My block king 'requested' me to ask you to do him a favor."

00π raised his eyebrows at me. I'm not sure what the look meant, but he clearly thought he was communicating something. "What's that?"

"Well, he, ah, wants you to attend his daughter's funeral rites this afternoon."

"I don't enjoy attending funerals," said 00π. "I've been responsible for too many in my day."

"This one promises to be a wild shindig," said Spaceside eagerly, "rife with impalpable presences and blasphemous hybrid anomalies. I didn't know the girl myself—not in the way she claimed in that nuisance suit she filed against me, anyway—but I plan to let bygones be bygones and check out the funeral just for the sake of a small dose of sentimentality."

"Then tell me, Spaceside," said 00π, scowling as the rock star lifted a thick lock of hair to adjust a tiny power pack implanted in his skull, "is your block king aware of my well-known disapproval of Aurelian religious practices, particularly mystery rites?"

"The block king said I'll look like Scorpion if I didn't do as he 'requested,' " replied Spaceside with a glazed look in his eyes.

"Does the block king anticipate the eruption of social discord?" inquired Scorpion.

Spaceside shrugged. "Naw, man. Well, not exactly an eruption."

"Then what exactly?" 00π was becoming exasperated. "I'll tell you one thing, Spaceside, you're a great singer, but your brain waves aren't going to be able to scan the police band if you don't cut out this powerpack jive."

"Did you say exactly?" Spaceside asked. "Oh yeah . . . well, by exactly, I mean nothing more than the usual. See, the king's been having his difficulties of late securing his boundaries, so sure, there might be an unprovoked incident, brought about by some rival faction. Nothing that his squad of shamans can't handle, I'm sure. It's the, ah, the other trouble that bothers him."

"What other trouble?" asked Yangtze, shivering.

"Well, normally the untimely demise of a loved one can be blamed upon rivals. But this particular daughter died, well, you know, differently somehow." Spaceside smiled enigmatically.

Yangtze fluttered her eyelids at him. "I just realized something, Spaceside. When the light strikes you in a certain way, you're almost handsome."

"Why, thank you," said Spaceside, genuinely flattered.

"Of course, when you open your mouth, the effect kinda falls down a little bit," added Yangtze.

"Glad to hear it," said Oliver, putting an arm around her. "Now that you've gotten over that essentially untalented individual, how's about you and me going off and possessing one another for a while?"

"No thanks, I've already got an asshole," said Yangtze.

"Aarrghh!" replied Oliver, reeling away. "Wheeze when you say that."

"I really must get him overhauled soon," I said to no one in particular.

"I'd throw his spare parts away, just to be safe," said 00π. Then, to Spaceside: "Let's try this again, shall we? Exactly what sort of unusual development is your block king worried about?"

"Well, I'm sorta leery about telling you," said Spaceside dreamily.

"Try me."

"Okay. Not to put too fine a point on it, 00π, 'cause I know how you disapprove of these things on account of the fact that you just reminded me of it for the umpteenth time, but normally when somebody dies, their relations tend to perform certain religious rites to ensure that their souls go to their proper destinations."

"So?"

"In this case, all the curses have been lifted, but for some reason the block king's not sure that's the end of it."

"I would think that would satisfy him," I said.

"That's because you're new in these parts, stranger," said Spaceside.

"I'm old in these parts and I don't understand," said 00π. "What is it about this death that's different?"

"Well, the symptoms, basically."

"Such as?" prodded Scorpion.

"The two holes in her neck," replied Spaceside, tapping his own artery there by way of example, "plus the fact that all the blood was drained from her body."

"*All* the blood?" asked Yangtze.

"Give or take a liter. The execution of this dastardly deed was really quite ingenious. It took several days, the block king recently realized with the advantage of hindsight. She wasted away before his eyes, and many shamans were cursed or slain outright while they tried unsuccessfully to help her. The holes in his daughter's neck, which she kept secret by wearing a scarf, stayed wide and fresh thanks to two microrobotic devices that could be plugged up when they weren't in use."

"Sounds to me like she knew what was happening to her all along," said Scorpion.

"Maybe," said Spaceside, "or maybe she was under the influence of a hypnotic suggestion that prevented her from telling. I'm not sure she was complaining though, seeing as how her last words, while she was delirious, were, 'There is no escape from the burning light you create! Bite me, for I cannot resist your fatal charms!' That's when she tore off the scarf and revealed the holes in her neck."

"I can see that the scientific method has gone into something of an eclipse here," I said.

"The block king was quite correct to slay his shamans for not noticing all her physical symptoms," said 00π. "But if her body was almost drained of blood, how did she stay alive long enough to utter even those last few words?"

"Ah, sweet mystery of life," said Spaceside, adjusting his power pack again. Gradually he became walleyed.

"Is there anything else unusual about her death that you wish to tell us?" Scorpion asked.

"Not really, not unless you count the fact that when the girl died, a bird flew in through the window and made a few circles over her deathbed before flying out again."

"Now that's interesting!" said Scorpion with a tiny smile.

"Why's that?" I asked.

"There are no birds on Aurelian," said 00π. "Other animal life, yes, but no birds."

"We had them once," said Yangtze, "but too many people complained about their toilet habits."

"Birds usually have good aim," said Oliver, with the gravity of one who knows.

"Well, I don't see what the big deal is," I said. "All right, so the girl's dead under mysterious circumstances, and that's one thing, and I'm sure that if 00π wants to investigate, he will. But I don't see why he or anybody should feel obligated to attend the funeral rites of someone he didn't know. After all, the girl's beyond caring about how many important people show up at her funeral. She's dead, for Seldon's sake!"

Spaceside snapped his fingers. "That's it! You've split the atom at the gluon! The girl is dead"—his eyes widened and he grinned malevolently, knowing I'd feel the joke was on me—"and her father wants to make sure she stays that way."

Chapter Six
The White Hawk Dreams

OU MUST REFRAIN
from thinking bad thoughts."

"Excuse me," Blather said tersely.

"You must not think bad thoughts. Our cubicle is overflowing with your negative vibes."

"Is that so?"

"It is."

"Well, that's great, but where I come from a man can think what he wants. He has to watch what he says, but he can think what he wants!"

"I and my fellow officers are very happy for you, but here on Nippon we have our own rules. Wha—? Wait. I am receiving a motion that while you are here on Nippon, you kindly respect our wishes and keep the negative vibes to a minimum. It has been suggested that they are too disruptive and are interfering with the thirty to forty other decisions and interactions I and my fellow officers happen to be making at this particular time."

"I'm still going to think what I want, bad thoughts or not, and there's nothing you can do about it."

"The motion is being called to question," said the officer, who stood at parade rest before the door leading out of the room in which Blather, Coryban, and Reina were being held prisoner. "Past experience indicates there will be little if any debate, so again I request you control the tenor of your thoughts. Perhaps if you recalled some pleasant time in your past, your mood might alter for the better."

Blather hunched his shoulders, put his legs together, crossed his feet, and then drew up his knees and wrapped his hands around them. "I wasn't thinking bad thoughts," he said defensively. "I was merely being frustrated."

"My fellow officers and I could tell."

"What fellow officers?" Blather asked impatiently. "There's nobody else here!"

Coryban sat between Blather and Reina on the couch. It was the sole article of furniture in the tiny room with off-white walls where they had been brought after the Space Police had transferred custody to them to the Thought Police. She stared in amazement at the officer. "You're in telepathic communication with them!"

"Naturally," replied the officer.

"Amazing. Are all you Thought Police telepathic?"

"Yes, every rookie's latent telepathic ability is electronically augmented as part of his initiation ceremony."

"You really can't blame Ensign Blather for being upset," said Coryban. "We've been cooped up in here for hours, with no food or water and no idea what's going to happen to us."

"My fellow officers and I cannot speculate with any degree of accuracy upon the particulars of your potential fates," said the officer, "because it has been many years since the Union has knowingly trespassed into the Avidya System. Our mind-reading techniques have of course made us aware of the extenuating circumstances, which fairly cry out for a merciful settlement—something that, frankly, runs counter to our spin. Overall, the situation is without convenient precedent."

The officer was a young boy, with short orange hair and big ears made almost comical by the tight fit and shiny, narrow brim of his translucent hat. His uniform consisted of a white militaristic tunic that came just above the knees, a wide black belt, gray breeches, and black boots. He seemed like a nice boy, Coryban thought, but he had a glazed, faraway look in his eyes, even though he otherwise acted very alert. It would not do, she decided, to underestimate him.

"Wise advice you have given yourself," said the officer with a slight smile. "In my opinion you should take it. Though I myself am personally lacking in combat experience, my mind is connected to the web during every moment, enabling me to draw at will upon the combined experience of the best officers in the Thought Police."

Coryban bristled with anger at the violation of her mental privacy, even though she hadn't been concerned when Blather's mental territory had been encroached upon. She was, after all, the highest-ranking officer among the captives, surely deserving of special treatment. "You heard that! You read my thoughts!"

"Naturally. That's why we call us the Thought Police. I can distinguish the thoughts of all three of you from one another quite adequately and without confusion. Furthermore, I can hear the buzzing of a thousand fellow officers in my brain, and yet feel no disassociation from my own personal self. I am unique, yet I am one with my peers—and with my charges," he added with a nod in their direction.

"What's your name?" asked Reina innocently.

"Corporal Roger Random," replied the officer.

Suddenly he blushed. Perhaps he appreciated Reina's thoughts.

"Well, Corporal, if you can read our minds, then surely you and the other Thought Police know that in our hearts we respect your laws and would be perfectly happy to leave at any moment," said Reina.

"That is so," said Corporal Random.

"Then why are we being treated with such distrust?" Reina asked. "All we ask to is have our own ship back again. Then we can go to the space islands and try to find Homer-B-Hunter. Or, if you prefer, we can just go away and leave him to find his own fate."

"An excellent suggestion," said Corporal Random. "But we in the officer's web don't make policy, we just enforce it—though truth to tell, we can make a good case that we should be making policy as well. It's out of our hands. What's debatable is the degree of personal sympathy that's acceptable for me to show you." Suddenly his already glazed eyes went totally blank, and he put a hand to his ear and tilted his head back as if staring at a shooting star. "Wha—? Oh, right. Sure. Okay, I'll say nothing more." Then he returned to normal. "Sorry, but it has been decided to trust you with as little information on the workings of our society as possible, as it has been theorized that you characters might not be up to the strain of dealing with such complex, sophisticated customs as our own."

Blather covered his face with a hand. "How do these people masturbate?"

"Actually, personal pride forces me to inform you that we do it with a lot of mutual cooperation, and often achieve simultaneous orgasms of global proportions," said Random testily. "However, involuntary second-tier memory examination of the one called Blather suggests that even that simple means of pleasure was denied him until he began to include in his somewhat nasty fantasy images the superior officer currently sitting to his left."

Coryban turned the complexion of a white tornado and, with great difficulty, restrained herself from choking Blather. "You've been *what*?"

Blather cleared his throat. "Yes, I confess, I have been."

"How often?"

"Occasionally."

"How occasionally?"

"Occasionally enough."

Coryban turned away and fumed, tapping her fingers nervously on one knee and tapping her foot furiously on the floor. "Well, I never—! You'll stop it, of course. Instantly!"

"Is that an order?"

"Of course, it's a goddamn order, you Plutonian Newt!"

Blather cleared his throat, then sighed regretfully. "Well, if you insist . . ."

"I insist."

"What sort of inspection do you intend to carry out later?"

"I will trust you," said Coryban between her teeth, holding back ever increasing amounts of anger.

"It's not exactly true, you know," said Random suddenly.

"What's that?" said Coryban in exasperation.

"That you've never masturbated," replied Random without the slightest embarrassment or hesitation. "You've masturbated googolplexian times. In fact, a great deal of it was accomplished during your spiritual training under the aegis of the Wouie Louie."

"Thank you," said Coryban. "Is there nothing you don't know about me?"

"Not that we can't find out," said Random. "We

of the web wonder, though, if you would enlighten us upon one detail."

"My pleasuure," said Coryban, folding her hands in a mock bow.

"Why you were so shocked when you discovered your fellow officer has engaged in activities so roughly parallel to your own?"

"That's because I've never masturbated using an ape like *him* as a fantasy figure!"

Blather was genuinely hurt at this one. "Colonel, forgive me, but I don't think of you as an ape, nor as only a sex object, either."

"How else do you view me?"

"As a superior officer, of course."

"And as a stepping *shtup* to power," put in Random.

"Thank you," said Coryban, leaning back and crossing her legs.

"What is it you mean by this term *masturbation*?" asked Reina. "It is not a deed I have found prevalent among the wild animals of the forests and deserts."

"I think in your case you should view it strictly as a warm up," said Coryban with clinical motherness.

"What a great bedside manner you're going to have," said Blather.

"Well, whatever masturbation is," said Reina, "they have a remarkably *open* society here, don't they, Colonel Coryban? I didn't know it was possible for humans to know so much about the private lives of others and still respect them as decent individuals in their own right." She stared raptly at Random, visions of the personalities behind his dancing like sugarplum fairies in her mind. "Isn't it wonderful?"

Reina still thought it was wonderful, in fact, several chrons later when she and her comrades fell asleep from the boredom of waiting to be escorted to the next stage of the legal process. Coryban had ordered Blather off the couch—she didn't want him to touch her even accidentally—and so he slept on the floor as the two women curled up on either half of the couch with their knees drawn up to their chests. Random, meanwhile, merely stood in position, apparently neither sleepy nor fatigued, and watched them as closely as ever.

Coryban dreamed. She had forgotten all about her anger and was completely relaxed. She dreamt of the time when she had been a white hawk flying through an alien wood at night. She swooped down on a scurrying rat-like creature, catching it deftly in sharp, strong talons that buried deep in the squirming body. She heard the drops of the creature's blood striking the dry leaves as she carried her twitching meal to a rocky crag that jutted out over a valley gleaming in the moonlight.

The white hawk tore at her meal with her talons. She plucked out the pieces with her beak, and shook her head to facilitate swallowing. She saw, but did not really comprehend, a flat spiral galaxy in the sky. It stretched from one end of the horizon to the other, but the light it emitted was too dull to illuminate the landscape. The world she was on must have been high above the galaxy's ecliptic plane.

Her meal finished, the white hawk flew up toward the heart of the galaxy. Up, up, up she soared, higher and higher. She flew as if she believed she could touch that galaxy, and her primitive mind, perhaps augmented by the consciousness that was Coryban, imagined the galaxy opening up and enfolding her into its cool white center.

And then—a bright flash of agony racked her breast, and a dagger of ice pierced her soul.

She plummeted, an arrow through her heart, its tip protruding from her breast.

The ground embraced her, and Coryban's consciousness was suddenly in the mind of a man wearing buckskins and a headband made from feathers. He had a grizzled, but not unkindly face. He was a hunter and the white hawk had been his prey. Slinging his bow over his shoulder, he walked from his place of concealment, picked up the hawk by the arrow that had pierced it, and carefully extracted the arrow. He tied the dead hawk by its talons to his belt, already burdened with three other victims of the hunt. He walked through the wood, unmindful of the great gods looking down from the sky.

But suddenly he stared in abject horror at the explosion of blood and guts that erupted from his chest with the impact of a bright red beam. He felt no pain, but that was to be expected, because he knew he was already dead. It seemed he looked down on his body lying in a pool of his own blood, and his last sensation on this plane was a whiff of his own charred flesh. Coryban stirred fitfully in her sleep as the consciousness of the hunter threatened to flicker out, ending the dream.

But then she saw herself advancing toward the fallen hunter. The smell of the burnt flesh and evaporated blood wasn't quite so overwhelming now: it was the sight of the fallen white hawk tied onto the hunter's belt, its feathers stained with its own blood, that truly sickened her. She experienced a wave of grief. As she reached out she noticed that her sleeve was very familiar, indeed, it appeared to be the sleeve of the fatigues she wore right now.

In fact, the entire uniform appeared to be hers. But the person in the uniform was someone else. She was smaller in stature, her muscles leaner but perhaps more powerful. She had pale red skin and raven black hair. Her name was Reina.

Reina in the dream gently untied the bloody white hawk from the dead hunter's belt and held it to her breast. With tears in her eyes she looked at the stoic galaxy above. She stepped into the air, and this time when the galaxy unfolded before her, it greeted her with the warm embrace of eternity.

At that point Coryban forced herself to wake. Though normally not a superstitious person who believed dreams could predict the future, she wasn't quite ready to find out what eternity was like.

At first Coryban's vision was fuzzy. Then she focused on a pair of eyes that looked exactly like hers. Reina smiled at her. "You had the same dream as I," she said.

"Yes, I suppose I did."

"Oh, give me a break!" groaned Blather from the floor.

"Spare us, Blather," replied Coryban tersely. "That's an order."

"Did he speak?" asked Reina, rubbing her sleepy eyes. "My homeworld has slugs who the old warriors say can mimic the language of the Heechie-Heechie. I thought that perhaps I had accidentally brought one offworld with me."

"The minister will see you now," said Corporal Random without warning, opening the door.

Blather instantly roused himself and bolted upright, straightening his wrinkled uniform.

"Slow down, Blather," said Coryban. "They've kept us waiting this long. It won't do to seem too eager now."

"I assure you, it will make no difference," said Random. "The minister has many things on his many minds."

They walked in silence as Random escorted them

down the first hallway, and then through a succession of many others, past an incalculable number of closed doors, undistinguished by a mark or insignia of any sort. Random seemed to know where they were going, though, and never hesitated for a moment.

At one point Blather mumbled, "At least we're on the right floor."

"Hmmm. This building does seem to be larger inside than it appeared on the outside," observed Coryban. "I wonder if the Nipponese have some sort of technology at their disposal that renders stairs and elevators useless."

"Well, I haven't seen any bathrooms, either," replied Blather.

"The old warriors say that the whole world is your bathroom, if you but know how to use it," said Reina.

"Don't take that advice seriously," Coryban told Blather.

Before the red-faced Blather could reply in his own defense, Random stopped before one of the doors and opened it. He stood in the doorway and saluted sharply. "Mr. Minister, sir!"

"It's ma'am today," said the fat man behind the desk as the three trespassers were escorted inside. "There seem to be more women augmenting my thoughts today than usual, and I must say, it's a most heady sensation," the minister added with a fluttering of the eyelids and a self-conscious brush at the lock of white hair that had fallen into his eyes. The minister did not stand but gestured at the three folding chairs before his desk, indicating that his visitors should sit. He was a bull of a man, whose immense girth dwarfed arms and hands that would have appeared considerably corpulent on any other individual, but which on him appeared extremely tiny. The exact number of his chins was hidden by a scraggly orange beard tinged with white, and his cheeks were so round they were on the verge of being Euclidian circles. His blue smock hugged his skin as if it had been sprayed on, and the folds of his body over-hung the frame and the arms of a chair enormous by normal standards. Coryban attempted to refrain from imagining an immense blueberry ice-cream tastee-freeze that had fallen out of its cone and was now melting on the ground, but of course once the picture was in her mind, she could not completely forget it.

However, if the minister noticed her thoughts, he was too busy, or simply too polite, to react. Maybe he believed he had plucked all possible visions of that nature from wandering minds before. As Coryban and the others sat, he waved Corporal Random outside while playing with some of the controls on his otherwise bare oakwood desk. The metal band he wore around his head had wires connected to some of the control panels which were equipped with arrays of colorful blinking lights. Like Corporal Random, he appeared both continuously alert and distracted.

The minister nodded, perhaps responding to some thought being transmitted into his brain, and then glared at Blather and said, "Of course I can think and chew gum at the same time, my good primitive. Furthermore, I surmise that during your enforced stay on Nippon, you'll find that even the worst of us have more control over our bodily functions than what you've demonstrated thus far."

Blather smiled meekly. "I could use a bathroom, sir, uh, ma'am."

"Discipline, discipline, Blather," said the minister, drumming two of his massive fingers on the desktop.

"Can we assume you already know the circumstances of our visit to your solar system?" Coryban asked, figuring the meeting might as well be called to order.

The minister leaned back. The chair creaked substantially and probably was recorded on all nearby seismographs. "You may assume that. My name is Minister Hoffman, though today you may call me Alyce. Tomorrow, assuming the configuration of the web forces me to reorient my personal conception of myself, you may call me Albert."

"Forgive me, ma'am, but I'm easily confused," said Blather. "For consistency's sake, can't I just call you Al?"

"No, but I can call you sentenced to seven hundred orbits in suspended animation, followed by thirteen lifetimes in somnambulatory labor," replied Minister Hoffman, without malice or pleasure. "Of course, any such sentence will have to be ratified by my fellow ministers of justice, who tomorrow, should the configuration change, might be more inclined to mercy. You know what they say about the female mind being inherently more cruel than the male. It's true, of course, and I've learned much of value from those of the female persuasion. Even the cross-dressers have their own unique viewpoint."

The minister pressed a button and a lamplike device rose from a panel on the desk. A stream of lights suddenly played across the band on the minister's head, and a red ray stabbed forth from the center of the device. In the field of the red ray appeared, as if from nothingness, a piece of pie topped with custard. The pie stuffing most resembled writhing, intermingling noodles, noodles with segmented bodies and tiny black eyes.

The minister looked down on what he had wrought, and evidently it looked good to him, because he licked his lips and rubbed his hands. "Hmmm, doggies," he exclaimed in anticipation. He produced a fork from his desk and began stuffing the writhing noodles into his mouth, swallowing with great loud gulps.

Reina looked at Coryban. Coryban looked at Blather. And Blather tried not to look at anything. Blather's complexion first grew pale, then took on a greenish color. When the minister belched with unabashed gusto, Blather covered his mouth and stifled an explosive reaction.

"Don't worry," said the minister. "I know how this must look to you savages. But this meal is entirely an illusion. The taste is what I make of it. Right now I've this hankering for chocolate and pickles, and this illusion is doing nicely." He laughed and tapped his head. "I suppose one of my comrades must be pregnant, don't you think?"

"Forgive me, sir, if I appear unsophisticated, but the smell is very real, at least to me," said Reina. "And while I have no idea what you mean by chocolate and pickles, the odor reminds me strictly of worms."

Minister Hoffman giggled as he stuffed in another mouthful. He ate vast quantities very rapidly, but it seemed that little, if any, of the illusionary concoction was disappearing. "I suppose that makes sense, little lady," he said kindly. "The taste is real, of course, so are the calories, and the feeling of a full stomach. Another of the neat little side effects from this satisfactory appetizer is that the waste will also seem real. But I assure you, it is all most unreal."

"But if it adds calories too, why eat an illusion?" Blather demanded to know. "You might as well be eating the real thing!"

"Real wormlike writhing noodles?" responded Minister Hoffman incredulously. "That would be disgusting. It's chocolate and pickles I crave. Besides, the calories are illusionary too; they simply act like real ones." He pushed the plate aside. "But perhaps it is rude of me to gorge myself in front of you. While you may be criminals, you do have rights, and it's up to me to see that you are treated politely during your—and our—enforced time together. So, if you'll excuse me for a second, I'll confer with my comrades and see what they think we should do with you."

And with that, Minister Hoffman folded his hands on his immense girth and rolled his eyes to the ceiling. He ignored his guests completely and began speaking to his mental cohorts as if they were present with him in the room. "Execution?" he said. "No, too messy ... Exile? ... No, that would be redundant. Any time spent away from Nippon is tantamount to exile in any case ... Hard labor at the noodle factory? ... Yes, a promising suggestion ... Already it is giving rise to bad thoughts on the prisoners' behalf ..."

Chapter Seven
The Prisoner in the Coffin

OMEONE THAT looked like a giant albino crab, but with more legs and eyes and a coral shell, once said that those who live from moment to moment live on the threshold of a dream; in their hearts, even the most grandiose monuments of civilization are just sand castles to be washed into the sea, eventually. Paranoia struck deep as I contemplated those words while entering the residential district where the funeral was to be held.

Sections of the district shimmered like sunlight reflecting off a mirror. Other parts were hunkered-down and mundane, as if they had grown under the dome like molds on a petrie dish. I surmised that most of the apartment buildings had been renovated several times during their existence, but probably never with great foresight. The builders had striven to meet only the needs of the moment with the goods they had on hand, sometimes erecting entirely new facades after shoring up the foundations and, as often as not, indulging their whims regardless of whether or not their vision conflicted with existing styles.

There was continuity in one district at least, where the architects had apparently taken part in an allout boycott of right angles. Corners had several angles, or they were curved or otherwise convoluted, but simplicity was never used if there was a more complex means to an end. The roofs were onion-shaped domes (sometimes with spires), or geodesic domes, or hexagonal astronomical domes with telescopes protruding from the openings.

Everywhere, billboards exalted the power of gods and goddesses, and often rival deities were celebrated with graffiti defacing the ads. Graffiti was also spray-painted on walls and stone fences. The subjects were not always religious; as Yangtze explained, some symbols proclaimed the superiority of one block king over another. Apparently the local power brokers on the space island always vied with one another for territory, whether the warfare worked to their advantage or not. It was an old story.

As all weather was strictly artificial, there were no gutters on the buildings, no drains in the streets. The breeze was slight, pleasant, scented with the faint odor of air conditioning. Energy sails beyond the sky dome deflected the worst part of the sun's rays, and the domes themselves cut out the ultraviolet rays. The streets, mainly deserted at this hour, were so quiet you could hear the rumbling of machinery underneath. The few people currently awake were headed to the subway entrances, toward the beckoning sounds of those incessant machines.

A few beggars, shamans, and magicians set up their booths at street corners boasting churches, mosques, and ziggurats. They did not attempt to hawk their wares. They looked respectfully, even fearfully at us, but otherwise left us alone. The crew consisted of myself, Yangtze, Spaceside, 00π, Scorpion, and Oliver. Though I had not slept for what must have been several cycles, I was not in the least tired. Indeed, I'd

grabbed a second wind, and every detail of my immediate environment was sharp and distinct in my mind.

Of course, the medicine Scorpion had given me
for my bruises and stiff muscles might have had
something to do with it. There had been a mirthful
light in his normally melancholy eyes, peering at me
through the vast chasm of his oversized helmet, as
he handed the pills over to me. Their chemical composition might have been partly responsible for my
paranoia, as I was deeply convinced that naked eyes
peered at me from the grout between bricks, from
behind plants, and through the cracks in Venetian
blinds in the uppermost windows. I felt the energy of
the entities empowering those eyes prickling my
nerves. Curious tendrils of thought nudged at the
boundaries of my consciousness. Concepts wavered
just beyond my abilities to bring them into focus. I
didn't quite know what was happening, but I did
know this: I liked it! *If this be paranoia,* I thought,
give me more, more, more!

Twice I caught glimpses of the entities who had
me under surveillance, at least I assumed they were
the same entities. The first was a tiny, butterflylike
creature that streaked across the street like a globule
of light. Even without a good look at her, I knew a
closer one could prove addictive. Something about
her black compound eyes and her tuft of green hair
and the semitransparent wings attached to her naked
back stirred dark emotions in my soul.

Where she might have come from, I had no idea.
I hoped to meet her again, and made a mental note to
ask her about the tiny pair of binoculars slung around
her neck.

The second sighting, a tad more dramatic, occurred a few minutes later. I happened to be, for
reasons that escaped me then as now, trying to draw
Spaceside into conversation. "So this district is home,

Spaceside?" I asked casually while we walked past a few buildings with split columns painted with a pit of mersnakes eating raw flesh. Fast-food joints were in the basements. I had no curiosity whatsoever regarding what might be served down there, not with those paintings about.

"Yep," Spaceside said, noncommittally.

"Lived here long?" I asked.

"Long enough."

"Hmm. Born on this island?"

"In a manner of speaking."

"Hatched?"

"Hey, man, I ain't no test-tuber," he said, grievously insulted. "I'm as human as you."

"That ain't saying much," put in Oliver.

"I'm just trying to be friendly," I explained.

"That's fine," said Spaceside, "but why did you have to try to be friendly with me? I'm a fucking rock star, man, and I don't have to be friendly with anybody unless they can get me a gig, or get me laid, or get me whatever. You grok?"

"How about if I were to say I could keep you from singing falsetto for a few more years?" I asked angrily. "How would that sound to you?"

"I already do falsetto," said Spaceside, missing the point entirely.

"Quiet," said 00π coolly. We had all stopped so Spaceside and I could carry on our discussion without the distraction of having to look where we were going. Ignoring us, 00π moved away and breathed deeply. Scorpion moved beside 00π and likewise breathed deeply. But while 00π was silent, Scorpion made a wheezing sound, not unlike that of, well, a falsetto exhaling a gulp of helium. "You smell it?" 00π asked him.

"Definitely," said Scorpion.

"What is it?" I asked.

"Death," said 00π.

"Fine, I'll see you folks later," said Spaceside, waving.

"You stay," said 00π.

"What's going on?" I asked Yangtze.

"Dad can sense these things."

"Well, of course he smells death," I said. "There's a funeral today."

"Death is invariably in the air, on any world," said Yangtze. "But I think Dad's point is the odor is somewhat more prevalent today than usual."

"There's nothing we can do about it now," said Scorpion, shrugging his massive shoulders. "Already the future has converged with the present. We've accepted the job, so we've got to accept the destiny that goes with it."

"No, we don't," said Oliver, rolling away.

"Stop!" I said, grabbing hold of him. "Don't you want to find Floyd?"

"Not by joining him!" said Oliver. "Besides, I don't see how this is looking for Floyd."

"Never underestimate the subtle machinations of fate, friend," said 00π sagely. "I suspect you are more to the point than you know. Besides, you can't achieve immortality by living forever."

"You misunderstand me," said Oliver. "I'm a robot. I can achieve immortality simply by staying out of trouble."

"When you asked us to come here," 00π asked Spaceside, "didn't you realize how dangerous it would be?"

"Look, sir, any amount of danger is too much for me. The only reason I asked you, remember, is because my block king expressly *requested* it."

"All right," said 00π, "but if we live through this, you and your band have got to add 'Melancholy Culture' to your repertoire."

131

Spaceside made a face. "That old saw?" He shrugged. "Well, if you insist, but I guarantee your gate's gonna suffer."

While they continued debating the matter, Oliver whispered, "Did I catch that? Did they really say they could smell death in the air?"

I nodded. "That's what they said."

"Well. I don't want to blow out the contents of my oil pan, but my info programming tells me the smell of death is usually accompanied by putrid, rotting, decaying flesh, filled with maggots and ants and other insects in quantities you generally don't find on space islands."

"Perhaps 00π was viewing things on another level," I ventured. "He is, after all, a superagent, and probably has a sixth sense about such matters."

"Now that's serious," responded Oliver, his eyes widening in annoyance. "00π and Scorpion were talking about the smell of death in the same definitive manner you or I might discuss the carcass of a Hogwallian horsefly crushed to death on the highway beneath the air cushion of a pneumatic automobile."

"I think that's largely a matter of interpretation," I replied.

"Look! There's the death!" shouted Scorpion in a high-pitched squeak that almost shattered my eardrums.

I and everyone in the vicinity, including a practically comatose, bearded, power-pack junkie lying against a building, looked in the direction Scorpion pointed at.

At first I saw only the billboard. On it was pasted the picture of a pair of eyeglasses, with a single purple and blue eye behind both lenses. The unseeing eye hovered over a cauldron of boiling lava. In the background were great fires, and the symbols on the left side of the billboard included a broken triangle, an infinity symbol, and a stylized heart with a stake driven through it. "What? That poster's death?" I asked. "I mean, the rendering's exquisitely awful, but I fail to see—"

"Behind it!" said 00π, an instant before the object of our scrutiny revealed itself.

"Great Seldon," said Scorpion.

"Holy ogu-balindjo!" said Yangtze.

"Left in!" exclaimed Spaceside.

"Will somebody please blow me down!" said Oliver.

00π and Scorpion silently put their hands over their holster flaps. Their fingers twitched restlessly, and Scorpion's tiny eyes darted back and forth suspiciously, but whether he feared or anticipated an attack, I cannot say.

My immediate impression of the entity was that he was some kind of man. Naked and roundish, with tiny arms and legs and a head that merged almost perfectly with his torso, he was stitched, glued, or otherwise connected to a semicircular, hollow flight unit. He had a single tuft of red hair, like the fibers of a worn-out brush, atop his oversized cranium. Thanks to the scores of tendrils around the border of the unit, plus the fact that it completely protected his back like a segmented shell, he most resembled a giant floating pillbox bug.

"Hi, guys!" he shouted out cheerfully in an electronically augmented voice that sounded a lot like the lonely wail of a guitar synthesizer trapped in a loop of feedback.

Scorpion unsnapped his holster as the newcomer flew down closer to us, but 00π detained the space hunter with a squeeze on the arm. "Steady, big fella," 00π advised.

"Right," squeaked Scorpion Mandando. "Thanks, π." I guess he had the right to call 00π just π because together, as fighting comrades of Aurelian, they formed a fraternity of two.

"Just let me do the talking," 00π told the rest of us.

"Aw, shucks," said Oliver. "And here I was hoping to find out if I'm related to the little scamp."

As the newcomer hovered in place about five meters away and three meters above us, 00π made a sign of greeting recognized in most cultures and said, "Howdy, little man. What brings you to these parts?"

The pillbox man shrugged, meaning his flight unit quivered a little; he apparently couldn't move his practically nonexistent shoulders. "A time machine brings me, of course," he quarbled in reply. "And I am not a little man," he added petulantly. "I am a male analogue, of massive stature for my race."

"And what race is that?" asked 00π.

"The future race of man, of course," he replied, as if it should have been perfectly obvious. Then he appeared to reconsider. "Well, one of the future races of man. That's why we invented a time machine, so someone with my unique masculine prowess could go back into time and manipulate events to ensure the evolutionary development of my people."

"I understand perfectly," said 00π, who was the kind of hero who could tell a lie. "But you're likely to run into trouble. We Aurelians like to control our own destinies, and even though we don't know exactly where we're going, we prefer it that way."

"That's what you think. Free will shall not be achieved in this timestream for at least another eon or so," said the pillbox man. Suddenly his beady blue eyes went wide in agitation. "Uh-oh! My fission clock's belatedly informing me that I've come too early. But you look like the right group. One, two, three, four . . . There are too many of you. I *am* early. Damn, sorry about that." He waved goodbye as he floated backwards. "Please do not permit this incident to influence your future actions, at least not for the next ten chrons or so. Things are complicated enough as they are, and who knows what's going to happen if the wires of the destiny get crossed any more than they already are."

Then he flew up and disappeared behind the billboard. "Oh yes!" he called out from the other side. "My condolences to somebody I can't reveal yet!" A mild yellow light flashed for less than a blink from the other side.

"He's gone," said Scorpion.

"How do you know?" I asked.

"Because the smell of death is gone."

"I think it was his flesh," said 00π.

"What? Are you trying to tell me that little guy was dead?" I asked.

"Yes and no. His flesh was dead," said 00π. "You might have noticed a peculiar pastel tone to his complexion, that of the subtle kind of makeup he used to make his flesh appear alive."

"I did notice that!" said Yangtze. "I just didn't know what to make of it."

"That's all right," I said. "I don't know what to make of it either."

"Don't you grok, Boss?" said Oliver. "The living part of him's sustained only by his cybernetic machinery!"

"He was a cybernetic zombie," I said, glancing at Yangtze.

"Is," she corrected.

"Will be," recorrected Scorpion. "In a little while."

"About ten chrons, I wager," said 00π. "Spaceside, are you still with us?"

"I think so, man," he said in that infuriatingly noncommittal tone of his.

"Is there something to this gig that you've refrained from telling us?"

Spaceside pursed his lips as if he'd just sucked on a fresh lemon. "Man, you heard my story. It's all I know. But you tell me: just based strictly on what you know already, don't you think there's a lot more to this gig than meets the eyeball?"

With that, Spaceside turned away and led us deeper into the district. 00π and Scorpion warily flanked the group. Occasionally one paused to sniff the air. Once 00π stopped us at an intersection as Scorpion scouted ahead. Finding nothing amiss, Scorpion waved us forward and Spaceside again assumed the lead.

The spaces between the buildings grew narrower as we progressed. Soon the people exited their buildings and disappeared down the subway entrances in waves. The scent of air conditioning became thicker, blowing past us in a steady breeze, ruffling our hair and sleeves as well as the leaves of the trees planted in the cramped spaces between apartment buildings.

Finally we reached a great square. In the center was a mansion, guarded by stoic-faced sentries in red-and-green paisley robes who stared straight ahead like men mesmerized, except for the one who nodded at Spaceside. We passed them and entered an arbor lined with trees and orange bushes. In the distance we could see a massive front porch with a great double wooden doorway.

"This is the residence of Wotan Amon, a powerful block king indeed," said 00π. "Regardless of what happens, or how you are treated, be respectful at all times. Unless you want to end up like Scorpion here." Then, to Spaceside: "I understand why you obeyed so unquestioningly. All is forgiven."

"I wouldn't say that," mumbled Scorpion in a stress-laden squeak.

Lifting the massive brass knocker on the door to

the left, Spaceside replied, "Oh, I questioned all right. It's just that there's a time for everything, a time to rebel and a time to obey, and it was definitely time to obey." He slammed down the knocker once and the door opened, seemingly of its own accord.

The sweet aroma of incense and consciousness-altering substances swept past us. We entered an immense foyer. "Nice trophies," said Scorpion, referring to the skeletons of alien warriors in full armor standing like statues against both walls, an exhibition of might that presumably warded off evil spirits.

At the end of the hall, on the edge of the worn yellow carpet, stood an old woman in a brown and purple robe. She wore a leather helmet decorated with horns and tusks of many varieties and she puffed madly on a huge reefer. Reaching into a pouch slung around her shoulder, she withdrew a white powder which she sprinkled on the carpet while uttering the words of a spell. *May happy days be here again,* she chanted. *O woe is me! May happy days be here again! O woe is me, Wotan! O bigger woe is you! May you bless these guests! May these guests bless you! May happy days come again! May happy days be here again!* She didn't stop chanting until we reached her, and then she had eyes only for 00π. "Come for another one of my hypnotic potions, big boy?" she asked in a rasping croak that strove to be seductive.

"Not today," replied 00π. "Only business today, and no pleasure."

Her beady eyes grew serious. "O double woe is me. Do you smell it too?"

"I think we saw it, but it didn't make much sense to us," said 00π. "It hinted that should we last the next ten chrons, we might know something."

"It is the kind of death that brings no glory," added Scorpion. "Only misery and dimness of mind and thought."

"Then enter," she said, opening the next door. "I'm staying here, trying to keep out of harm's way." She winked at 00π. "And when your business is over, come visit me. I've got a new diaphragm that's an interdimensional tesseract—it's definitely got a few surprises in store."

"I'll remember that if I survive the next few surprises," said 00π gently as she closed the door behind us.

"Daddy! You haven't really fucked *that*, have you?" exclaimed Yangtze in a stage whisper.

"She has potions you wouldn't believe," said 00π with a dreamy expression in his eyes. "Some of them make her as beautiful in your mind's eye as anything you're capable of imagining. Even more so. After all, sex doesn't happen to the body, just in the mind."

"Pervert," mumbled Yangtze. "My old man, the space hero, is really a goddamn pervert. What's this galaxy coming to?"

I didn't know the answer to that, but it was immediately obvious we had come to an empty room. The walls were lined with cheap wood paneling, and there were a few wrestling mats on the floor and several lighting fixtures in the ceiling. That was all.

But that was also when I smelled death, really smelled it, as brilliantly as I had encountered the overwhelming odor of rotting flesh on the battlefield of the Transcendenticons. It permeated my saliva and sweat glands; it clung to Yangtze and 00π and Scorpion and Spaceside and it even invaded the oil pan odor of Oliver. The smell was part of the memory of the psychedelic drug *ka* that Reina had twice given me, and it was part of every dream I'd ever forgotten. The smell was like the flip side of life.

Death and life are in perfect balance in this room, I thought, trying not to tense overmuch as a panel slid over the door to prevent us from leaving. *I wonder if—no,* how—*our presence here's gonna up-set things?*

00π and Scorpion gave every indication of enjoy-ing the situation. In addition to leaving his laser pistol unholstered, Scorpion withdrew a hunting knife from concealment in his boot. 00π remained unarmed, at least obviously so, but he walked tensely and war-ily, like a great cat ready to spring. Surely his body alone could be counted as a lethal weapon.

Yangtze stayed close to me, and Oliver practi-cally attached himself to Yangtze. Spaceside walked apart; perspiration beaded on his forehead and he shivered involuntarily. He actually turned his power pack down. Then he calmed completely, almost in-stantly. He appeared strangely relaxed and confident. I thought perhaps he had decided to accept his fate and that he was fighting to stick to that decision.

I was wrong. The decision had been made for him.

The results weren't pretty. But then again, pos-session never is.

Spaceside suddenly froze in place and trembled as if having an epileptic seizure while being sub-jected to voltage at the electrocution threshold. Saliva dribbled out of his mouth, and when his convulsions reached an incredible intense peak, he sprayed the immediate vicinity so thoroughly with that fluid that the rest of us recoiled from him in self-defense. After a few moments he walked mechanically about in cir-cles, like a toy boat with a broken rudder. His fingers were splayed far apart, as stiff as sticks, and his elbows bent back and forth like rusted springs trapped in motion. He swayed left and right, and his eyes grew wide with the sight of a nameless horror just beyond my range of perception.

I *felt* the horror, though; a chill had entered the room that hardened the marrow in my bones. I knew instantly, as the others must have known instantly, that Spaceside's ego had been displaced by another, originating from a place we did not know.

"Uh, does this happen often on Aurelian?" I asked.

"It can if you're a believer," said 00π, "which I happen to know that Spaceside isn't."

"It doesn't matter, though," said Yangtze, "if the deity wants a host bad enough it will find one."

"What do we do now?" I asked.

"I, for one, would like to say for the record that we should run like the blazes," said Oliver.

"Where to?" asked Scorpion, pointing both his knife and pistol toward Spaceside. Never taking my eyes off the posessed man, I asked Scorpion if, while in this condition, Spaceside could do harm to anyone but himself. "Depends on how powerful the deity riding him is, old bean. Some are just tricksters. They have just a little bit of power. Others have great power. Seeing as how we're in Wotan Amon's abode, I'd say the latter is the more probable."

Suddenly Spaceside's convulsions ceased and he stood straight and tall. As if from nothingness a cane had appeared in his hand. He held it before him with both hands on the top, the tip flat on the floor between his feet. He smirked and giggled. **Hee-Hee-Hee. Baron Hardehar Cohen bids you greetings.**

"I didn't know the baron had degenerated to the point of using *loa*," said 00π.

"Nor did I know he was in league with a scumbag like Wotan," added Scorpion.

Ooh, watch yourself, said "Spaceside" in mock seriousness. **You are, after all, a guest.**

"Only temporarily," replied Scorpion.

The gods have chosen to stitch together the destinies of the baron and Wotan for a short time, said "Spaceside," leaning against an invisible column and twirling his cane like a man on a holiday walk. As for me, I am but an unworthy *loa*—a lowlife deity mainly interested in having a good time—doing a few favors for the baron in the hopes that my divine superiors may look more favorably upon me during the lifetimes to come. And as for the baron's sudden willingness to strike a deal with the religious sector, well, let's just say it's been coming on for a long time, and right now he needs all the help he can get.

"Oh? Tell us more," prodded 00π.

He's become a close personal friend of the Farce—that is to say, he's been seduced by the Frothy Side.

I think at that moment you could have knocked 00π over with a gluon. "By Seldon's knickers!" he exclaimed. "That explains a lot. Is the Baron involved in what's happening here?"

Only by accident, said "Spaceside," throwing the cane into the air and catching it a few times. He seemed bewitched by his own activity; the *loa*, whatever it was exactly, seemed overjoyed with its presence on this physical plane. He treated his conversation almost as an afterthought. **That's why he requested that Wotan permit his house to be used for a test, and why Wotan accepted. They too do not appreciate the intertwining of their fates, and they desire oh so fervently that the beings responsible have their fates brought to quick, untimely conclusions. To this end, my orders were to usurp one of you, so that your group's worthiness to face the fate that will befall you could be judged. Personally, I don't get it. When the gods demand a soul at a certain time, they will have it then, no sooner, no later. It doesn't pay, you see, to show up early at an appointment with Death.**

"So this means the Baron is somehow connected with the death of Wotan's daughter?" I ventured to observe.

"Yes, but not necessarily as a result of design," said Scorpion, who had relaxed a tad. "If the Baron's been seduced by the Frothy Side, then I can almost feel sorry for the floating fat jerk. I'd wager what's left of my brains that the Baron wishes he'd kept his fat fingers in the economic sector!"

"I tried the Frothy Side once," Yangtze observed. "You notice your friends doing it so you think it's cool. At first it seems like fun, and so you try it again, and again. But after a while the average, everyday, ordinary absurdity doesn't satisfy you, so you need more, and more, and more. Absurdity compounds upon absurdity, and pretty soon nothing in life makes any sense at all. Living on the edge is all that counts. And finally you discover you've completely lost control of your life."

"So that's when you decided to go into religion, eh, babe?" asked Oliver.

"Well, yeah," replied Yangtze in perfect seriousness. "Now that the goddess Marie has favored me, I feel my life's resting at last on a smooth sphere."

00π covered his face, evidently thinking otherwise.

"Spaceside," meanwhile, had begun concentrating so hard on twirling his cane that he appeared to have forgotten all about us. Scorpion got his attention by firing a short laser burst between his legs. "Spaceside" nearly dropped the cane, then motioned as if to throw it at Scorpion. The space hunter just grinned as "Spaceside" reconsidered the matter and said, **You boys got something on your minds?**

"We saw a flying entity today," said 00π. "We think he was a cybernetic zombie from a time line in the future, maybe even a time line that hasn't been laid down yet. Was his presence related to the baron's activities?"

I cannot say. I can say, however, that some cybernetic deceased flesh has been making the rounds lately. You see, the baron believed he could predict with certainty when an absurdity would work in his favor, so he secured the services of certain renegade scientists who had done some research into the, ah, deeper mysteries of existence. There's no point in going into detail now—you'll just have to take my word that they came up with some fairly intense absurdities that infected the mainstream of society long before the baron intended, thus putting the kibosh on the baron's higher ambitions pretty damn quick, let me tell you. Now he's made a score of new enemies, and his old ones feel renewed hatred for him. But he sincerely believes his responsibility for the unforeseen disasters is strictly limited.

"That's what all the Farce-users say," replied 00π grimly.

True, but sometimes you find the absurdity, and sometimes the absurdity finds you, said "Spaceside." The cane changed into a shower of yellow flower petals with a wave of his hand.

Now that's interesting. It may be that Floyd's predicament is one of those absurdities! I realized with a rush of excitement. *Maybe this Farcical Force you can't explain without giving away the punch line of life isn't so bad after all!*

"Well, you've certainly given us something to chew on, Mr. *Loa*," said Scorpion, "but the smell of death still reeks in this room. What's going to happen to Spaceside Hodgson when you stop riding him?"

The same thing that was always fated to happen, he said with a mirthful grin. **Those who**

are about to croak, I salute you. You shall go to your death knowing more, but perhaps less, than you otherwise might have.

00π said philosophically, "If you villains only knew how many times I'd indulged your kind, just to have a little more information that ultimately made no difference whatsoever . . ."

"If we did," said Yangtze, "we'd be as old as you!"

This interlude has been brought to you by the gods, said "Spaceside," shaking like a branch of a tree in a hurricane. **You may now resume your normal destinies, already in progress.**

"Terrific," said Oliver. "Now one of us is going to die."

00π narrowed his eyes with steely determination. "Not if I can help it!" 00π stepped up to "Spaceside" and struck him on the jaw, decking him instantly. The possessed rock-and-roll singer plummeted down like a bevy of asteroids.

You scumbag, said the *loa* from the unconscious mouth.

"Wow," said Yangtze, looking up at her father in awe. "You knocked him out before he could do anything."

00π smiled smugly and nursed his bruised knuckles. "Yeah, I did."

Suddenly an incredible flash of blinding orange light came into being around Spaceside, causing every stitch of his clothing to go up in flames. The flames disappeared in an instant, leaving behind not a burn or even a singed hair.

"Wow," said Yangtze, looking down at Spaceside's naked body. "I think I can find an entirely new respect for this guy."

The rest of us just watched in a mixture of horror and fascination as every hair on Spaceside's body stood straight up. And that wasn't all the *loa* left standing. "Yeah, definitely a new kind of respect," added Yangtze.

"Does this mean we've passed this particular test?" Oliver asked.

"Possibly, but perhaps it has yet to begin."

That last was spoken by a person or thing in a black, hooded robe, standing in the doorway on the other side of the room. His voice was immersed in a permanent phase distortion. His hands were hidden in his sleeves, as were his feet beneath the hem, but we saw, thanks to the open buttons below his neck, that his torso consisted of a computer bank. His face was a numbered clock; the hands on the dial indicated it was half-past first chron. Close enough, but I wouldn't have set my flight procedures according to that face.

"It's U-Shant Eye!" snarled Scorpion. "I might have known you'd show your steel face around here! Absorbed any raw hearts lately?"

"Only those of my enemies," replied the clock-faced entity. "That is why your own heart has not passed through my admittedly unusual digestive system. It is also why you still, in a manner of speaking, have your own head upon your shoulders. You see, Scorpion Mandando, you and I are not enemies; you are in my view merely the perpetrator of a heinous transgression."

"All I did was kiss a girl," protested Scorpion, lamely.

"It's the girl you tried to kiss, and more," replied U-Shant Eye evenly. "You are as aware as anyone of the high value of virgins on this island, particularly when they are the daughters of block kings." He held up a tentacled hand to cut off Scorpion's next protest. He had rows of gray, undulating suction cups on the bottom of the tentacles; they were perhaps the external organs of the unusual digestive system he had referred to. "Please, spare me the obligatory wry observation about virgins being a rare and valuable commodity throughout the entire galaxy. The point is, you threw a complex political arrangement, to be sealed by sanctified marriage, into chaos, and thus may be held partially accountable for the violence the omens have indicated may be visited upon our fair block later this day." U-Shant Eye paused, rubbing the dials on his face as if they itched. Maybe they really did, but I wasn't in a hurry to know. "Believe me, Scorpion Mandando, Wotan and I bore you no personal animosity when we punished you. We merely acted to restore the balance as we perceived it must be. That was why we also cast upon you a spell of haziness, to confuse and frustrate your natural inclinations toward seeking revenge. How could you fight back against that which you could not truly remember?"

Scorpion absently rubbed the outside of his helmet as if it was his chin. "I understand. I thank you, sir, for this information. Already my mind is eased as I grok the motivations for my strange acquiescence to the fate that has gripped me since the onslaught of your heinous, subhuman spell."

"*Post*human," U-Shant Eye corrected.

"But I reiterate," protested Scorpion lamely, "all I did was kiss a girl."

"Ah, but it's *where* you kissed her," replied U-Shant Eye.

Yangtze rolled her eyes toward the ceiling; Oliver and 00π smiled, while Spaceside on the floor just groaned. We had all been amused at how Scorpion's story invariably changed to suit the needs of the moment.

"All right, I'll co-operate with you and Wotan for the time being," said Scorpion after mulling things over for a millichron. "Besides, I'm just tagging along with 00π."

"That's what the faces of the clocks I broke against the wall last night during my prayers indicated would happen, but I thought it might be best if we cleared this matter up before proceeding," said U-Shant Eye. "I cannot help but congratulate the lot of you, by the way, for so nicely circumventing the most recent whims of fate. The odor of death can no longer be detected by my mystical sensors."

"We can't help but grok we've had a slight reprieve," said 00π, putting a protective arm around his daughter's shoulder.

"This is all well and good," said Scorpion, idly twirling his laser gun around his finger, "but what's in this security racket for me?"

"The satisfaction of a job well done?" said 00π.

"I need something more than that," said Scorpion.

"Of course," said U-Shant Eye. "Another spell will be cast after the funeral, a spell of redress."

"Great!" exclaimed Scorpion. "But when you change me back to my former self, can you fix my nose? It was never the same after it was smashed by that banth back in '42. Or was it '47?"

"Is there any aspect of your new body you'd like to remain as is?" asked U-Shant Eye slyly.

Scorpion grinned. "Some sacrifices I can make."

Spaceside groaned again and sat up, nursing his jaw. "Anybody get the frequency of that shuttle?" Then he looked down at himself, and his eyes widened in shock at the sight of his proudly erect member. "I'm naked! What's more, I'm excited!" He looked around, becoming paler by the millichron. "At what? Who did this to me?"

U-Shant Eye helped Spaceside stand. When the posthuman grabbed the rock star's arm, the suction cups on his tentacles made squishing noises, leaving tiny little bruises in their wake. "Do not fret, my friend. Your response to the proximity of your demise is a natural enough thing."

"You mean I almost died? And it turned me on?" He pounded his power pack as if a circuit had shorted out.

"Do you know the address to your fan club?" Yangtze asked, her eyelids fluttering.

"It was in my pocket!" Spaceside took U-Shant Eye aside in a vain effort at privacy and said, "I can't go on naked!"

"Oh look, he's got a birthmark on his ass!" exclaimed Yangtze, pointing.

"I guess if he's got a twin somewhere, they'll be able to recognize each other, eh, Boss?" said Oliver.

"U-Shant, I need some clothes," insisted Spaceside. "My dignity depends on it."

"Strange, how you humans care so much about your thin veneers of civilization," said U-Shant Eye. "Oh well, if you must have clothing, you must have clothing."

"I notice you're wearing clothes, Mr. Eye Person," said Yangtze.

"Ssshh!" said 00π. "It's better that he does."

"Your father speaks truth," said U-Shant Eye. He stiffened his tentacles and slapped them together, twice. "One feat of atomic reconstruction, coming up!"

A whirlwind began to spin in the center of the room. In a matter of moments a black mass coagulated in its center. At first I thought it was just some dust lifted from the floor, but as the size and density of the blackness grew, I realized it originated from other, deeper sources.

The wind died suddenly without so much as an instant of slowing down—one minute it was turbulent and the next it was absolutely still. But where once there had been dust, there hung suspended in midair an exact duplicate of Spaceside's clothing, down to and including a pair of white and blue polka-dotted briefs. Then the clothing fell to the floor.

Spaceside eagerly began dressing. "This is fantastic. U-Shant! Uh, are all my hidden amenables intact too?"

U-Shant Eye shrugged wearily. "Yes, of course, though why a mind such as yours feels the need to alter its mode of consciousness, I shall never understand. I should think that for you, the mere act of functioning would be difficult enough."

"Who wants to function? I'm a rock-and-roll star." As he put on his shirt, he withdrew a joint from a pocket. At least he had the good sense to tie his shoes before he lit it. "Besides, I've got to keep in shape. I mean, after the funeral I'm due to sing the blues!"

"When do we get to meet Wotan?" I asked.

"Not until the funeral," said U-Shant Eye, "though it will behoove you to pay your respects to the corpse first. Wotan sends his regrets, by the way. According to our beliefs, a grieving father must exclude himself from society before all burial ceremonies."

"What's this business about his daughter not wanting to stay dead?" Yangtze asked. "I didn't think corpses had much of a choice."

"All your questions will be answered in good time," said U-Shant Eye, turning away.

The AC kicked on just in time to keep Spaceside's face from being completely obscured by the reefer smoke. He should have been nicknamed Smokestack. "Nobody gets off this plane alive," he observed as he staggered to a standing position.

"They usually don't want to after hearing your music," said 00π, helping him remain upright.

U-Shant Eye then led us through a series of winding corridors broken only by a succession of unmarked, undistinguished intersections. We had entered a maze beneath the mansion, a maze so convoluted, so masterfully laid out, that our only hope of returning to the surface quickly lay with our guide.

Now I never did receive an adequate explanation as to what U-Shant Eye meant by "posthuman." Perhaps Wotan's main shaman had been a man before replacing his anatomy with cybernetic devices and alien organs. One thing was certain. Such an entity, who had committed such a radical desecration of his own body, was likely to revoke his word at his convenience and therefore could never truly be trusted. For this reason I was glad that Scorpion, for all his willingness to forget and forgive in light of their new arrangement, did not take his beady little eyes off our guide for an instant. Nor did his fingers ever stray from the flap of his holster.

Oliver, for his part, kept a surreptitious record of our travels by pointing his eyes in separate directions, and tracing outlines on his palm as a visual aid. I'm sure he needed it. Mechanical logic problems, such as retracing his steps, weren't meant to be among his major functions.

Spaceside, meanwhile, puffed madly on reefer after reefer. I was getting a contact high that buzzed like a sun bee, and Oliver made sure that he always walked directly behind the rock star. How Spaceside managed to conceal such a mammoth supply of drugs on his person, by the way, was a mystery to me. I'm still surprised that the THC molecules had been able to get it together long enough to reconstitute themselves at U-Shant Eye's command.

Perhaps 00π regretted having brought his daughter with him. He paid more attention to Yangtze than to anything else, almost doting on her, but always speaking tersely. She didn't seem to mind and always answered him with a friendly wisecrack. It probably wasn't easy being the daughter of a galactic legend, even a retired one.

00π took pains to conceal that our pace was a tad too brisk for him. His famous stamina was a thing of the past. Occasionally I debated asking the others if we could take a break, ostensibly for my sake, but I doubted 00π would have permitted it. He had his pride. He wouldn't let us slow down for his sake until he was in the grip of a coronary.

As for U-Shant Eye, he glided across the floor. Either he didn't have feet and was really gliding, or else he indeed had feet and I was better off not knowing what they looked like. In any case, his robe concealed his mode of transportation.

Finally, after an indeterminate time, we picked up a pungent scent capable of holding its own against the sweet aroma Spaceside was manufacturing. It was a familiar scent.

It was the smell of death.

"Seldon, that's grotty to the max!" exclaimed Yangtze, perhaps summing it up for us all.

Scorpion nodded. "You never get used to it," he said.

00π grimaced and said, "This is one curse a five-day deodorant pad will never cure."

"Daddy! Don't tell me you wear . . ." Yangtze whispered.

"Just kidding," 00π said wryly. "Don't even know what they look like."

"I've always doubted cleanliness was uppermost in your mind," said U-Shant Eye. "I thank the gods I was permitted to give up such frivolous pastimes when I was transformed."

"We noticed," said Oliver.

"Afraid you'd oxidize your private parts?" asked Scorpion.

"He's a man who misses his lust, thanks to his rust," said Spaceside.

U-Shant Eye put his tentacled hands to his clock-face as if to tear out his dials. "Will you people stop it with those one-liners? There's a dead woman in the next room, and she needs peace and quiet!"

"Say what?" asked Oliver, doing a perfect Spaceside Hodgson imitation.

I'll tell you what I say! shouted a voice from the next room. **I'm a deceased devil-woman with a red dress on, a living-dead monstrosity who says set me free, set me free! Do it today, before my Prince Charming does the job for you!**

We were all, I am certain, immediately cognizant of many things in regard to that voice: it spoke proudly, defiantly, and with remarkable enunciation despite a certain lisp that I, for one, was certain to be caused by a rotten, swollen tongue, an unavoidable side effect of its state of decay. And yet, despite the lisp, the voice boomed quite clearly.

"Even in death, you remain quite the pushy broad," mumbled U-Shant Eye with annoyance as he glided to the door and the foretentacle of his right arm wrapped itself around the doorknob. Yangtze squeezed my arm, and Oliver huddled behind me. 00π simply glared piercingly at the door, his bushy white eyebrows scowling so low, they were in danger of slipping off his nose. Having finally achieved the mental state he thought necessary to survive this leg of the journey with his sanity intact, Spaceside pursed his lips in an attempt to look nonchalant, but only succeeded in looking awfully smashed.

From the first moments the dead woman had spoken, Scorpion's eyes had grown steadily wider and by her last words they had nearly achieved normal size. His fingers drummed incessantly on the flap of his holster. His breath came in an audible wheeze. I had the distinct sensation an emotion stronger than fear, deeper than pride, had begun to get the best of him. He gritted his teeth in anticipation.

U-Shant Eye twisted the knob and the latch was released. The door swung open and he glided inside, gesturing for us to follow.

We didn't. We just looked at one another. "Well," said 00π, gesturing impatiently at Scorpion, "you always said you'd give anything if you could talk to her again. Go inside."

"You first," Scorpion replied. "I can't be objective about this."

"I'll go in," said Yangtze determinedly. "No one who's really dead can be as decayed as she sounded and still talk."

Spaceside bowed with a flourish, urging her inside.

"You go," Yangtze suddenly said to Oliver. "You're a robot, you can't die."

"Obviously you haven't been keeping up with current events," said Oliver.

What's the matter? said the voice inside the room. **There's nothing to worry about. I can't bite.**

Not in my current state of repose, anyway.

U-Shant Eye, meanwhile, had turned to face us from inside the room. If he was amused or otherwise had a reaction to our reluctance, he of course had no way of showing it. His expression was truly as blank as those of the primitive robots built during the First Empire, now only seen on exhibition in museums.

Evidently able to restrain himself no longer, Scorpion brushed past me. That was exactly the inducement the rest of us required, and we found ourselves wedged in the doorway. Oliver and I stepped back to permit the others to file in ahead.

Yangtze was the first to react, gasping and choking as if she'd just swallowed a Janissarian vapor bug. All the blood drained from her face, leaving her with a pasty yellow complexion. "Da-da-daddy . . ." she managed to stammer.

"An abomination!" exclaimed 00π, his face red, the muscles of his neck wound up like the cords of a rope. "A blasphemous scourge! By the gods, if this is what civilization has come to—!"

"Possibly civilization has already come to worse," said U-Shant Eye casually, "but M'Bell's our very own scourge, and since she was Wotan's daughter he insists she have a decent funeral."

I'd rather have a decent burial, said the dead M'Bell slyly.

Without so much as a glance between them, Spaceside held out the latest reefer to Oliver. Evidently my faithful robot companion had decided to join Spaceside in his vain attempt to escape from reality, and with an almost telepathic sixth sense, Spaceside had responded to my friend's need like a true good Samaritan. Oliver, who was equipped with a powerful air ventilation system operating through his speaking orifice, turned the joint into a tiny cinder in a matter of moments.

"Impressive," said Spaceside, as Oliver returned the roach to him.

Scorpion tried to wipe a glistening tear from his eye. Once again he had forgotten he was wearing his helmet. He stepped forward like a sleepwalker to the coffin where the dead woman lay chained in repose.

00π grabbed him by the arm, detaining him. "Don't do it, Scorpion," he said grimly. "Don't get any closer to her."

Why not? said M'Bell. **The results can't be as bad for him as they were the last time.**

"This is her?" asked Spaceside incredulously. "This is the dame you got your head shrunk for?"

154

Scorpion nodded, but did not take his pathetically plaintive eyes off her. It was very clear that the sight of this woman brought forth a rush of memories and emotions that Scorpion had been doing his best to actively suppress, even without the assistance of a spell of forgetfulness.

Oliver whistled in amazement. "Extreme obligation, bipeds!" he exclaimed.

"That's heavy—" began Spaceside. "Oh, never mind."

If you think I'm fetching now, said M'Bell, drawing her own conclusions, **you should have seen me when I was alive. But in a way my beauty was wasted. I didn't know how to use what I had to my advantage. I was so much more naive then; I'm wiser than that now.**

"I didn't think you naive, not at all," replied Scorpion. "During our brief time together, you brought me more light than I had seen from a thousand suns."

You sweet-talker, you, she said, drawing back her lips. Her unnatural grin revealed two elongated canine teeth as sharp as needles. Her straining to achieve perfect enunciation indicated she hadn't yet adjusted to those metamorphosed canines, but otherwise she had taken to being undead like a Gullian balloon-flyer takes to a methane atmosphere. The process of skin decay had been arrested just beyond the initial outbreak of rigor mortis. Her complexion was waxen and gray, while the epidermis was like an overripe fruit whose rind was on the verge of bursting open. A cross of flour marked her forehead. Her basically hexagonal coffin rested on a slab leaning against the wall at an angle of approximately forty-five degrees; the coffin was wider at the top to accommodate her curly, black hair, fanned out and pinned to the boards in what struck me as an unintentional parody of a stylized halo. Her eyes gleamed with an energy precisely the opposite of the essence we associate with life.

"Do not touch her," U-Shant Eye warned Scorpion, wrapping a restraining tentacle around the space hunter's hand, thus preventing him from grasping the thin gray fingers chained to the dead woman's side. "Her touch may prove impossible for you to resist, and resist her you must if her soul is to survive."

He is an adult quite capable of taking care of himself, said M'Bell. **Let him find his own way.**

"I warn you now, devil-woman with the red dress on, stay your unholy powers, lest I be forced to burn out your eyes before the ritual, thus dooming your soul to an eternal deprivation more terrible than extinguishment." From concealment in his robes U-Shant Eye withdrew his own personal laser weapon, spinning it on his tentacle with a finesse the grittiest space bounty hunter in the baddest mining colonies might have envied.

She replied with a grin, **I shall respect your wishes . . .**

The blaster disappeared back into the folds of U-Stant Eye's robes.

For the moment.

"I have heard stories of such unfortunates who waver between the planes of life and death," said 00n. "I have heard them from shamans and crones throughout the galaxy, as well as hardened outposters who need a grisly story with their drink to send shivers of pleasure down their spines. In fact, the motif of the undead is well known to serious students of galactic lore. Still, no cases have been purported to have happened recently, save perhaps as some kind of prank. And still, the spiritual agony she endures is a torture

I wouldn't wish on the Baron himself. U-Shant Eye, I understand Wotan's urgency. The burial ceremony must go forward today without delay!"

"Is it like they say in the stories?" asked a timorous Yangtze. "Is it true *this* can happen to anyone?"

"Unfortunately, the answer, as things stand now, must be yes," said U-Shant Eye. "The whereabouts of the culprit responsible have yet to be pinpointed. Rest assured, though, Wotan has enlisted the services of every thief, prostitute, addict, and lowlife on the island. Even now, his army of spies is stationed throughout the length and the breadth of the tunnels, on every level and in every social stratum. The culprit whom the Baron accidentally inflicted upon our frail colony will be found and will be dealt with as the legends instruct."

And for those reasons you will burn out my eyes before the mind transference? Well then, do what you will—see if I care. You will never find your culprit. My lover is invincible. To me he is no fiend, but a shining beacon of light where all else is dark. And he is of noble blood. The roots of his unholy lineage can be traced to the mother planet, long before the dawn of the First Empire, and yet he is utterly comfortable with the frenetic pace of the most rad elements of modern city living. And he has other advantages, U-Shant Eye, advantages even you haven't thought about, advantages not even the tortures of the living could force me to reveal. She paused. **Go on. Try me.**

"Your words are specifically chosen to cause me to doubt," replied U-Shant Eye evenly, with only a trace of anger. "But do not delude yourself for a moment into thinking I regard you as the M'Bell I once knew. Therefore, how can your most vicious insults possibly sting? I cannot be wounded by the wind."

What a pathetic syllogism. How futilely you attempt to deny that which you have no choice but to acknowledge! Look at me! I freely admit it, I am dead. If I wasn't, do you think I'd be shackled up this way? Futilely, she rattled her chains. Made of a tungsten-silver alloy, they were wrapped several times around her body and allowed her precious little movement. Many links were pinned to the coffin by large staples, splintering the wood. Some of the splinters had ripped into her red dress or dug into her skin, causing bloodless wounds. **What do you think of these chains, Scorpion? They give you any ideas—remind you of any suggestions you may have once made to me?**

"I like this woman, Boss, even if she is dead," said Oliver. "She's got tremendous imagination. I bet she's chock full of possibilities."

"I'm not sure you and she would be shooting for the same possibilities," I replied, "so you keep away from her. She's dead, for Seldon's sake! Don't you have any standards at all? Any sense of pride?"

"Boss, why should her being dead have anything to do with my standards? Dead or alive, she's nonetheless composed of organic matter, which is what my attention monitors seem to be focusing on these days."

Blood or oil, it's all the same to me, you little creep. Crom, I hate robots. They are the true abominations of our galaxy. They only masquerade as the caretakers of life. Don't get me wrong. I am not now, nor have I ever been, a mindless bigot. My condition dictates a certain degree of open-mindedness. A few metal parts tacked onto organic matter are okay, even pleasurable; they make you feel like you've grabbed

onto something substantial. But a metal meal devoid of flesh is like a diet soft drink without carbonation—it lacks pizzazz!

"You're so bitter!" Yangtze exclaimed. "Is death so terrible that it naturally results in such rampaging cynicism?"

You must be kidding. I am not bitter. I have merely perceived the truth of things beyond the veil. And as one dead, I have no need of reaching a philosophical compromise with the conditions of my environment. Come to me, my dear, let me stir you. Permit me the honor of opening your eyes. You have been as one asleep, but after one chron in my company you shall learn the true meaning of life, and drink deeply from the well of pleasure.

"Don't give in to her. It's all a scam," said 00π, his hand blocking Yangtze from the coffin. She looked at her father, first in annoyance, then with the realization that she had actually taken a step forward, had almost been willing to give in to the dead woman's exhortations. 00π nodded in confirmation.

"That was a mean thing to do," Yangtze accused M'Bell, though she now refrained from looking directly into the corpse's eyes. "I was only trying to be friendly."

I've no need of friends.

"Just what do you have need of?" asked Spaceside suspiciously.

You might do . . . for starters.

"No thanks," he replied, taking yet another toke. "I got my career to look out for."

"This is all my fault," said Scorpion, shaking his head sadly. Little flecks of black skin fell off his neck, working their way under his helmet and resting on his shoulders like ashes floating in from a distant bonfire. Things definitely weren't airtight in Scorpion's cranial container.

"It is the fault of no one," replied 00π, his voice cool and steady. "She cannot help being the thing that she has become. She is not responsible for her own evil. No, if it must be the fault of something, then let it be the fault of the universe itself, forever indifferent to the plight of intelligent life, forever merciless and neutral."

"Oh, I see, Daddy," said Yangtze, "you're trying to be poetic."

"And a damn fine job he did too!" exclaimed Oliver. "For when you think about it, do the moons and the stars really care about all the confusion and suffering we poor deluded mortals undergo during the simple day-to-day struggle? I, for one, seriously doubt it. The moons and stars don't care if we live for a higher purpose or simply to make a buck and experience fast times. No, they don't care if we should die by fire, by ice, or by earthquake, or by the light of two lamps or three. And in the end, I think that's good. Where would this galaxy be now if we let our rulers guide us by the moons and the stars?"

"Don't mind him," I told 00π. "He's a twerp."

"I noticed," said 00π, "but he does have a point, however vague. The artisan who fashioned that picture on the wall probably felt much the same way." And 00π gestured at the mosaic above the coffin. Complex and colorful, it depicted a three-horned god, half man, half buffalo, raping a virginal priestess. But instead of the erect penis you would normally expect, the god proudly displayed a blazing bunsen burner. Both god and victim possessed strangely passive expressions. The god did not even look at the woman; though tied prone to a cross resting on the ground, she did not appear to be remotely concerned with the imminent event. *Let the universe do to you what it will*, the mosaic seemed to be saying. *Soon enough it won't matter anyway.*

The rest of the room was a bare grotto, with coarse rock walls that scraped the skin off your knuckles at even the slightest brush. The chipped concrete floor was covered by a single straw mat. A few tiny but bright light bulbs embedded in the ceiling gave off a harsh glow, and the air conditioning blew in the faint scent of peppermint and garlic incense. The complexity of the mosaic, contrasted with the otherwise austere decor, suggested that during less interesting times, people came here to make prayers and offerings to their personal deities.

"Come on, try to remember what you must have been like before you died," said Yangtze persistently. "What was your favorite color?"

M'Bell's lips pulled back and she hissed. Black vapor jetted from her nostrils. She laughed. **I like you. I think I'll make you my pet.**

"Don't you remember those happy chrons we spent together?" Scorpion implored, realizing Yangtze had attempted to reawaken whatever spark of humanity might remain in M'Bell. "When nothing was as important to us as the love and passion and need we felt for each other, when we actually thought we might overcome all odds and become soul mates for eternity?"

That still might happen, though the ground rules have changed somewhat.

"Don't do it, damn you!" exclaimed 00π, reaching out to detain Scorpion once again. "Don't go near her!"

"Sorry, I forgot," said Scorpion, putting his hand to his helmet as if to wipe away the perspiration now beading on his brow. "It's just that she's still so beautiful. It's so hard to believe that so much has happened in the last year . . ."

"Remember always that your eyes, however shrunken they may be, do not deceive you," said U-Shant Eye.

This is all your fault, U-Shant, said M'Bell with a hiss. **It was you who inadvertently consigned me to my current fate. I do not grieve for myself, that is beyond me now. But I cannot refrain from commenting that even by your standards you should be racked with an agony of horrific guilt; what you had foolishly believed would be only a punishment suitable to the so-called crime, in fact resulted in a disaster for which Wotan will certainly, sooner or later, hold you personally responsible.**

"Wotan and I have an understanding," the posthuman replied with a distinct lack of emotion.

Without warning, Scorpion grabbed U-Shant Eye and threw him repeatedly against the wall. U-Shant Eye's clocklike visage lost a screw or two every time Scorpion struck him. "What did you do?" Scorpion screamed. "What did you do to her?"

00π appeared more interested in the fact of Scorpion's anger than he was in the act of violence itself. Spaceside and Oliver sarcastically muttered phrases of approval, then started giggling. I stepped closer to the door for a quick getaway in case things got out of control.

U-Shant Eye's metal head quickly began reeling. Scorpion obviously wouldn't have shed any tears if he cracked U-Shant Eye's engine block, which remained a distinct possibility until Yangtze calmly stepped under Scorpion's arm and gently put her fingers on his chest. Now her father looked really amazed. She had moved in as quickly as he might have, established her presence, and stared Scorpion down with wide eyes positively exuding the sort of authority one

normally associates only with—why not admit it?
—galactic heroes.

For several long moments Scorpion did not know
what to do, but he finally did lower the staggering
U-Shant Eye.

M'Bell hissed, disappointed. I think she wanted
to see the posthuman break his universal joint.

"What did he do to you?" Scorpion asked the
dead woman in a voice that was a little dead itself.

**What he thought was appropriate. After our
tryst was discovered, he and Father agreed that
your head should be shrunk and a spell of haziness cast over you, and that I should be en-
rolled in Baron Hardehar Cohen's Divinity School
for Young Women. They knew it was an unusual step for a block king to take—men of Father's stripe generally prefer personally educating
their children, but Father had to admit that, in
this case, his indoctrination had failed. Father
especially regretted the huge fees that would
go into the baron's already bulging pockets, but
that too could not be helped. And there would
be advantages. Only the most wealthy send their
daughters to the Divinity School. There the education is strict and the grounds isolated and
drug-free. It seems the rich are no less senti-
mental about their daughters than are block
kings. They don't mind debauching themselves,
but they prefer that their daughters refrain from
debauchery for as long as possible, at least until they're married and then have no choice but
to act like everybody else.**

So off I went, to Divinity School. I didn't
mind it so much, after I got used to the idea. In
fact, the monastic existence, surrounded only
by those of my own sex, soon appealed to me.
The mystic training was interesting, as was

the instruction in arts and music. The gym was a nice place for a hearty workout, and the camaraderie proved adequate for the time being. Besides, whenever I was bored enough, I could always count on a one-night stand with one of the other girls. Everybody did it, and as a daughter of a block king among the bored children of the rich and famous, I didn't want to be a total outsider. Just a partial one, with the reputation of being reasonably discriminatory.

Even so, as time passed and I had almost forgotten the reason why I had been exiled to the Divinity School, I came to realize something was missing in my life. Something significant. Something that would give me a reason for living.

I knew it wasn't because of my burgeoning mystical education. It wasn't because I was exposed to the finest music, the greatest arts and crafts, and the best bodies on campus. It wasn't because I was going insane. It was because I was heeding the call.

I didn't know it then. Then I was only alive, a silly young girl on the verge of what living society calls maturity. Now that I am dead, I always hear the call, quite plainly. It permeates the ether. But back when I was alive, I heard the call only intermittently. It was like a whisper in the back of my mind. My studies faltered, my friendships lapsed, and the world I had inside my mind became infinitely more vivid than any other I had previously known. In time, a legion of counselors passed before my eyes, advising me to renounce the seductive lure of the Farce but by then it was already too late. I had already given in to the Frothy Side, gladly, utterly, without even knowing it.

And so one night, when the Nipponese moon was full in the sky of the space island that is the Divinity School, the call became like a symphony in my breast, and there was no civilized will left in me to resist.

I slipped from my quarters, evading the robomatrons. Bordering my dorm was a well-tended garden with flowers and plants from all over the galaxy. Nurtured by the lunar rays, the nocturnal flowers were in full bloom, their pale colors especially beautiful as I wandered, searching for the source of the call, searching for someone I knew with utter certainty would cut me entirely loose from the existence I had known.

He did find me. At first I thought him a man of unnatural beauty. A closer inspection proved I was right about the unnatural beauty, but about little else.

He beckoned me to come closer. I complied, standing with my hands at my hips, the artificial breeze caressing my skin through my flimsy nightgown, and breathing heavily with a desire I could then barely fathom.

He touched me. I realized then, with a curious acceptance, that he was neither man nor alive. He was dead flesh made animate by his cybernetic machinery and it was his intention—his right and his need—to see to it that I would never breathe heavily again.

But my desire, he promised as he opened his mouth and kissed my soft warm neck, would live forever.

The last sensations I experienced as a living entity were those of falling helplessly into his arms and feeling my hot blood stain my gown.

Having concluded her tale, M'Bell laughed. To say her tale had chilled me to the marrow is an understatement.

Scorpion and 00π exchanged one of those looks whose meaning, by now, could not escape me. After today's funeral, the hunt would begin in earnest.

"Her story's over!" exclaimed Oliver disappointedly. "I wanted to hear what happened next!"

"You already know," said U-Shant Eye.

"Does this mean we can go now?" asked Spaceside eagerly.

"We may leave the immediate vicinity," replied U-Shant Eye, "but our task is far from over."

Chapter Eight
Passing through the Flame

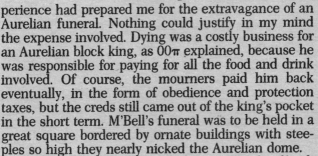

NOTHING IN MY EXperience had prepared me for the extravagance of an Aurelian funeral. Nothing could justify in my mind the expense involved. Dying was a costly business for an Aurelian block king, as 00π explained, because he was responsible for paying for all the food and drink involved. Of course, the mourners paid him back eventually, in the form of obedience and protection taxes, but the creds still came out of the king's pocket in the short term. M'Bell's funeral was to be held in a great square bordered by ornate buildings with steeples so high they nearly nicked the Aurelian dome.

Having permitted Spaceside to rejoin his band, 00π, Scorpion, Yangtze, Oliver, and I cased out the square. Technicians climbed atop the steeples and flying buttresses, preparing for the fireworks exhibition. Volunteer staff members hauled in truckloads of food and drink and set up snack counters down one length of the square, while on the other side a long, long bar with seating suitable for most life-forms was being erected. If the variously colored powders in the plastic bags were any indication, drink was not fated to be the sole conscious-altering substance to be handed out at the bar. Most of those dry substances were technically illegal, but I soon saw that the authorities here, as elsewhere, didn't mind looking the other way so long as they were allowed to pocket whatever they could carry inconspicuously.

A scruffy band of teenagers, mostly power junkies who wore their electric packs on their hips or over their ears, set up the equipment of Spaceside's band on the giant platform already erected in the center of the square, near where the materials for the bonfire had been stacked. After the teens were reduced to hanging around the bars, the cameramen arrived and plugged their equipment into outlets revealed by opening up metal shields on the macadam. Someone who must have been the director shouted out an order to someone on a flying buttress, and then four immense video screens slid down from the highest ledges. Regardless of where you stood in relation to the platform during the upcoming proceedings, you could count on several simultaneous Olympian views of something!

A few spectators—known as the oldsters—trickled in. They were the old, the wretched, and the medicated. The women covered their thinning hair with plain, translucent shawls. The men had skin so wrinkled and haggard that shaving of any sort, even with dissolving creams, was simply too painful and complicated to be accomplished effectively. Many of both sexes pulled themselves along with the help of pneumatic walkers, the bars interwoven with wires connected to the wrists and ankles. And many of these, though relieved of having to lift their walkers, were still too weak to hold on without their arms quivering and knees buckling. What sustained them, and all the others, was obvious: it was constantly being pumped into their varicose veins.

Their clothing consisted almost entirely of modest robes and sandals, but from the great variety of facial types and skin hues—not to mention all the genetic and medical restructuring—it was possible to deduce that they had, like so many on this island, originated from a variety of worlds. It was possible that for many, the reasons why they had come to the Avidya System was locked away in long forgotten memories. What broken dreams, what ash-bitter goals they might have harbored in their souls I would never know, but it was clear there remained one dream which they clung to tenaciously—the dream of holding on to life, no matter what the cost.

These oldsters said nothing to one another. They spoke only to themselves. I overheard one fine old lady complaining about the inconvenience of attending another funeral so soon after the last one. "Why are these people here?" I asked Scorpion.

"You mean in addition to the fact that attendance of a noble's funeral is *de rigeur* to the ultimate in these sectors?" he said, tipping up his helmet to light a foul-smelling cigarillo. "Wotan demands a certain degree of respect from those who reside within his boundaries, but he attempts to be considerate as well. The oldsters are given the privilege of arriving first because Wotan appreciates how difficult it is for them to get around. He figures anybody who's lived as long as these people have has earned the right to pick and choose the exact spot where he wants to stand. It's been my opinion that if Wotan really wanted to demonstrate cosmic altruism, he'd supply the oldsters with chairs, but he wants them to stand like everybody else. But again, you'll notice he's still managed to give them extra consideration. See those power packers serving drinks and hallucinogens to the oldsters at that end of the square? Well, eventually the power packers will see to the needs of every oldster in the crowd."

"What service!" exclaimed Oliver. "What are these oldsters complaining about?"

"They prefer to receive their hallucinogens in the comfort of their cubicles, several levels below the real world," said Scorpion.

"It's only fair that they get some extra consideration," said Yangtze. "After all, their elixir-pack taxes go a long way toward balancing Wotan's budget."

"Spoken like a genuine heathen," said her father with mock pride.

"You'd better hope so," snapped Yangtze. "I know who and where to turn to when the need arises."

"All right, let's stow that topic for a while," said 00π with a curt wave, "and concentrate on our mission here. Oliver, you stay with me in this area near the platform—" 00π then separated Scorpion from Yangtze and me, positioning us in opposite corners of the square.

"I've just thought of something," I said. "How come *we're* doing this security gig and not the Brain Police?"

"Because, sir, this kind of funeral is strictly illegal," said Scorpion.

"The Brain Police used to try to break them up," said Yangtze, "but since they and their families generally live in the tracts of block kings, an unspoken truce eventually evolved."

"Yeah, live and let live," said 00π. "Much as I hate to see the forces of law and order give in to crime under any circumstances, I have to admit I'm glad to see it's happened here."

"Hey!" Yangtze suddenly shouted, waving at someone in the thickening crowd. She put two fingers in her mouth and whistled shrilly. The sound echoed off the buildings with such piercing vibrations I feared all the stained-glass windows looking down on the square would shatter. "Over here!" she shouted at the approaching members of Spaceside's band.

Usually oldsters stood their ground, once they found it, but they gladly put up with moving to avoid being too close to Spaceside's crew, even for a moment. And who could blame them? When I saw Mike Chane, his vid-bass grafted to his body, coming my way, I wanted to do a little edging away too. The fact that Mike was accompanied by Sulphate Eddy, with his glistening slimy head, the black-tentacled Yep So Wha, the gigantic semihuman Tiny Habibula, and the sharp-toothed Jive Electro, who frequently tipped his Space Cowboy hat to the grandmas, provided the oldsters with that extra burst of incentive.

Except for Jive, the band laughed and talked strictly among themselves, and were completely oblivious to Yangtze's efforts to get their attention. Every effort she made was immediately doomed by the sudden presence of Spaceside's voice, booming from every speaker in the square.

"Hey you dirtbags!" he drawled. "About fucking time you got your fat lazy posteriors in gear." The ends of his echoing words died off slowly, with long fades. "Hey, Jive, wait'll you see the bitch we're gigging for today! She's got canines almost as sharp as yours!"

I was shocked that Spaceside had so crassly disrupted the solemn atmosphere; hence I experienced a vicarious thrill when Jive Electro responded with a grin and an obscene gesture.

"Oh yeah?" sneered a leering Spaceside. I knew he was leering because at that moment the director snapped his fingers at a technician and the immense vid-screens were switched on. The camera caught Spaceside just as he was grabbing his crotch. In every direction I looked I could see him squeezing his jewels with tender macho gusto. It was like being in the center of the eye of a fly watching a greasy porno movie.

Yangtze fumed as Oliver got what little attention the band bestowed upon our group. Tiny picked up Oliver and they banged heads, making a sound like a gong's. Back on the ground, Oliver weaved like a bowling pin struck, but not felled, by a succession of bowling balls. Mike Chane pressed his attached vidbass against Oliver and let him create a few "found" notes and color schemes with his weaving. Yep So Wha simply wrapped a massive tentacle around Oliver and, releasing him with a snap, spun him around like a toy top. Jive Electro tossed his hat onto Oliver's head, and then caught it when it flew away as if yanked on a string. Sulphate Eddy concluded the progression by helping the very dizzy robot stand upright for a moment, and then leaving him to tumble smack against a grievously insulted Yangtze. Eddy also left a few streaks of green slime on Oliver's head.

Yangtze looked down in horror at the bit of green slime that had rubbed onto my shirt, which she still wore (by now augmented by boots and blue jeans). I'm afraid she took out her frustration on me. She snarled like a rabid Sirian Odd Dog and barked, "What the hell of kind of robots do you have in your damn Patrol anyway? Who ever heard of a robot who gets dizzy?"

A good point. I made a mental note to ask Oliver about it someday.

Spaceside, meanwhile, mugged for the cameras, undulating his hips as if threatening to perform a strip tease. "I see Spaceside's being a class act, as usual," observed 00π. He clapped twice, just loud enough for those he wanted to hear. "Places, everyone!"

Yangtze was dour and silent as we wove our way through the people to our position. Imagining why she was angry was a little difficult. In any case, her relationship with the band, assuming she had one, was fated to remain a mystery, at least to me. Before I could broach the subject, I was distracted by what I saw on the immense screen before me: a puff of green smoke suddenly appearing behind Spaceside on stage. When the smoke dissipated, there stood U-Shant Eye, seemingly materialized from out of nowhere.

"Well, throw my undies against the wall and watch them stick," exclaimed Spaceside over the loudspeakers. "That's one heck of a trick, U-Shant Baby."

"I wish to have a word with you concerning your sense of decorum," said U-Shant Eye, unmindful, no doubt, of the titterings in the crowd.

"Ooops! Shouldn't have used that word 'heck', huh?" replied Spaceside, just before someone killed the sound. But no one killed the cameras, and so the people made catcalls as they witnessed the two stand face-to-clockface and, presumably, present to the other his side of the story as forcefully as possible.

By now the representatives of virtually every population in Wotan's domain had made an appearance. The majority of the latest arrivals fit the profile common to all the ethically conservative, technologically sophisticated classes I'd encountered previously on my other-worldly travels. That is, their bodies were washed, and their shoes were polished. They were clean-cut even when their hair was spiked and green. Some had pointed ears, and/or pins stuck through their nostrils. Whether male or female, young or old, rich or poor, a natural humanoid, an altered one, or an offshoot, they carried themselves with the self-assurance of those who believed themselves to be the very philosophical underpinnings of society, as well as the ones who did the grunt work necessary to keep all life functioning at its current luxurious materialistic level. The uncomfortable-looking guys with flattops and clean shaves were probably Brain Police in civvies, relieving the rest of their families of the arduous duty of religious service. Wotan had to be one of the wealthiest, and hence most powerful, block kings on the island. No wonder the baron had been forced to enact a truce with him when his experiment, whatever it was, went awry.

Other categories of political and cultural affiliation were present, of course. In a few pockets of the crowd congregated a cross section of the lowlifes typical of the secular district; there aliens of a dizzying variety consorted with a plethora of muggers, lovers, and thieves—all especially moved to laughter by Spaceside's confrontation with U-Shant Eye. A few shouted, "Shoot him a moon, Johnny!"—leading me to believe there was some precedent for the remark.

But make no mistake about it, a palpable layer of grief was in the air, not to mention a certain level of tension and a sense of forthcoming release. "They say the girl's not quite dead," remarked a corpulent woman to her steady whatever as Yangtze and I took our positions nearby beside a domed streetlamp. The woman wore a white T-shirt and had a black mohawk with flashing light bulbs in it. Her whatever wore a collar and she held the chain. He had floppy ears with silky brown hair and a long snout with a triangular black nose on the very tip. Obviously his earliest ancestors had been illegal mutations, perhaps a cross-species mix. The whatever said, with a slight howl in his voice, "I imagine she'll be finished off before the ceremony."

"Don't be too sure about that," said the woman. "They also say she's succumbed to the plague that defies death."

"Then why have a funeral at all?" asked the whatever. "Why not just cremate her and be done with it?"

"Idiot!" she said, punctuating her epithet with a slap. ("Thank you!" he replied.) "There's still the afterlife to consider! The soul must be folded, spindled, and mutilated with the proper procedures, lest it find itself lost in a maze juggled by the Farce!"

"Who cares about the afterlife," said he smugly, "when I can do all the suffering I want here?"

The woman cuffed him again. "Thank you," he said.

Suddenly the buzz of the crowd diminished, and heads turned. The picture on the screen cut to a wide shot from another camera, positioned on the highest peak of the wooden tower behind the platform. The shot was of the crowd—"us," the people realized with calls of delight. The solemnity of the occasion dissipated, and looking at the nearest picture of "ourselves" packed like nuclei in an atom compressor, I began to wonder if 00π hadn't accidentally set us up at a sporting event.

The picture changed again, to a close-up of U-Shant Eye stepping up to the mike. Behind him stood three vestal droids, with lilacs interwoven throughout their metal tiles, throwing tiny handfuls of petals on the stage; they delicately balanced the baskets of petals as they performed a series of ballet steps and pirouettes, only occasionally smashing into one another.

U-Shant Eye said, "Friends, Aurelians, fellow worshippers, direct to me your aural capacity. Today we come to bury M'Bell, not to lust after her. Her ugliness has lived on after her, while her beauty, as is generally the case, has fled with her soul. So let it be with M'Bell. She was my block king's daughter, and hence was always jake with me. So, she was impetuous, and vindictive when she didn't get her way. What else could you expect of the daughter of Wotan the magnificent, Wotan the great, Wotan the wonderful, Wotan who has lent his name to so many righteous and charitable telethons that his name has become practically synonymous with disease . . ."

And so on. I confess I completely lost track of it after a while. I also got tired of watching the vestal droids banging into one another; so must have the director, because as U-Shant Eye droned on, the picture on the screens cut to an aerial shot of the crowd, then to a succession of other shots. In one I saw Scorpion, sitting on the ground with his back against a lamppost, pretending to be drunk. *Why drunk?* I wondered, just before I noticed how many in the shot weren't pretending.

In fact, many in the crowd, young and oldster alike, were furtively consuming the consciousness-altering substance of their choice, a ritual probably commonplace at these ceremonies, but which was, like so many other commonplace things, officially frowned upon. Postures and expressions changed as the drugs took effect—some entities becoming buffoonish while others became serene, depending on the properties involved.

"This is it," said Yangtze, jabbing me in the ribs a tad more roughly than was necessary (perhaps as revenge for all those times I'd jabbed her), a moment before the picture changed to what appeared to be a tunnel below the surface of the square as seen from over someone's shoulder. I judged from the feathered cape and the black mane with the row of shrunken skulls tied to it that it was Wotan. The sudden restive nature of the crowd led me to believe I was entirely correct.

"And so, without further ado," U-Shant Eye said, holding forth a tentacle toward the wings, "may I present to you the wounder and the healer, the destroyer and the savior, the man for whom life is death and death is life."

The picture on the screen cut to a wide shot of the platform just as the big fat man with the skull-laden mane and the feathered cape strode onto the boards. Some people whistled and others cheered. The more devout simply bowed their heads, some in silence, some mumbling chants that merged into an undercurrent like the hum of a horde of Meadean Sap Bees, lifting the whistles and catcalls to startling new heights of discord.

"He's big, he's bad, he's wonderful," said U-Shant Eye in tones that, despite his effort to be cheerful, were oily and obsequious. "He's the man of the chron, the main man on the main street of life—"

"All right, already, let's get this show on the road," said the big man, slapping U-Shant Eye on the back with such uninhibited might that the ring of skin against metal echoed in the square like the detonation of a bomb.

That's when the folks went wild, cheering madly, shaking their fists and waving their arms, throwing gloves and hats and power packs into the air. Wotan accepted their approbation with confident appreciation, waving to the people even as he helped U-Shant Eye stand. The vestal droids knelt, overturning their baskets and spilling the remaining petals. U-Shant Eye bowed and exited quickly and deliberately, his shoulders hunched over, indicating that now that the introductions were over and done with, he did not want to call excess attention to himself. The star, after all, had arrived.

Seldon, had he ever! The big man beamed at the crowd. I did not need the screens to see the flashing of his metal teeth; they glinted so often I could almost imagine him signalling me. The big man rustled and rattled his staff—the rustling caused by the layer of serpent feathers running down the length of the staff, and the rattling caused by the pebbles in the shrunken head of the *Pachydermo sapianus* adorning the top. Wotan moved like a monolith holding itself upright during an earthquake. He directed his smile toward each of the three cameras at the foot of the stage, and the director cut to each in turn.

Then, as if on cue, the big man twirled his staff—if the serpent feathers had rustled restlessly before, now they rustled mightily, and the pebbles in the head rattled like buckshot ping ponging off the interior walls of a barrel that stretched into infinity. The speed of the staff made it a blur, creating a wind that shook the skulls in the big man's hair. "Thank you, thank you, thank you," he said rapidly. "Glad you good people could take time out from your busy schedules to make it. I know most of you have attended funerals before, and so you're probably thinking you already know what to expect. After all, since everything is done in a certain order and a certain way during a ritual ceremony, a certain amount of repetitiousness is involved. We're going to be striving to achieve that repetitiousness today, but because of the special nature of the deceased, a few special features have been added. I think you folks are in for a real spiritually rewarding experience today." He beamed again, spread wide his arms, and tossed his spinning staff high in the air. The camera followed it up then down again as the big man caught it and said, "But what else can you expect from a ceremony brought to you by none other than the illustrious individual known as me? Hallelujah! Glory be to me! Glory be to Wotan!"

If I had thought the crowd had gone wild earlier, I was sorely mistaken. The earlier cheer had been only a warm-up for this one. People didn't just shout, they roared at the tops of their voices. Instead of throwing just their hats and gloves in the air, they threw other bits of clothing as well, and a few cyborgs threw their smaller body parts.

Wotan bowed. His smile, once so expansive, was now merely humble, as if the overwhelmingly favorable response had caught him by surprise. His military tunic was open at the top, exposing a manly chest with a manly expanse of hair. His belly was too large for such a tight-fitting tunic, but his obvious weakness for food added to the overall impression he gave of having a robust lust for life in all its forms. His trousers were pressed jodhpurs, heavy on the starch, and the shine on his black boots rivaled that of his metal teeth. Even at his most humble, then, he exuded an air of authority and command, and I wagered he would have done quite well in the Stellar Patrol, if his troops didn't frag him first.

Wotan held up a large palm to indicate his desire that the applause fade away, which it did. Tucking his staff under his arm, he turned to the vestal droids and clapped twice, briskly. They commenced to clumsily step and turn as they attempted to move out of the way. (I could almost hear Oliver comment on the shoddy workmanship.) Then Wotan clapped thrice. From behind a blue curtain walked a procession of four young girls with boyish figures, carrying blazing torches that caused the black sequined emblems on their white bodysuits to glitter like stars. They walked past the vestal droids and stood on the left side of the pyre with statuesque poise. Wotan regarded them with an approval that struck me as being more than merely fatherly.

Then his expression grew more serious; it in fact grew quite pained. He waved weakly, as if all his strength was drained and even this minor movement cost him a great effort.

U-Shant Eye emerged from the wings. He floated across the stage like a regal barge on an invisible river. He was tugging M'Bell from a rope attached to her coffin, which had been equipped with wheels. M'Bell had a wooden gag stuck in her mouth.

Wotan then proceeded to explain to the crowd that while the individual about to burn might appear alive, the reality was that she was very, very dead. She had succumbed to the same nameless disease that had recently become depressingly familiar in the territory.

At that point the voices in the crowd ceased to be solemn or jubilant, they became angry or uneasy. Since I really didn't need to hear Wotan's explanation, I let the ceremony go to the background of my attention and concentrated on what I was supposed to be doing—checking out security.

I paid particular attention to an alien whose eyestalks changed color for some reason; to a naked woman with hooves and an equine tail; to a scruffy, sullen young man with two rather obvious unsleeping eyes; to a pair of little creatures accosting various members of the crowd, saying, "We want to conquer the world" and "Can we have a cookie?"; to a humanoid totally invisible save for his circulatory system; to a creature of controlled flame best described as a matchhead; to an energy entity contained only by the confines of his transparent compression suit, revealing the swirling colors that were his essence and being; and to a cyborg who was literally bisexual, that is, his right side was male and his left side was female. All these and more I paid attention to, but not necessarily in the order stated, because I kept coming back to that equine female. It wasn't just her nakedness that so enticed me, it was the way she neighed and shook her mane of blonde hair. I was totally mesmerized by her until some of Wotan's words moved her to leave a very substantial critical commentary on the macadam. Then she strode proudly off the square, unaffected by the irate stares she received from those who happened to be standing too close to the commentary for comfort. Evidently the equine female was every bit as wild as those creatures her ancestors had been genetically spliced with.

Then Yangtze jabbed me in the ribs. "Check this out," said Yangtze, pointing to the nearest screen.

On it was a shot of Wotan standing between his futilely struggling daughter and a female of the startling-human variety. Fully as tall as he, she at first glance appeared a giantess, thanks to her magnificent feathered headdress shaped like a great basket of fruit—blue MacCreigh bananas and crimson Padgett artichokes, to be precise. At second glance she was merely built like an antediluvian outhouse. She had incandescent blue skin, long silky yellow hair, and luscious green lips. Her clothing consisted of a black bikini augmented by a series of long white veils.

"I'd like to introduce you to Miss Golem," said Wotan. "Isn't she something?" (There was wild applause.) "Miss Golem was a gift from Baron Rebop Redux a few cycles back."

"A rival of Hardehar Cohen's," Yangtze whispered to me. "He's dead now," she added sanguinely.

"Not a big player on Aurelian any more, then," I said, making an effort at sarcasm.

Yangtze shrugged. "You never know."

"Miss Golem is an expert at transchanneling," Wotan was saying. "And since my daughter's spirit is no longer with us, having been mercilessly displaced from her body by some parasitic thing that feeds off her memories as well as her physical residue, Miss Golem has kindly consented to vacate her mind—"

"That shouldn't be difficult," said Yangtze.

"—and reach out to a point beyond the beyond, to a place where even the gods are afraid to look, and there she shall reach out and touch someone—someone who was once my daughter!"

Suddenly my own mind flooded with a wealth of ideas, all derived from the shred of hope that what I was about to see had some grounding in reality. For it was immediately obvious that all I had to do was to get Miss Golem, or someone like her, to "channel" for Floyd; then he and I might finally get to the bottom of that pit of limbo he was trapped in.

Wotan continued: "And once you hear from my beloved M'Bell, whose corporeal mask you see struggling right here, right here on this stage, then for the first time you shall be as aware as I of the great challenge our whole neighborhood faces. You will agree with me that you, the good people of our neighborhood, must sacrifice your civil liberties and submit to martial law for an undisclosed length of time. We've got to face reality—the Brain Police can't stop this kind of crime. The perpetrators have got the kind of brain waves that can't be traced or controlled. So it's up to us. Only the people can stop these criminals from corrupting our youth with the song of the undead!"

"If I didn't know better, I'd think he was making a power play," I said.

"A block king can parlay that kind of control, even for a brief period, into a lot of social advantages," said Yangtze. "And he can do it while legitimately protecting the people."

I noticed from the cheers that a lot of folks agreed with those sentiments. But I also noticed that the mood of many had turned rather ugly. A few verbal altercations broke out, and here and there B.P.'s in civvies had to step in to break apart the overenthusiastic. With his next words however, Wotan immediately glossed over the discrepancy between the conflicting reactions before most had really figured it out. He

bowed with a flourish, absently knocking down a
vestal droid with his staff, and shouted, "And now,
folks, a treat you've all been waiting for—whether
you knew it or not! Because now we're going to hear
from a gentleman who's kindly consented to help
Miss Golem reach the exalted state necessary to channel for the true soul of my M'Bell. Ladies and gentle-
men, humanoids and aliens, insects and slugs, it is
my pleasure and privilege to introduce a man whose
devotion to his musical instrument knows no limits.
That's right, you got it, I'm talking about the man of
the bass, the Fender bender himself, Spaceside Johnny's own main musical throb—*Vibratin' Mike Chane!*"

Then the crowd went really nuts. Chane stumbled distractedly through the curtains as if someone
had pushed him. A moment later it struck him—
mentally he probably had a three-microchron delay—
that all the applause rattling his eardrums was meant
for him. He beamed, then played a few grateful chords;
the sweet sound complemented itself with rosy-hued
spirals.

M'Bell trembled in her coffin. Miss Golem squealed
in delight, and Wotan's smile, wooden at first, became expansive and natural. I had the feeling Miss
Golem's squeals were among her most delectable as-
sets. Chane began playing a serious of long, lilting
tones that rose like the tendrils of a fog. They struck
an emotional chord deep within me, and if the initially cheerful, then contemplative reaction of the
audience was any indication, the effect was universal.

The music reminded me of how the pink sun
reflected off the waves in the bubbling seas of Tachyon
VI, of how the ring system of Reilling's World resembled giant smoke rings from the vantage point of the
forest moon, and of how the parasitic globules on the
vibrating trees of Telluride sparkled and glowed in
accordance with the songs the trees sang to celebrate

their molting. At last I began to understand, however dimly, the bond that must have grown between Chane and his bass, and it became less of a wonder to me that he would seek to push the bond to the ultimate limit.

Miss Golem was deeply affected by the music too. Gradually we became aware that she was humming along. Wotan modestly stepped to the back of the stage, as Miss Golem knelt by his dead daughter who was writhing in profound spiritual agony. Miss Golem threw back her head; her hat slipped off—although no one seemed to notice. Every sufficiently open-minded, basically licentious individual in the square was too busy being thankful for the camera providing us with a massive close-up of Miss Golem's cleavage as she undid the strings of her bikini top and pulled it down slowly, teasingly. No one breathed as she cupped one breast tenderly and ran a finger delicately around the rising nipple.

Her song became louder. Chane's music simultaneously became sharper, and the lights assumed the color of jade. Miss Golem rolled her head, letting her hair caress her body. Her free hand reached into her briefs.

An audible, predominantly masculine gasp went through the crowd.

M'Bell roared. Or she would have, if she hadn't been gagged. As it was, her protestations emerged as a series of gurgles trapped in her throat, and I feared the very violence of her utterances would tear through her decayed skin. She worked her jaw furiously, as if she hoped to shove the gag out with her dank tongue.

. Suddenly Chane's music reached a climax and then leveled off on an emotional plateau. At exactly the same time Miss Golem and M'Bell closed their eyes, the former doing so voluntarily, the latter snapping her head with the motion of a dog being jerked on a leash.

When Miss Golem opened her eyes a few bars later, they were gone. In their place were two black wells, of infinite depths and of dubious powers of observation. Somehow they made her beauty, which before had been merely voluptous, sublime. And her heavy breathing and perspiring body, not to mention what she was doing to achieve those effects, had transformed her level of sexual charisma from the magnetically irresistible to a point off the scale entirely.

"Steady, big fella," said Yangtze, squeezing my arm to induce me to cease trembling. It didn't work. Perhaps she should have kicked me.

Miss Golem removed her hands from her naughty bits. She remained on her knees, her head thrown back, her arms at her sides. Wotan came to her and gently set her head aright. "Her soul is thrown out," he said in reverent tones. "It has gone seeking. Keep playing, Mike Chane. Keep playing until her soul returns" —he glanced at his unmoving, undead daughter, whose eyes had opened to reveal blank white slates— "and brings with it a soul long since fled."

Wotan's eyes widened as Miss Golem groaned. A complex series of emotions played across his face. His hands hovered over her shoulders, as he resisted the urge to grab and shake her for fear that he might interfere with the channel. It was clear that unless something gave soon, he could tolerate this waiting no longer. "Play, Chane, play!" he snapped, for no reason other than to distract himself by giving someone an order.

Chane had given no sign of stopping. His eyelids hung heavy, and the color of his eyes sparkled, apparently glowing with an urge to follow the transchanneler's into never-never land.

Suddenly Miss Golem jerked as if she'd been

struck, and the blank places that should have been her eyes widened almost imperceptibly. Then she smiled, as if in ecstasy. Ooooh! she said, and then her manner completely changed. She threw herself on the floor, rolled over, crossed her ankles together, swished them back and forth, made a steeple by putting her palms together, and twisted them through imaginary waters. She went glob, glob, glob, her mouth dilating like a cyclops gill, and then she suddenly stopped in abject terror and stared at the audience with pure, raw, naked fear. She threw back her head and emitted a series of panic-stricken screeches that promptly began shattering the windows of all the nearby buildings.

People who had been standing beneath the falling glass swarmed into the body of the crowd, pressing everyone together. Yangtze and I were both taken by surprise as we were suddenly jostled about, with the result that we lost one another temporarily. The director, never one to lose a dramatic moment, cut to a close-up of a pane of glass bursting, then to an overhead shot of the crowd taken from the top of the dome.

Judging from the number of bodies lying on the ground where the glass had fallen, many entities hadn't been too lucky. The director felt obligated to drive the point home by showing us quick cut after cut of those bleeding and, in some cases, dying from having been pierced by shards of glass.

Miss Golem, meanwhile, still screamed those high-pitched squeals while Wotan and the vestal droids looked on in amazement. Chane continued playing his sensitive, melodic chords, oblivious to all.

"By Seldon, I know what that sound is!" I said to Yangtze, the moment we found one another again.

Yangtze grimaced and put her hands over her ears. "What's that?"

"It's a sound dolphins make! I heard it once, on a history tape!"

"Dolphins? Isn't that the other intelligent species that originated on Earth?"

"Yes," I said as regretfully as I could at the top of my voice. "They've been gone since the dawn of the First Empire, exterminated by mutations who believed that ground dolphin brain powder was the most potent ingredient in some bullshit formula that would increase their intelligence. They accepted no substitutes. It's too bad, but that sort of behavior was typical of those unenlightened times."

"Oh, no," replied Yangtze, also at the top of her voice. "We wouldn't *think* of behaving so illogically!"

Onstage, Wotan booted Miss Golem in the back and sent her flying face first onto the boards. The screeching stopped immediately. Wotan stood over her like a conquering hero and glared at the crowd. The only sounds were those of a window belatedly shattering from the cracks it had sustained earlier and the engines of the Robo Medics administering first aid to the wounded. "Is anybody going to laugh?" Wotan shouted, his voice trembling with barely controlled rage.

Nobody did. You could cut the crowd's silence with wayward photons. Wotan glared in various directions until he was certain that everyone, especially that subset of everyone who could see the whites of his eyes without the aid of the video screens, had been subjected to a direct dose of his regal charisma. Once he was satisfied, he clapped twice, distinctly beckoning someone to step from the wings immediately.

The someone did, a second femme, rather obviously a Vixen from Viros, despite the cosmetic surgery that had been performed to bring her more in line with human standards. But there hasn't been an epidermic dye invented that can disguise that distinctive scarlet hue, as shiny and bright as the wings of a ladybug. And as spotted. This one had gray and white spots. The Vixen certainly exuded something sultry. You could catch a faint whiff of that something sultry all the way back where I was; Vixens' scents can get mighty intense close up, and they were known to get especially intense after you'd been close up for extended periods, the way Wotan had obviously been. He must have been addicted by now.

Despite all her cosmetic surgery, deep scars had been left behind after the removal of her tusks. Her nose was too lumpy, the set of her eyes too lopsided, and her jawline a little too nonexistent for her to be thought of as decently humanoid, but she was lovely all the same. Her horns had been filed down to a delicate, if pointed, shape, and her style of dress, in this case a simple yet elegant green slip, appealingly revealed just enough hints about the true state of her figure to make it interesting.

"You like her?" Yangtze asked, mischievously.

"Say, isn't that your mother shrieking?"

"Vixen scent makes most of us normal females want to projectile vomit," she said sternly. "I hope you realize that. Also, it's been known to ruin some men for all time, and face it, Homer, with your luck, there's probably not much left to ruin."

"So what's protecting Wotan?" I asked playfully. "What is it that Wotan has that enables him to flirt with the most sexually potent aroma in the Empire, while I have to take my chances with the rest of the crowd?"

"Wotan has a clock-faced goon who supplies him with special potions," Yangtze shot back.

I pointedly returned my attention to the events onscreen. "Silence!" commanded Wotan, unnecessarily, his palm raised as if he was making a proclammation. "Her mind is about to phase out!"

That was all right with me. Usually the mind is the last thing a person involved with a Vixen is concerned about. Such is the terrible price sexual addiction can extract. At least, that's how I'd always imagined it. In any case, I thought I spied an uncharacteristic flicker of intelligence in the Vixen's eyes before they slated out and her mind went tripping in the great spotted beyond. Wotan seemed especially pleased that she had phased out so quickly. The vestal droids resumed their dancing, the crowd seemed relieved that a certain tension had been released from the air, and M'Bell just appeared bored. Evidently this wasn't the kind of coming-out party she had envisioned upon becoming undead.

I'm here! the Vixen exclaimed delightedly. **I can see her. I can see the soul of M'Bell. I can almost touch it. It feels so white, and it sounds so soft, so . . . I don't know how to say it. Everything is so mixed up here.**

"Go on! Touch her!" urged Wotan. "Touch her and let me speak to her. Go on. Touch her."

What's in it for me?

Suddenly Wotan appeared embarrassed, as if the cameras had unexpectedly caught him with his codpiece down. He leaned down, apparently unaware the director had ordered an extreme close-up so we could see plainly how his eyes darted back and forth in a suspicious mode. He kissed the Vixen on the cheek. He hesitated, then gently nibbled on a white spot. "Do as I say," he said, altering his tones into a little boy voice, "and Big Daddy will make nicey nicey tomorrow."

We do the nasty?

"Only thirteen, and you know how to nasty," he said admiringly.

The Vixen considered the matter, then said, **Okay,**

I'll do it. But remember what happened the last time Big Daddy didn't keep his promise.

"That was a rotten story to spread around," he said between his teeth, straining to hold his smile in place. A neck muscle twitched, the fist at his side trembled. "And a lie, too. You know I could never have such a disease, that I'm routinely examined by a robomed after every encounter."

Yes, but the entire harem believed it, didn't they? You didn't get laid for a—

The block king grew pale and stopped her with a gesture not unlike the one a man makes while twisting the neck of a chicken.

The Vixen, evidently deciding their disagreement was best resumed in private, returned her full attention to the task at hand. She stared into space and attempted to be firm, as a mother might with a wayward child. **M'Bell, come to me. M'Bell, I say, come here, girl!**

I noted that the M'Bell in the coffin stared at the Vixen with narrow eyes, almost, I thought, as if she suspected some kind of scam was going down.

As with the first transchanneler, the Vixen's eyes suddenly went blank and her head snapped back. She'd made the connection! **Boss!** the Vixen shouted, her natural quasi-chameleon powers enabling her to widen her eyes into the shape of discs. **Boss! What's shaking? I've been trying to reach you, but I haven't been able to get through. All the lines must be tied up. Metaphysically speaking, of course.**

There was something disturbingly mechanical about that transchanneled voice. "Floyd," I whispered.

And even though the Vixen could not possibly have heard me, she said, **You got it, Boss! This is me, Floyd, come to you to sing the lament of we who ain't got no time for Hucka-Bucka-Beanstalk**

**today. By the way, we ain't got no time. Have I
got some news for you—!**

"Homer?" Yangtze asked me, as the crowd tittered nervously at the painful incongruity of this voice, so totally out of place with the rest of the proceedings. Even the dolphin's squeals had fit in better, somehow.

"Floyd?" demanded Wotan. "Who the fuck is *Floyd*?"

I had just enough time to notice M'Bell squirmed violently in her chains, as if trying to press *inside* the coffin boards.

For some reason I panicked when M'Bell closed her eyes.

And then a bomb exploded. I had the distinct sensation I was right in the thick of it before I blacked out.

When I woke up the experience proved to be a lot more subjective than I imagined it would be. Time dragged on while it was happening, so my brain obviously wasn't up to processing information in the proper order. Consequently I saw the people flying up in the air long before I heard them screaming. The bomb must have been planted under the street, because vast chunks of macadam and steel rained down on the crowd, expanding the radius of the injuries inflicted.

I actually felt relieved—I had made it through unharmed. A surge of adrenaline warped my soul, creating a wave of unholy delight in the fact that while others might be injured or dead, I was alive! Alive and whole! I prayed with all my heart an identical observation could be applied to Yangtze. I couldn't see her for all the smoke and confusion; she was lost in the jumble of people scattering about like a mob of mice trapped in a burning cage.

Then a second bomb went off, and the screaming worsened. I put my hands over my head and hugged the ground. My hands moved sluggishly, their touch weak and distant, for some reason. *Holy Seldon,* I suddenly thought. *What if I'm lying right on top of another one?*

I lacked the time to contemplate subtleties because a third bomb exploded, then a fourth, and a fifth.

It was a good thing that most of the glass in the square had already been shattered, otherwise the damage, already of unthinkable proportions, might have been even worse. I didn't open my eyes. I didn't need to see it. All I had to do by then was hear it, and there was plenty to hear.

Starting with the thuddish splats of various body parts hitting the ground, admist the rain of gravel.

And the crying.

And the sound of flesh burning.

Beneath it all, there was the laughter. A hideous cackle of unearthly delight, buried in the background of the horror like a whisper. A whisper that was like a scream.

If this be the Farce, I thought, *then let it laugh on—laugh on! I'm still here.*

There came a lull in the rhythm of the bomb blasts, and I called out for Yangtze.

There was no answer.

I strained to hear a cry or a moan that might belong to her, and I heard nothing.

Just that laugh. It was so low, so quiet, yet it threatened to overwhelm everything else.

After what seemed like an eternity, the laughter was drowned out by the sound of approaching sirens. Help was on the way. The Cyber Docs would soon have their way with the living and the near-living. The dead had a more predictable future ahead of them.

I noticed I was sweating; my body was surging with panic. I wondered why. The bombs had stopped, for the moment at least, and I was still alive. Why couldn't I get my fear under control?

The stage weaved back and forth in my vision. I attempted to focus on it and try to get everything straight. The stage appeared to have survived basically intact, with only a minimal number of bodies lying around. So far it appeared that no one on the stage happened to be harmed.

Some people scurried around, others had frozen in place.

I saw a fire hydrant standing next to a man waving his arms about. People appeared to be responding to his directions, whatever they were.

Good, I thought. That would be 00π and Oliver. *They've made it so far.*

Suddenly I got this centrifugal feeling, centered in the small of my back.

I shot up into the air like a rocket.

I twisted around real slow, head over heels.

A moon was in the sky.

A blast of blue-green light inundated the stage.

A moon was in the sky.

The light was gone. The stage was intact but somehow emptier.

The moon was in the sky.

I hit the ground and the space island spun like a dynamo, rolling over and over in a mighty pool of weightiness too vast to see, too thin to touch. I imagined that pool with all my might and I clung to the island with trembling, numb fingers.

The moon in the sky was beautiful.

It occurred to me that I might be wounded.

I realized I might have been thrown into shock by the first blast, but that second one . . . I might have been wounded in the second blast.

I tried not to think about it.

If I didn't think about it, it might not have happened.

I tried not to think about it, but I did. I couldn't stop rationalizing about it.

Most people who lie down close to where an exploding bomb's been planted usually get wounded.

I didn't *feel* wounded. I felt *whole* enough.

The moon had a motherly face with high cheekbones. She had the presence of intelligence. Beyond the dome, in the moon pool. I reached out to touch that face . . .

. . . And touched a tentacle on the ground. Nothing to speak of was attached to that tentacle, unless you counted a few stray muscle parts and those few drops of blue-green plasma substance still oozing out.

I tried not to think about it.

The tentacle felt incredibly warm, which was odd because my hand felt incredibly cold.

And my hand was still attached to me.

Without meaning to, I started checking out the spare body parts that happened to be lying around. Something about the boot on a nearby disembodied leg disturbed me greatly.

I tried not to think about how the disembodied leg was wearing a regulation Patrol boot.

Finally I recognized it as belonging to me.

I tried not to think about how much I had to get my leg back. I reached out again but couldn't lift my arm.

I knew I wasn't going to get it. I heard Blather speaking, somewhere in my mind. "The Patrol has to pay for that boot, Hunter, with taxes that come out of your salary and mine! You've cost me money, Hunter!"

He went on and on. I tried not to listen to him, but it seemed there was always a part of him with me. Watching me.

There were more explosions in other parts of the

square. Some had sounds, while others were just light, like that blue green light that had inundated the stage.

That light belonged to a kind of bomb I hadn't seen or heard of before. It made compact groups of entities disappear, but didn't seem to do any other kind of damage.

Luckily for me, it was by then too hard to think. I simply stared at my boot, gradually experiencing a twinge of regret I was as yet unable to understand.

It was strange how numb I felt all over. The only genuine sensation I was capable of feeling was the wiggling of my toes.

Over there. In that boot I was looking at.

I pressed my toes hard against the shoe. Seldon, how good it felt!

And look, there was another part of my uniform! I wondered if I managed to tug at the front pocket of my regulation shirt lying over there, covering that headless torso, if I would be able to feel my heartbeat.

Of course, my heart was where it was supposed to be. And so was my shirt.

I tried not to think about it, but I couldn't help crying uncontrollably.

I had lost nearly all trace of consciousness when suddenly I was snapped back to the purgatory of the living by the sight of someone reaching down into my field of vision and picking up my leg.

The someone laughed mechanically. It was a familiar laugh.

He had a black sleeve. The flesh of his hand was so gray and lifeless it seemed it could hardly remain intact beneath the pressure of gripping my ankle. But it held firm as the other hand reached out to bear the weight of the rest of the leg. That sleeve was also black but the hand was cybernetic, half fully mechanized and half entirely dead flesh, somehow arrested at an early stage of decay.

The undead cyborg held my leg up and brought the end of the severed thigh to his fetid lips.

He was dressed in somber colors, with red ruffles on his collar, breeches, and codpiece. In fact, it was a jim-dandy of a codpiece, augmenting the predominantly artifical torso and legs by being stitched together with computerized plexyester of an ever-changing array of shades and colors.

I realized that whatever happened, I'd have to find a new blood supply, fast, because the man in the codpiece was drinking what he was squeezing out of my thigh. He squeezed it like a sponge, and out poured my blood in rivulets.

After a long time, the rivulets slowed to a trickle, and he was done.

That's when he looked me in the eye for the first time.

Bright red lights flashed in his eyes, and with a grin he tossed my leg aside. He licked the points of his teeth. The canines were long and sharp, just like M'Bell's.

I don't know what I'd expected him to say. Something profound, perhaps, or at least a hint of why he was involved in what had been done in the square. I was doomed to disappointment. He merely smacked his lips and said, simply, **Tasty, tasty, Mr Hunter.**

He narrowed his bushy green eyebrows and took a step forward. He had a lean face with an exaggerated bone structure; all in all, he most resembled an insane harlequin.

I should have been afraid of him by then, but I wasn't. I was ready to accept whatever might happen. What else could I do? All my strength was taken up by my crying.

A sudden flash of purple and black light distracted the cyborg in the codpiece.

Where once there had been nothingness in the sky, there now hovered the little man in the pillbox suit. Two complex rifles with their own miniature power packs swung out above his shriveled shoulders. He touched a button and the rifles moved into firing position with a whirr.

"Aha!" exclaimed the pillbox man. "The Supreme One was right! Chronometic explosions did take place here—and as for you, undead one—!"

The pillbox man bore down on the cyborg, firing silent silver beams that cut little holes in the already cracked and shattered concrete. He kept missing his target, though, even at that close range.

Well, I guess you caught up with me, said the cyborg, standing his ground despite the barrage of fire. I couldn't be sure, of course, but it definitely appeared a few beams had passed directly through the cyborg, burning a few holes behind him. **I suppose I'll have to surrender and die here,** he said wearily.

And then he threw my leg in the air. It spun, slowly at first then gathering speed, toward the pillbox man.

The pillbox man's tuft of red hair suddenly stood straight up in the air, as if it'd been electrified.

My leg hit the pillbox man.

Right between the eyes.

Squish! went the end of my severed thigh.

"You geek!" shouted the little man, rubbing the blood from his eyes.

It's true, said the cyborg. **I admit it, I am the geek. But you, sir, are the chicken!**

He pointed a mechanical finger at the distracted pillbox man and sprayed him with what at first appeared to be jet black ink.

But which upon contact turned out to be a liquid that immediately began eating away at the pillbox man's face, while spewing forth tremendous clouds of rancid yellow smoke.

The pillbox man screamed. "Yaaah! That's not supposed to happen!"

How do you know? gloated the cyborg. **Maybe you're still too early.**

The pillbox man's flight suit trembled in sympathy with his agony. It shot up and down in the air at all angles like a basketball caught in an invisible box, trying desperately to bounce its way out. "Damn, you're right!" he rasped—how he knew that I had no idea, but his input valves apparently hadn't yet been damaged. "I told those scumbags my temporal time synchronizers needed to be checked out. Fart breaths! They wouldn't know a good time travel piece from an antimatter vibrating ray!"

The pillbox man exploded. Pieces of already dead and decaying flesh, along with an amazing number of mechanical parts, rained down on the square, while in the place where the pillbox man had once been, a faint wisp of red smoke dissipated.

That red smoke was the last thing I saw for a while.

Chapter Nine
Meanwhile, Where the Big Ships Go

ADMIRAL BOINK'S
robe dropped to his feet and he dived belly-first into
his hot tub, which was laid out in the symbol for
infinity. He stretched out luxuriously on his back in
the steaming water and kicked his way backward
through the twisted course. Lately Boink had been
thinking of changing the shape of the tub, since he'd
overheard one of the crew referring to it as the perfect
shape for the perfect 8-ball. But at the moment he
was as happy as he ever got. The water had relaxed
him almost immediately. The sheer opportunity to do
nothing, to not even think, took the edge off the day.
He sighed, delivered another kick, and blissfully closed
his eyes as he twisted around another bend.

And promptly banged his head against the edge.
"*Damn!*" he exclaimed. He sat up and stared in
disbelief at that edge. Luckily, he hadn't drawn blood,
but already his head throbbed like a pulsar.

He couldn't remember having done *that* before!

Logic told Boink that he should remember having done it. He remembered having had this bath for
a long time, almost from the very beginning of his
tenure on *Our Lady's Hornblower*. Surely he must

have struck his head against the edge at least once—even a slight impact, far lighter than the one he'd just endured, would have forever alerted him to the possibility.

Maybe he had, so long ago he had forgotten. Yet his body was reacting as if this had happened for the very first time. The blush in his cheeks, the indignation running rampant through his spleen, the quivering of his muscles—all told him the sensation was exactly like the many he'd experienced on those dimly remembered occasions when, as a raw Patrol recruit, he'd initiated some remarkable snafu through sheer ineptness, awkwardness, and naiveté.

And now he could not have been more dumbfounded had he peeled off the skin of his wrist and discovered he was a robot. Which, considering how things had been going lately, wasn't all that ridiculous a possibility.

He pinched himself, just to make sure, and then returned his undivided attention to being dumbfounded at the edge itself.

Then he got tired of that and stared at the faucet. For an extended moment he marveled at how hard and solid it was. He visualized the vast fields of nothingness between the atoms, and thereupon thought it nothing short of miraculous that solid objects weren't always slipping and sliding out of place. Because when you looked at them microscopically enough, they weren't really solid at all! What a thoroughly craftsmanlike piece of work the universe was!

If only his head would stop throbbing. It was as if the pain was trying to remind him of something.

Of something that might have been, once.

Another bathtub? Another faucet?

If so, then what about the memory of that crewman's remark?

Boink washed himself quickly, almost furiously. *If only Coryban were here,* he thought forlornly. *She'd know what was real and what wasn't. And if she didn't, she'd fake it adequately.*

Boink stepped into the pneumatic drier and wondered what he should do next. When you've been in space long enough, traditional biological sleep rhythms become pretty academic, and though he'd been awake for an unholy number of chrons, Boink had no desire whatsoever for shut-eye. Furthermore, as of the moment he had no idea whatsoever how he wanted to spend his scheduled free chrons. Too bad Coryban was still away retrieving that Hunter chap. He would have gladly turned off his brain and let her do his thinking for him, which was exactly the way he liked it.

He wondered why he needed to see that Hunter chap so badly, anyway. Oh well. It didn't matter. Coryban would remember.

Thanks to an unprecedented fit of inspiration, which came to him like a nova flash, Boink decided where he should go. He also decided to take the long way around.

Boink began walking through the outermost corridors at about the same time Dr. Proty did, albeit from opposite ends. If Boink was preoccupied with metaphysical conundrums forever beyond his talents, then Dr. Proty had been spiritually pole-axed by emotional conundrums of daunting complexity. Circians such as Dr. Proty had been thus daunted throughout the ages, ever since the first of their formless kind had slithered upon the lava coasts of methane seas. During the early millennia of Circian civilization, the quest for the answers to those conundrums consisted of exploring various spiritual and physical avenues, generally carrying the searchers to the heights of exaltation or the depths of despair, and to the extreme limits of both pleasure and pain. Eventually, as the Circian culture evolved, a rather complicated philosophical construction, a sort of spiritual maze, became the sole groundwork upon which civilization was supposedly based.

The maze became known as the Hierarchy of Shapes. For the Circians' ability to alter their shape and mass at will became, in time, their entire basis for communication. Within any given shape, they saw meaning, nuance, and music. By judging one's ability at grading contours and delineating textures, they gauged the quality of one's mind, thus passing judgment on the social worth of one as a whole.

Even social outcasts, whose control over their shape was untalented in the extreme, were imprisoned in the maze. For should an outcast ever need to speak to his fellow Circian, he had no choice but to resort to the vocabulary dictated by the Hierarchy of Shapes. Communication was simply impossible without it.

Dr. Proty was descended from the founders of a religious cult whose denunciation of the Hierarchy of Shapes had been without precedent—the cult had sought the answer to their race's perpetual identity crisis elsewhere, by taking what were then innovative options. Up and down the lava coasts they formlessly traveled, disdaining all shape-changing methods of communication in favor of those employed by the lower, physically static life forms. It was from these static life forms that those of the cult took their communicative cues, and hence they were the first intelligent creatures on their world to excel at speaking through an orifice.

Of course, this method of communication, by necessity, conflicted with their fidelity to genuine formlessness, but they believed that as long as they otherwise remained blobs of white protoplasm, then the invention of a spoken language would more than compensate for the philosophical inadequacies. This allowed Circians to explore abstractions that had no need to be presented in a physical shape, thus preparing them, however tentatively, for the event which soon befell their civilization: The coming of the bipeds.

These were members of the Diplomatic Corps, who invited the Circians to take their proper place at last in the full sweep of galactic history. They brought with them all the pleasures and terrors of the higher civilized arts, and with a few generations all that was known of the Hierarchy of Shapes resided in the minds of a few reactionary scholars who yearned for the security and order of the Old Ways.

Otherwise Dr. Proty's people took completely to the stellar winds. They often repeated among themselves certain phrases that, for them, had special meaning: "It stands to reason, after all, that shape changers would be so adaptable to the Ways of the New and would so irrevocably cast aside the Ways of the Old." The key phrase there is "it stands to reason." Before the coming of the bipeds, Circians had never heard of Aristotelian syllogisms, the scientific method, the lower and the higher forms of geometry, games, tactics, or, for that matter, a joke with a complicated setup. True logic had eluded them down through the millennia. *What need had they of logic?* they'd protested when first confronted with the mysteries of rational thinking, *when for all this time they could change with the whim of a thought.*

Rational thinking was only the first change bipedal civilization wrought upon the Circians, and the average Circian now dealt with a truly major identity crisis, one not only personal but racial. After all, who was a Circian, exactly, when one could look like anyone else? And, considering the same question from another point of view, who did the bipeds at large regard the Circians as being, when a Circian could look like any intelligent entity, biped or not, as he chose? So mightily did these questions weigh down the race that entire generations went through some awful bummers. Many were the Circians who decided they couldn't take it any longer and threw themselves pseudopodlong into the embrace of death. But many more reacted to their experiences by learning to improvise, to overcome, to adapt.

And within a few generations, some Circians were confident enough to wonder openly if those who professed to be the kings of rational thinking were all that rational in the first place. Those more prone to feats of deductive reasoning took it upon themselves to study the problems and contradictions of rational thinking seriously, to apply the scientific method for the first time to the realm of logic itself.

These scientific Circians quickly discovered some shortcomings in the minds and methods of the so-called rational thinkers of the galaxy. Actually, it took precisely fifteen chrons at the first scientific conference for them to reach that conclusion—unanimously. They knew at once, even without the aid of logic, that they had their work cut out for them. It would take lifetimes to get to the bottom of things, and would take them down avenues hitherto unfathomed in the Circian consciousness.

And as a result, some pioneered in the science of gritology—that is, studying the sex drive, which seemed to be a major motivating force behind the behavior of most life forms in the galaxy. Of course Circians had always had their own peculiar form of sex drive: they reproduced by emitting a smoky cloud laden with their semen and immersing themselves in it for a while. The act in itself gave them pleasure, and any impregnation that might occur as a result was up to the individual. *What use was a partner,* they always asked themsleves before the coming of the bipeds, *when you could blow smoke up your own ass?*

Needless to say, the average scientific Circian's conception of his role in the galactic social order expanded to the infinite power when he discovered the possibilities of sharing favors with actual sex partners, as opposed to just thinking. And what favors the average gritologist shared, especially when he found an entity willing to help him make the next logical deduction available from the compatible body parts at hand! Not one avenue of sexual pleasure was so base, so depraved, so perverted, or for that matter, so commonplace as to be considered unworthy of in-depth study. Possibilities existed for the sole purpose of exploration. Variety existed for the sole purpose of being exhausted—at some far-future date. The gritologists quickly became famous for their perseverance and insights in the name of science. What papers were written, what reports given at gritology conventions! The Circians were proud that at the last convention, pornographers from all levels of the Third Empire posed as busboys and "companions," all for the avowed purpose of picking the Circians' brains for what they knew about the infinite varieties of turn-ons that some feared, if permitted to continue, would one day cause the political and cultural collapse of the Third Empire.

Until today, Dr. Proty had been proud of being a gritologist. Until now he had assumed it meet and proper that as a scientist he had extended his pseudopods and gotten down to plumb the secrets of the universe in the most personal way possible. Once he had believed he did it in the name of science, that what pleasure he might have derived from his studies had merely been a fringe benefit.

Yet now, for reasons that escaped him as he walked down the outermost corridor, he perceived his reasons had been far less idealistic than he had ever supposed. The acts he had performed down through the years had hardly been scientifically motivated; they had been personally motivated. If Dr. Proty, and any number of gritologists like him, had really wanted to study sex in a clinical manner, they could have done so the way others studied murderers and drugtakers—with morbid fascination for the activities involved, but no desire to participate themselves. Perhaps all that sexual activity, so lovingly reported in hypnotapes for the benefit of future generations, reflected a spiritual need only disguised, or mollified, by physical gratification.

The word that summed up the need, in all its pleasures and pains, glories and humiliations, was simple. The word was love. To the best of Dr. Proty's knowledge, it had never figured prominently in the literature, perhaps because cross-genus sexual relations had little to do with idealism and a lot to do with a passionate desire to flaunt social taboos. *Love!* The word explained so much. Now that he had admitted it, the extreme desolation of spirit he was currently experiencing was logical indeed. The worst part was, had his destiny proceeded the way the fates had originally dictated, his love would have been a love fulfilled. For the first time Dr. Proty would have been a Circian with a whole self-image, no longer in need of constant change.

Eyes of all shapes, sizes, and levels of perception stared at Dr. Proty as he rolled on his skateboard down the starship corridors. Surely the more sensitive of the onlookers could see the waves of heat, anger, and embarrassment radiate from him like a corona of pain. So overwhelming was his inner angst, his id screamed silently in his mind like a raw wound.

Dr. Proty estimated that at this rate, he had approximately thirty chrons remaining of relative sanity. He knew full well that to stand out as mentally unstable among this crew and party of passengers took some doing, an indication of how desperately he needed to break his spell of emotional desolation. Strangely, his mind was gradually divesting itself of the underlying reasons for his angst in the first place, while grasping onto the angst itself with renewed tenacity. The pain had become the most important thing.

Proty wondered if he was becoming a masochist. It was at this moment of his wanderings, during which he felt his spirits at their lowest ebb, that he happened to spot Admiral Boink walking down the corridor—coming straight toward him!

All manner of irrationalities suddenly plagued Dr. Proty. He was convinced Boink had somehow connived to plumb the depths of his Circian soul and was annotating his deepest, darkest insecurities for future reference, probably with the intent of leaking them to the shipboard gossip columnists so they could be plastered across commissary holorags. Proty easily envisioned the headlines. *"What's so Bad About Feeling Out of Shape?—Proty Knows!"*; or *" 'Why Can't I Be You?' Proty Asks!"*; or, worst of all, *"Scientist Admits He's Had Sex With Creatures Who Don't Even Have a Sex!"* Any one of those headlines could conceivably put the kibosh on Proty's reputation for lifetimes to come.

Boink, for his part, glared suspiciously at the

little Circian. It would have been easier to justify his suspicions if he could recall what reasoning he'd used to justify having suspicions in the first place. But fortunately Boink possessed a species of mind that, once it had justified regarding someone suspiciously, continued to do so long after the initial reasons had been explained away. Perhaps, Boink thought, if he could find some new reasons to be suspicious of Dr. Proty, he might also provide the powers that be additional proof that he should be advanced to the rank of Fleet Commander as quickly as possible.

The two came to a stop and faced each other in the corridor. This, then, was the confrontation both had dreaded, when Proty would be forced to confront Boink with a litany of the degradations he had suffered aboard *Our Lady's Hornblower,* and when Boink would have the opportunity to justify, once again, that which required no justification. Boink glared at Proty, and Proty created two beady eyes near the top of his cone, the better to glare at Boink with.

Each waited for the other to be the first to break the ice.

"Hi," Boink finally said, when he could bear it no longer.

"Hi," said Proty.

"How you doing?" Boink asked.

"Fine," said Proty, immediately hating himself for letting the opportunity slip away.

Boink moved past Proty. "Great. See you around, okay?"

"Fine. See you," said Proty, and they both went on their ways. The dreaded moment of confrontation was over, a minimum of damage inflicted.

So lost was Boink's mind during the next stage of his wanderings that he was almost startled when the sole path remaining to his destination was the direct short one. He could have dallied, by speaking to any number of diplomats milling about the lounge area, but propelled by some impetus he would not thoroughly comprehend for the next several moments, he decided not to wait. He walked down the long, narrow corridors that led to the Navigation Room.

It takes a special kind of cosmological nun to master the intricacies of space-time geometry in the void, he thought with a special kind of *déjà vu* as he came to the dilating door and walked inside. The odor of incense assailed his nostrils, the jingling of arcane percussive instruments assailed his ears. *I just hope Justine O and her crew are everything they're cracked up to be,* he added, recalling the more spectacular particulars of the navigational crew's collective résumé. He had to admit that the sense of eroticism in the room as a result of their group arousal was not only impressive, but contagious. Now Boink knew why it had been so essential that he bathe before making this visit, and with a mighty effort he restrained himself from taking off his trousers.

"At ease, ladies!" he said before a single nun had actually noticed him. He didn't want to take the risk of distracting them in the void. A few nuns did glance up and smile, and one even wiped the sweat from her brow and seductively licked her lips, so Boink was almost content with that. Already he found it difficult to breathe. It was a good thing he'd ordered the room off-limits to passengers and crew; so overwhelming was the eroticism emanating from every molecule that only a mind with the unique properties suitable for command was capable of resisting. And then only barely.

Forty-five nuns were seated, reclined really, at the forty-five auxiliary terminals in the room. Each nun was clad in a cowl, a merry widow (white or black), and fishnet stockings. Most were completely human (a few cyborgs or xenoborgs counted among them), and all were drenched in their own perspiration. All wore bracelets and necklaces replete with symbols representing various religious factions in the Third Empire, and all were attached to the terminals at the jugular and the belly button with semitransparent wires that glowed and sparkled with changing intensities in response to cosmological conditions. Judging from the exhaustion most of the nuns exhibited between their cosmologically-induced spasms of orgasm, Boink deduced this shift had been on for several decachrons, maybe a few too many for *Our Lady's Hornblower's* own good. Boink was especially concerned about a blonde near the door. The cut of her merry widow not only provided indisputable proof that she possessed a natural shade of blonde, but that her large, dark nipples were capable of bold erectness.

"Admiral, so good of you to come," said Justine O, the Mother Superior, rushing to greet him. Her presence caught him off-guard. "Please do not be concerned about what you were thinking," she said, squeezing his arm and digging her long nails into the fabric of his dress jacket. "It is only natural, and perhaps may one day even be proper, should the more radical factions of the Guild have their way at some future Council Gathering."

Boink laughed weakly. "Sorry, Mother Superior, I guess I'm just feeling a bit randy."

She tsk-tsked and shook her head sadly, but not without an affection that made her subsequent chiding easier to take. "You older men always have so much to prove. My sisters and I already know fully what you are capable of. But, really, Admiral, how can a mere mortal satisfy any of us, when oneness with the cosmos is ours for the taking?"

Boink tsk-tsked back. "And all that mental and sensual training gone to waste. It's all right, even Mother Superiors must retire someday, eh?"

She smiled sweetly. "And when I do, perhaps I will think of you, and plead with you to fill the void which by then would overpower all my pride."

"Is that a compliment?"

"Possibly." Now her smile wasn't so sweet. Of all the nuns, the Mother Superior was the only one mobile. Not for her the typical reclining posture on the divans before the terminal consoles. Not for her the mere sifting through of cosmological data, nor the fevered concentration upon a single aspect of the complex tapestry of space and time. For the Mother Superior was an elderly female with a lined face and a handsome body and bearing that were in their way far more erotic than those features possessed by her charges. The softening and rounding of age granted her a character the youthful nuns could only emulate but never equal.

The Mother Superior's clothing matched that of her charges in every respect, save that the symbols on her necklace and bracelets were indicative of the building blocks of matter, and that instead of a cowl she wore an Alpha receptor that enabled her to listen in to, and actually experience, the thoughts and sensations of as many charges at once as she chose. In fact, the ability to lock into the mind waves of all forty-five nuns simultaneously and remain rational, in order to gauge the ship's position in the ether, was a prerequisite for the Mother Superior position. To be a successful nun, you not only had to have a pleasure center in your brain capable of overriding all other worldly concerns at the slightest whim, you not only had to be so metaphysically curious that you would risk all personal *separateness* from the universe for the vaguest avenue toward enlightenment, you had to possess a Kirlian aura so serene and balanced that it affected every entity within a radius of several meters. This particular Mother Superior mirrored her inner serenity with every expression, and her Kirlian aura was so pronounced as to be practically visible. After a moment her smile sweetened again. She blinked her wide eyes, and for a moment he was lost in a sea of gold-flecked blue. "After all, each of us must live in the future someday," she said. "Who knows what unexpected pleasures it might bring? Perhaps we shall even be rewarded in a manner commensurate with our worth."

As she spoke, Boink could have sworn this was his first visit to the navigational room, although his memory and his long history of bantering with the Mother Superior informed him otherwise. His reply, whatever it might have been, was lost in the ripples of nonexistence when his concentration was suddenly disrupted by a scream from one of the nuns.

Boink and the Mother Superior immediately rushed to the nun's side. She was a green-haired lass with freckles on her shoulders, crimson polish on her nails, and several rips in her stockings, evidently part of a rebellious new style of dress favored by nuns of certain religious orders. The poor girl spasmed violently, caught in the throes of an uncontrollable sustained orgasm. She bled profusely at the neck where the wiring had been inserted into her jugular, and the connection at her belly button sparked dangerously. She rolled her eyes and, instead of attempting to yank the wires from her neck and belly, pulled at her hair, tearing it out in great tufts before Boink grabbed her by the wrists and held her down on the couch.

The Mother Superior's Alpha receptor glowed

incandescently as she moved between Boink and the nun, gently stroking the girl's face until she calmed down. "What is it?" said the Mother Superior soothingly. "What do you perceive?"

The nun dug her nails into the Mother Superior's bare shoulder, drawing blood. "The horror . . . the horror . . ." she gasped, then promptly passed out.

"Whew, that must have been some orgasm," Boink said.

"That was no ordinary orgasm," said the Mother Superior, "that was a celestial climax of unholy proportions. If we'd had gotten to her a nanochron later, her brains'd be fried and her ovaries baked like a cake."

Boink perhaps knew whereof she spoke. He'd seen burn-out cases before, tragic losses to the navigational craft and to the sexual potential of mankind. But something about this near-miss disturbed him more greatly than had all those incidents combined. " 'The horror,' " he repeated. "What could she possibly have meant?"

The Mother Superior frowned at the pale nun, already sinking into a blissful state of unconsciousness. "I don't know, but I intend to find out."

The forty-four remaining nuns, an admirably disciplined bunch, had reacted only slightly to the incident, and once they saw that the Mother Superior had everything under control, had returned to their assigned tasks. They knew from the bitter experience of reliving disasters via hypnotapes how entire ships had fared in the past whenever too many nuns had been distracted from their sexual fervor and celestial orientation. The consequences of failure were simply too great for them to be overly concerned about a comrade. Even so, those nearest to the unconscious nun, who had heard her exclaim, "The horror . . . the horror . . ." scowled with worry and were possessed of considerably less sexual excitement.

Boink looked helplessly at the Mother Superior as she drew herself up to her full height and closed her eyes. She pressed a finger to her temple and held her other hand high. Her Alpha receptor suddenly radiated a cascade of colors that included some primary shades new to Boink's experience. "Ladies," she said, "the time has come to . . . *mindlink!*"

A group orgasm practically shook the room. Boink couldn't guess how the rest of the ship might have been affected, but his crotch all of a sudden had gotten incredibly damp, and he had the distinct sensation his synapses had short-circuited.

The Mother Superior's eyes fluttered with ecstasy, but they remained clear and piercing nonetheless. Boink realized what was happening, that her mind had enveloped all forty-four conscious nun minds in the room. She was now sifting through the vast amounts of information in order to get the best fix possible on what might have been too much for one individual to perceive directly.

"Look there!" commanded the Mother Superior in a barely audible voice.

Boink turned toward the hologram display above the terminal in the center of the room. The matrix of dots representing real space was undergoing some kind of transformation.

The Mother Superior screamed once and swooned into Boink's arms. So warm and soft was she to the touch, and so magnificently did her touch fulfill one of his most potent fantasies, that he almost forgot the ship might be in dire danger. "What is it?" he asked. "What do you see?"

The Mother Superior replied in a whisper that

was not just a single voice, but a chorus of voices, as if all the minds of all the nuns were speaking through her simultaneously. . . . *I see the fabric of space being ripped asunder. I see wheels within wheels, lives within lives, universes within universes. By Seldon, the possibilities! I had no idea there were so many possibilities! . . .*

"That's very terrific," said Boink, "but can you tell what *that* is?"

That appeared to be a thousand pinpoints of light emerging from a single point in space. What the pinpoints represented Boink could only speculate, but the magnitude of their mass was beyond doubt for it bent the very grid of the map out of shape.

The pinpoints sped past the dot in the matrix representing *Our Lady's Hornblower.*

The ship lurched. Boink fell directly on top of the Mother Superior. *Hot cha!* Boink thought.

"Invoke emergency measures!" she shouted in her normal voice, as she kicked Boink off with her kneecap.

As the ship steadied itself, several of the nuns crawled from their couches and onto those of their neighbors. After the most perfunctory of foreplay, they crawled directly upon the neighbors themselves. Boink was shocked. He'd had no idea women enjoyed doing those sorts of things, even in the line of duty.

But as provocative and as perhaps illegal as the nuns' methods were—and the Mother Superior later confided in him that what he had witnessed was a secret of their Guild and was revealed to an outsider only because it was an emergency—they succeeded in keeping the ship on course.

"What in the name of Seldon's happening?" Boink asked.

Racked by the ecstasy growing exponentially with

every passing second, the Mother Superior gasped, shivered, and fell to her knees. Propelled both by gravity and lust, she grasped Boink's crotch. Suddenly the admiral cared naught for the rest of the ship. By Crom, destiny was destiny, and Boink's impending destiny flashed in his mind's eye as Justine O opened her mouth, licked her lips sensuously, and then bit down, at first gently but slowly with more force. Fortunately, she hadn't bothered to unzip the Admiral, so her biting down was accomplished while she was . . . a little blind. Pretty soon Admiral Boink experienced the extreme delights of exquisite agony. It quickly became too much for him, and he screamed at the top of his lungs.

He found himself looking straight up at the ceiling.

The back of his head struck the floor, but the Mother Superior managed to slip her palm underneath it while it was on the rebound. *"Admiral!"* she exclaimed. *"Are you all right?"*

"What's happening?" he inquired, standing, his voice sounding unnaturally low in his ears, the words taking an unnaturally long time to finish.

"Something's emerging from another space! They're huge! The mindlink senses fragments of what once must have been vast, imponderable intelligences! Even the fragments dwarf the mindlink! Inklings—I'm picking up inklings of cognizance from their subconscious identities. They call themselves the Transcendenticons. They are the survivors of a future war that blistered the surfaces of a thousand worlds, and have come to the past in search of an opportunity to change the fate of their future conflict. Their mind tubes are suffering incredible intellectual breakdown even as I speak!—But wait—! Fragments drift apart, like splinters of wood eon-soaked in a turbulent sea! Their minds are going, Boink. The pain, the agony! Aaiieeee!"

Boink slapped her around so she could get ahold of herself.

"Thanks, I needed that."

"What else can you tell me?" he demanded.

The Mother Superior frowned, her mindlink evidently deep, as two nuns nearby rolled off the couch, groping madly. A chorus of groans and gasps droned in the background as she slowly said, *"Their bodies are so hard, like a hundred thousand tons of cold, driving steel, glistening in the sun. Nice. Oh baby, oh baby. I never knew nirvana could be this good . . . that the dissolution of my personal identity could be so . . . so . . . horrific! They're slipping down the time stream, into the past! Holy moley! I've no idea who I am any more! Aaiieeee!"*

Boink decided he'd had just about enough of this nonsense, so he decked the Mother Supeior. His knuckles throbbed in intense pain, but otherwise he felt very smug and serene as he stood above her, almost as if a sexual conquest was imminent.

For her part, the Mother Superior looked up at him with cold eyes behind which a single intelligence again resided. She wiped a trickle of blood from her face with the back of her wrist, smearing it, as the Alpha receptor gradually ceased to glow and the nuns on the couches gradually disengaged to resume their normal duties. "Next time, try a kiss," she said.

Boink nodded and said, "All right, but I didn't want to overstep my bounds." He glanced at the holomap. The massive objects were gone; only a few slight indentations in the lines of the matrix marked their passage. "Mother Superior, tell me exactly what happened, from the top. That's an order."

"Yes, sir!" said the Mother Superior with a breathiness he'd never heard before. "The mindlink sometimes has a metaphysical dimension beyond the control of its component parts—that is, my nuns and I—and in this case it gravitated toward a vast intelligence in a manner analoguous to the way a comet is caught in the gravitational pull of a star. We were sucked in, sir, all of us, before we could do a thing about it. There we learned that once upon a time there will be these big cities, bigger than any city we've ever seen before, cities that walk around and change shape into battle configurations whenever the need arises. And they were falling into the past and breaking up thanks to being caught in the unexpected rapids of the timestream . . ."

"That's strange," mused the Admiral aloud. "There's never been any archaeological evidence of any massive artificial intelligence ever having existed."

"And that's precisely the point, sir," said the Mother Superior through gritted teeth. "There never was . . . had been . . . until now!"

"You mean—?"

"I don't know. The mindlink sensed disruptions in the timestream, both in the future and in the past. For some reason things are in flux. The future may change. The past may change. Everything may change. Even our own present may be in danger. I don't know. It may have already changed. Several times."

"Hmmm, I see," said the Admiral, nodding, even though he really didn't understand very much. "Well, they're probably out of our story now, eh?"

"Probably. It's difficult to say."

"Just let me know if any noteworthy changes happen in our present, all right?"

"Yes, sir," said the Mother Superior, rubbing her chin, staring openly at Boink. "Maybe we can get together later, and discuss our possible futures, eh?"

"Mother Superior . . ."

"Call me Justine," she said in a breathless whisper.

"Justine, it isn't like you to even discuss breaking taboos."

She shrugged. "What's a taboo for, if you can't break it every once in a while?"

Saluting smartly to the Mother Superior . . . no, to Justine as he walked out the dilating exit, Boink thought it possible that Coryban had by now forgotten the reasons for her mission, but not the mission itself. Her mind was too tenacious for him to believe events could proceed otherwise.

Even so, he resolved to return to his office and look up Coryban's name on the files, just to make sure she still existed.

Chapter Ten
Dream On, Little Dreamer

CORYBAN NOTED with silent approval that Minister Hoffman's experiments in fashion—to better relate to the web gestalt—were becoming more stylish, if no less jarring. Today his black tie outfit, instead of exaggerating his porcine presence, subdued it, making his appearance almost elegant. Of course, Coryban wasn't sure she could keep a straight face whenever she looked at his day-glo pink tutu, especially whenever he curtsied and bowed in an effort to be delicate.

But Hoffman didn't take kindly to being laughed at. The punishment Coryban had endured the last time had been sufficient to deter her for the time being, so when the temptation became too great, she glanced up at the rafters high above them in the prison's experimental playground. The playground was huge, as large as an indoor stadium. It was where the Nipponese tested the IQs of their children, but since Coryban, Reina, and Blather were adult trespassers, they were at the moment the only three subjects on the entire floor.

Hoffman shook his shoulders in accord with the silent music in his brain as he knelt on the other side of Coryban's playpen and scowled at the half-finished design she had made from the puzzle pieces she'd been issued. "Nice work," he ventured in detached tones.

Coryban left her lotus position in the dirt long enough to reach out and grab a purple non-Euclidean ellipse. She smiled. "Nice of you to notice."

"And what is that object supposed to be?" inquired Hoffman, as if to a little girl.

Coryban held the three interlocking pieces before her eyes and scowled. "Whatever you want it to be, I suppose. Isn't that the purpose of the game?"

"No, no, no!" exclaimed Hoffman, forgetting his lady-like poise as he pounded his flabby fists on his knees. "You must know *what* you're making!"

"Really? And all this time I thought the intent was to conceive of something utterly abstract."

"No, no, it must have some practical function!"

"I thought that was to come later."

"No, how can we know if you're qualified for ambulatory punishment if we don't understand for certain what was on your primitive, amorphous mind in the first place?" He paused. "You're doing this deliberately, aren't you, to foul up the web? You know it's hard enough for so many brilliant minds to deal with so many clear and brilliant thoughts at once. It doesn't help if you subject us to muddy thinking."

Coryban refrained from comment. Unfortunately, she couldn't refrain from thinking, and the Nipponese had been very good about tuning in to her wavelength lately.

"But it *is* your problem!" the minister exclaimed, his complexion reddening. "If the web believes there's not a comet's chance in Heck that either you or any of your partners in crime can adapt to Nipponese society, then you'll be sentenced to suspended animation until our goshdarned sun goes nova!" Out of breath due to the sheer exertion of talking, he panted heavily.

Coryban waited until Hoffman was about to stand, and then said, "Wait—I remember what I was doing!"

Hoffman relaxed. "How could I have ever thought otherwise?"

She held forth the piece. An exaggerated half-crescent disc protruded through a glowing red square with a narrow cone sticking out from the top and the bottom. Coryban smiled, not at the artistic validity of her endeavors, but at the remembrance of the satisfaction she'd felt once she realized that some of the pieces could slide in and out of one another, as if bonding between the atoms was, thanks to a science beyond her ken, provisional. "It's a new kind of W.C.!" she proclaimed.

Minister Hoffman was clearly confused. "Is it the building—or the fixture?"

"That I haven't figured out yet!" Coryban replied cheerfully. "I think we should build both. We can stand the building on the side like this—and the cones of the fixture can extend into the ground, be part of the plumbing maybe, so that the whole enterprise will be aesthetically pleasing on the blueprint page, if nowhere else." Coryban waited impatiently for a response. "Well come on," she said, "don't you have any opinion whatsoever? There are at least forty others in there with you today."

The minister brought an illusory candy bar from his pocket and took a huge bite from the end, wrapping and all. Illusory caramel ran down the side of his mouth. It screamed as it fell from his chin. As each scream died it was punctuated by a little slap.

"Come on, out with it, man! Or men, or women, or puppy dog tails and whatever else goes into making Nipponese ministers these days," demanded Coryban. "Tell me the truth. You promised you'd always tell us the truth—though you advised us you might deliberately leave some out—when you said we'd have to endure educational conditions for a time, to see if any of us might serve Nippon in a useful capacity."

"Fortunately for your rather pronounced sense of propriety, our telepathic abilities rule out the possibility of testing your capacities in the fashion men have found the most useful since the dawn of time."

"Ha! It would never do for a minister to accidentally let down his guard and let his mate know that he savored an illicit pleasure," Coryban said with a sneer.

"Ay," said Hoffman, nodding knowingly, forgetful of the presence of others, "even when this one did, once, solely for the vicarious thrill of a fellow whose pull was needed on a certain voting matter of some import, this one's mate responded by giving us all a vicarious pain in the crotch."

"I knew it!" said Blather, looking up from the mess before his playpen. "The fat geezer's pussy-whipped!"

"*Quiet!*" Coryban hissed. Then to Hoffman: "What about an illusory pleasure? Surely if the illusion of food can be whole, then why not an illusion of the object of one's desires?"

Hoffman looked her straight in the eye. "Forget the W.C. You'll go far on this world." He stood up with a grunt, did a playfully clumsy step, and danced on his toes over to Blather's playpen.

Blather, meanwhile, looked scathingly at Coryban. "I see you'll say anything to get ahead."

"It's true, but unlike some people I could name, I won't *do* just anything."

"Are you implying there's a distinction of some sort between us?" Blather protested.

Coryban stuck her tongue out at him. Hoffman executed a miserable pirouette. He appeared to be deliberately delaying. Coryban and Blather always said exactly what was on their minds whenever it took Hoffman a long time to traverse the short distance—ten meters—between them. During any subsequent conversation the minister generally had little idea of the content raised. Coryban theorized that he was taking advantage of the brief break to catch up on what the rest of the web was doing at the moment.

Reina sat at a playpen beyond Blather; she too played with peculiar objects in both Euclidean and non-Euclidean shapes, both colorful and drab, tangible and semitangible. So far she'd been concentrating entirely upon her composition. While it had taken Coryban precious chrons to deduce the properties of the pieces, Reina had rather quickly come to an instinctive understanding of their potential and had already completed a substantial portion of a work that had come, essentially unbidden, to her mind. She worked quickly, trying this part and that to see if the actuality resulting from their junctures matched her ideal. She worked urgently, afraid that if she faltered, the vision would dissipate and she would be forced to work from but a fragment of memory. Her only enemy was her frustration—whenever a potential avenue did not work out to her satisfaction, she felt a wave of anxiety that in and of itself threatened to distract her. She was learning to use the anxiety to her advantage, however, and soon realized that a misstep was not an accident revealing a shortcoming on her part, but was instead essential to the completion of the project. Not since she had stalked game in the woods, making use of the warrior secrets she had stolen from the males of her tribe, had she felt so close to her totem of the White Hawk. It was strange, but putting together the pieces of the puzzle she had created in her mind brought forth sensations of harmony with her environment that corresponded almost exactly to those she experienced during a hunt in the night, when her senses were on full alert and the slaying of game was inevitable.

She felt especially confident she was on the right track when two pieces merged together into an aesthetically pleasing shape and began to *hum,* as if she had created a machine where before there had been only uniformity. Yes, Reina was on to something all right, and she was completely undaunted by the fact that so far she had only begun to work on the *inside.*

"So what do we have here?" inquired Hoffman of Blather, kneeling and holding out his hand impatiently. When viewed from one angle, the object Blather had jerry-rigged together resembled a pentagram with a circle inside, and from another angle a spherical triangle; Coryban noted that as Blather turned it in his hands it assumed still more shapes or aspects of shapes: Cassinian ovals, hexagons and octagons, and spirals and Bowditch curves. The colors changed constantly but always remained in the crimson and blue range of the spectrum.

Blather scowled. He held it close to him in both hands and pouted. "I'm not finished yet. It's only a rough draft."

"It's very interesting," said Hoffman. "What is it?"

Blather shrugged.

"Don't you think that after our words with Coryban you should at least pretend to have a definite idea in mind?"

Blather shook his head.

"Why not?"

"What difference does it make? You bureaucratic bozos are going to do what you want anyway."

"Are you sure of that?"

"Sure enough."

"Perhaps the web and I might approve of your intuitive powers, if not your reasoning abilities."

"I don't see what was so intuitive about it," replied Blather. "I just sorta lucked into this thing. Pretty neat, though, isn't it?" He turned it around a few more times; this time the shapes included cycloids and a Reuleaux triangle, which was formed by the colors resulting from the three intersecting circles.

"You too might go far on this world," said Hoffman, "particularly if you cooperate with Random the next time he asks you nicely."

Blather nodded. "Maybe I will."

"Blather!" Coryban exclaimed.

"What's the matter?" he asked. "If stringing Random on helps us get off this Seldon-forsaken planet any quicker, then it would seem that I'm doing my duty."

"Blather, duty requires propriety, and propriety requires standards!" Coryban said.

"Something you've never accused me of having," said Blather. "Besides, what difference does it make to you? You're always thinking of Hunter!"

"I am not," Coryban said lamely.

"Naughty, naughty," said Hoffman, who had stood back to enjoy their altercation. "You should know by now that outright lying is impossible here. You've got to learn how to hide the truth a little bit."

"I'm thinking of him in a professional capacity," said Coryban. "After all, my mission is—"

"We know what the mission is," said Blather, angrily throwing his composition on the ground. "The fact is that I'm always thinking of you and you never seem to care."

"I told you to always avert your eyes whenever you think of me that way!" Coryban ordered.

"So what? I can always see you here," said Blather, tapping his temple. "And then I can think of you whenever I want."

"Maybe I should have your hand cut off," said Coryban.

"It won't make any difference," said Blather.

"The lust-struck gentleman is correct on that score," said Hoffman. "There's nothing you can cut off that we can't replace."

"We'll see about that," Coryban said.

"I'm finished!" Reina suddenly exclaimed. Five centimeters above her palm floated a purple and white geodesic dome.

"By the blazing bowels of the Utod," said Hoffman, rising and moving toward Reina with a speed Coryban hadn't imagined possible, "I can't believe you've done that!"

Reina backed away. "Neither can I—it was just an idea I had." The dome moved with her. When she playfully gestured up and down, it bounced in place like a basketball in an antigrav field, but always managed to stay directly above her palm. "Isn't it wonderful?"

"My dear," said Hoffman with cloying condescension, "I am afraid that not even a mind as open as yours possesses the vocabulary for me to communicate what you've done."

"Why? It's not like I did something that was impossible or anything; otherwise I couldn't have done it."

"You haven't been keeping up with the latest equations of our mathematicians and philosophers; otherwise you wouldn't have made a statement of such stunning naiveté," said Hoffman, gesturing impatiently. "Give me that thing."

"No, it's mine."

"It was made from Nipponese parts. Therefore I am the caretaker and you should give it to me."

"Do as he says, Reina," said Coryban.

"Why?" asked Blather.

"Because I've been keeping up with the latest equations that the Nipponese mathematicians have been leaking out lately," said Coryban.

"What leaks?" demanded Hoffman.

"Uh-uh," admonished Blather. "You'll get only part of the truth from us, especially where state secrets are concerned." Actually, he knew none of it, but he couldn't resist the opportunity to make Hoffman's skin crawl.

"Give it to me," said Hoffman to Reina.

"Why?" Reina asked.

"Give it to me before it goes off!" the minister said.

"Before it *what*?" Reina asked.

"Be . . . be . . . be . . ." said Blather, suddenly quite pale.

"Before it goes boom-boom," said Coryban. "The greatest theoretical minds on this planet aren't even sure what kind of explosion you can make with that thing."

"How? There's nothing in it that could possibly explode," said Reina, backing away from the slowly advancing Hoffman.

"It uses part of the space-time fabric, doesn't it?" said Hoffman. "Then it can explode."

"Only space and time will explode," said Coryban, "but we don't know exactly how or why. We only know that an object with the unique capabilities your composition gives every indication of possessing will also have the capability of exploding."

"*This?*" said Reina.

Hoffman lunged forward, though whether his intention was to strike her or merely to grab the dome never became clear.

Because Reina threw the dome at his face.

And scored a direct hit on the nose. Blood sprayed to the right and the left. Hoffman screamed. He turned about in agony, and Coryban realized with horror that his nose was completely gone, vanished as if it had never existed!

Reina, meanwhile, caught the dome on the rebound.

He's not that loud, Coryban thought, covering her ears to shut out the sound of what was threatening to become a perpetual scream. *What am I hearing?*

And then Coryban knew. She was hearing the sounds of forty-four other screams in her mind. Laid on top of the litany was a single, overpowering thought: *Corporal Random, get your lazy ass in here!*

Coming, Boss! Random thought, from a distance.

"Stop the screaming!" Reina yelled, running away with the dome. "Stop it!" Evidently she could hear what was happening as well as Coryban, but because she was still unfamiliar with all the implications of a telepathic society, she wasn't clear on everything that was happening to her.

"Reina—come back here!" Coryban yelled. Damn! She knew the spineless Random would stick his pasty face out from somewhere in the room, and Hoffman chose that moment to faint and fall into her arms. Coryban grabbed him only instinctively, but she'd have to let him go if she wanted to stop Reina.

"Colonel! Look out!" Blather hissed in a stage whisper that couldn't have fooled anyone; he might as well have shouted it.

Still holding Hoffman, Coryban turned to look in the direction Blather pointed: Random's pasty face was indeed in view, not five meters away; he was rising up on a platform beneath the floor, his laser gun already pointed!

Coryban heard Blather scurrying on his hands and knees and stopping behind her. *Terrific,* she thought in disgust.

"Halt or I'll shoot!" Random shouted. But though his words might have been meant for Reina, they were directed at Coryban, and that's whom he stepped toward warily.

"I hate to disappoint you," Coryban said, "but I'm not going anywhere." Then she turned Hoffman in Random's direction.

Random fired in panic, exactly as Coryban had hoped.

The laser blast shot Hoffman in the shoulder, splattering instantly baked tissue and splintering instantly scorched bone throughout the vicinity. "Gross!" exclaimed Blather from behind Coryban.

Random dropped his gun at once and put his hands to the sides of his face. His eyes practically bugged out. "I've shot the minister!"

And Coryban let the wounded minister drop. He landed like a dwarf ball in a playpen; the placement of the pieces inside was disrupted like a salad being tossed by a massive earthquake.

"I've shot the minister! I've shot the minister! I've shot the minister!" Random wailed.

Coryban walked calmly to Random with long, purposeful strides. And though her intent was plain, Random was too upset by what he had done to notice the fist speeding directly toward his face.

Coryban plucked his laser gun from the air as he fell backwards toward the ground. She turned. Blather was still on his knees and Reina was just a tiny figure racing toward a distant door.

Suddenly Reina halted. Two more Thought Police stood at firing position in the doorway. Suddenly there were Thought Police in every doorway, pistols drawn, shields out, and helmets strapped.

"Uh-oh, we're in for it now!" Blather exclaimed.

"We'll have none of that! How's Hoffman?"

"He'll live, but I'd hate to be part of his web right now." Evidently he heard none of the web's screams.

"Don't do anything, Reina!" Coryban shouted. "Just stay there! I'll handle this!"

"How? These guys are ready for a shoot-out!" Blather protested.

Reina fell to her knees and put her hands over her ears, vainly trying to block out the screams.

"I'm coming!" Coryban shouted, but a single word—*"Ready!"*—from a commander with a transparent face helmet froze her.

The Thought Police got ready, and the commander waited.

And in the silence that followed, a wisp of gray smoke materialized in the air above Reina's head. It erupted in a silver-bordered blaze of green flame, and a bronze hawk-faced humanoid in a purple outfit, with great white feathered wings fanning out from his shoulders, leapt from the hole of empty air.

"Aim!" shouted the commander, and Coryban did not have to see, she *felt* the barrels of the lasers edging away from her toward the hawk-faced humonoid.

But the new arrival did not seem to notice. Nor did Reina. She was huddled over, her face buried in her palms, racked with sobs from the pain of the web. Coryban could not even be sure Reina realized what was happening. The geodesic dome hovered over her. The hawk-faced humanoid took it and stood close to Reina; he would protect her with his body, if it became necessary. He snapped his beak open and shut a couple of times, as if to ward off any of the Thought Police who might foolishly be thinking of closing in, spread his wings to their full length, which was considerable, and then folded them over Reina, completely hiding her and most of his own body from view.

Something Coryban couldn't quite conceptualize was disturbingly familiar about the humanoid—if not in appearance, then perhaps in the way he moved. He vaguely reminded her of someone she had known, though she realized it was open to question if she really had known him or if his appearance had sparked the existence of a new memory that, disturbingly, had never been part of her past before.

Meanwhile, Coryban braced for the commander's order to fire.

But before the order could be given, both the humanoid and Reina disappeared—blinked out of sight! Not even a wisp of smoke was left behind to remember them by.

"Ah . . . ab . . . ab . . . ah!" said the commander softly, looking at his men. They looked at him. Then the commander, evidently not knowing what else to do, stiffened back into attention and pointed his laser pistol at Coryban and Blather. "Ready!"

"Uh-oh! We're going to eat feces in the meadhalls of Hades tonight!" Blather exclaimed.

"Please control yourself," said Coryban, waving to distract their attention as she walked in a little circle, faking her way closer to the playpen in which Hoffman lay. "And just do as I say!"

"Aim!" shouted the commander.

"Hold it—we've got a hostage!" said Coryban at once, even as she knelt, pulled Hoffman up, and positioned him like a shield before her.

The commander blanched and waved both arms desperately. "Hold your fire! Put down your weapons! Hold your fire!"

"As a matter of fact," said Coryban as she stood, clearly refraining from making a jerky move, "we've got forty four hostages! Blather, get thee behind me—now!"

Chapter Eleven
Limbs for the Man

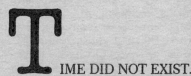IME DID NOT EXIST. Place did not exist. I did not exist.

Suddenly this ultimate in negative space came alive with the sound of music. It swelled with magnificent sound. Sound that gave me something solid to walk on. Soon I traipsed over the sonic terrain like a pagan satyr boy. Never before had I felt so happy. Not even the huge deadly flying glove—a jet-propelled rocket-powered, radar-equipped, supersonic nasty Thing—coming down again and again to smash me into the musical hills dampened my irrepressible joy. I simply dodged it, hiding in the two-dimensional, red and yellow jet trails it left behind or dancing over its perpetually pointing forefinger, until at last I reached the relative safety of the sea of holes.

I was in little danger of slipping into the holes, as long as I avoided their razor-thin edges. Evidently the glove didn't know, because almost immediately upon entering the sea, it fell through the first hole it encountered, leaving behind it only a red and yellow trail. I half-expected to see the glove, transformed somehow, emerge from another hole, but that never happened.

Then I woke up. Time existed after all. And so did place, after a fashion. I was in a hospital bed. I was still alive, and Seldon, did my feet hurt. I looked down at my legs. "Where's the rest of me?" I cried piteously.

"Right here," replied Oliver cheerfully, holding up a metal leg. His other arm was in a sling. "The rest of you just hasn't been installed yet."

The leg's plexiglas epidermal shield was sleek but dull. The segmented banks of display lights on the artificial leg's thigh reflected the fluorescent lighting fixtures from overhead; those banks would remain dormant, and would retain that dull luster, until the unit was activated. Perhaps due to some dubious rationale I've never been able to figure out, the foot was designed to be interchangeable with a right leg or a left. Maybe it was all a matter of economics.

Hot, salty tears ran down my cheeks. "Holy Kinnison, Oliver, what happened to me?"

"Boss, you got blown up real good," he said with as much tenderness as his metallic voicebox could muster. "You also got blown up pretty much in half. And the half of you that got blown off was broken by shock waves, burned by the blast, and sprayed with pieces of concrete like buckshot. Even if the robomedics had been able to save your real legs, they would have been seventy-five percent metaplastic anyway." He put down the leg and took me by the hand. "Relax, Boss. You'll feel as good as new soon. Eventually you won't even be able to notice the difference, and most of the time it'll never even occur to you that you're a cyborg, except when you need a lube job, that is."

"Yeah, and I'm going to be stuck with sonic showers for the rest of my life. No more baths with painted women for me."

"Boss, you never did take baths with painted women." Before I could explain that it was an attempt at humor, a pronounced lump came to his throat, as if he had accidentally swallowed a rodent. "Boss, I've got some more pretty bad news for you."

Now what could be worse than losing my legs? I thought. Then: "Tono Bungay! What happened to Yangtze?"

"She's dead, Boss. She was torn apart by the initial impact—couldn't have known what hit her." He released my hand to wipe a greasy tear from his eye. "At least she didn't suffer."

"It's all my fault," I said, my lower lip trembling. "I shouldn't have brought her along. We knew there might be violence!"

"How were we supposed to divine the degree?" Oliver retorted impatiently. "According to the local media's biased reports, what happened during the funeral was due to a rivalry between religious factions, so it wasn't our fault. We couldn't possibly have done anything about such an underhanded, dastardly deed."

"Just because you can say it so easily doesn't mean I have to believe it."

"Listen, Boss, would you feel better about it if someone had dropped a hydrogen bomb on the premises? Then we would have gone up in vapor, too."

"I think that might have been more bearable," I said, experiencing intense agony in my nonexistent toes. A glance down to see if anything happened to the sheets when I "wiggled" them demonstrated nothing, but I did notice how close to the torso my limbs had been severed. (And with that observation, a vague nagging settled upon my writhing soul.)

"Boss, there's more."

"Oh god, tell me quick," I said, gripping the covers with all my negligible might. "I want to get this part of my life over with."

"Well, Spaceside and the band, they completely

disappeared. There was a whole series of blasts all over the intersection, you see, and just between you and me and the biased media, not all of them were the sort you could easily pin on an irate religious faction."

"Meaning?"

"Meaning some were planted by mysterious outside forces the various Space and Brain and Thought Police are unaware of, at least as far as the general public is concerned. Some of the bombs blew holes in the space-time continuum, under cover of the rest of the carnage, and Spaceside Hodgson and the Ashton Gluons flew into a real beaut of a space-time hole, let me tell you!"

"Say what?"

"You should have seen it, Boss. For a few minutes there it looked like a sea of holes had materialized in the square. I don't know if anybody besides me realized it—the Aurelians are nice people and all that, but they're somewhat conventional in their space-time outlook."

"Their plagues are hardly conventional."

"Yes, it isn't often you encounter a plague in which the victims defy the laws of life and death," he said thoughtfully. "In any case, I'm convinced someone knew there was going to be trouble during the funeral and used it as a cover for achieving their own hidden agenda."

"Maybe they wanted to get rid of Spaceside and his music," I said, desperately trying to ignore my misery. I had this overwhelming urge to scratch between my legs which weren't there anymore, only I was too afraid of what else I might not find.

Oliver nodded thoughtfully. "That crossed my mind too, but I eventually dismissed that explanation as being too extreme."

I raised my eyebrows.

"Yes, I confess that Spaceside's music could conceivably arouse a degenerate into a murderous frenzy," said Oliver chidingly, "but I hardly think an attempt at low humor is appropriate while we're discussing the incident that resulted in poor Yangtze's senseless and untimely demise. Tsk-tsk. And she had such a cute little ass too. Such a waste."

"Uh, excuse me, Mr. Holy Spectre, maybe you don't know this because when all is said and done you're just an inhuman robot, but that was an exhibition of a quality we try to cultivate back on Gallium. We call it being comically dour. Some people who don't understand it call it sick humor, but it's not. At least I don't think it is. I think there is something strangely heroic about a man who can joke about the horrible. I'd rather see a man laughing at horror than crying in hysterical terror because he can't face it. And, when horror is inevitable, when a man cannot escape from the unpalatable, then he can only do one of two things. He can pretend it doesn't exist, or he can decide with what kind of emotional defense he can meet it. The type of emotional defense I would choose for myself would be laughter. I am not the crying kind. My laughter may be grim in the last resort. My humor may be what some men would describe as sick, but I'd rather have the sick joke than the ostrichlike refusal to accept reality or the hopeless collapse of the hysterical weeper."

"What do you do when the humor's over?" asked Oliver.

"This." I pulled the sheets over my head and wept piteously. I cried until I realized I might accidentally open my eyes and despite the comforting darkness see what probably wasn't there anymore. So I controlled myself as best I could, uncovered myself, and asked, mainly just to be asking something, what made Oliver think Spaceside and the band weren't just dead.

My faithful robot companion sadly shook his head. "Your synapses must not all be working yet. It's obvious when you consider that even the remnants of their personal energy fields were completely untraceable by the most sophisticated surveillance devices. They had to go *somewhere*, and through the process of elimination, a trip in time is the only reasonable explanation."

"You know, Oliver," I said sarcastically, "when you put it that way, I almost believe you."

"Thank you. Furthermore, the technology required to produce time-space bombs is currently nonexistent, even in the Avidya System, but obviously the technology had to have come from somewhere. It couldn't have come from the past; it had never existed until just before the incident. So the heinous terrorists must have originated from the future, when the technology could be available *and* they could go back into time *before* it was invented, all the better to tip the scales in their favor with a carefully selected strike to influence the circumstances of the still-unborn. You know, you really should start reading more science fiction, Boss. Otherwise, how are you gonna know the future has happened when it sneaks up on you?"

"I'm planning on keeping you around for a long time, little buddy. I hate to nolt, but what's the story on 00π and Scorpion?"

"00π took the demise of Yangtze pretty hard, so he's been consuming vast quantities of recipes from the Book of John Barleycorn."

"He's not even after those responsible?"

"The terrorists the Brain Police think were responsible accidentally got blown up by one of their bombs. Or else they've returned to their own time, beyond the reach of the most dogged operatives. Thanks to his need to punish himself in the pits of degradation and despair, 00π has chosen to go along with the official story, thus letting him off the hook when it comes to pursuing revenge."

"I'm willing to bet that not all those responsible come from the future," I said. "What about Scorpion? Does he think there's a connection between the plague and the attack?"

Oliver shrugged. "Maybe. But he just as maybe might be dead. He's disappeared too. The reconstructors found a pool of black blood that might have come from his head, mixed in with some plexiglas that might have come from his helmet. But the genetic samples indicated the blood might have just as easily come from somebody else. A few other shrunken heads were spotted in the vicinity that day. In any case, conclusive evidence has not been found, so his fate is likely to remain one of those niggling little mysteries that will drive us bonkers for the rest of our lives."

"The reconstructors . . . were they able to piece enough of Yangtze back together for a funeral?"

"No, not even close."

My stomach twisted into a knot. No wonder 00π had taken it so hard. I asked Oliver about the cybernetic vampire I'd seen.

"What cybernetic vampire?"

"The one who squeezed all the blood from one of my legs and drank it."

"Boss, your legs were completely shattered by the blast. Otherwise the reconstructors would have sifted out your pieces from everybody else's! There was no way enough of your leg held together so a bloodsucking undead person could squeeze its blood out."

I wonder what happened to Yangtze's parts? I

thought idly, even as I responded with, "Ah, no, I think my molecules were destined to take a digestive hike away from the vicinity. Sure you didn't see any unusual entities wandering around after the blast?"

"No, I'm afraid I ducked underground and stayed there until it was safe. I'm sorry if you think I'm a coward."

"That's okay. I would have done the same, if I'd been able."

"Hmm, come to think of it, a cybernetic vampire might explain your missing cells—and M'Bell did make several allusions along those lines, I recall—but I sure didn't see one."

"Your faith in my veracity never ceases to astound me."

"Oh, Boss, thank you!" Oliver exclaimed gratefully. "I never realized how much faith you have in me! I promise I'll never let you down again!"

I rolled my eyes, laid back down, and stared at the ceiling. It was cruel of me, I know, but I couldn't help but wonder if Floyd had ever been that dumb while he'd been my faithful robot companion.

The answer, of course, was a big yes. From that observation of consistency I derived a sense of comfort, while so much else had changed too rapidly for me to grasp. I had been just getting to know Yangtze, and now she was gone forever. My body was about to be changed forever. One of my lifetime heroes had hit the sauce, apparently in a big way, and I know that were I in his position, I'd be doing exactly the same. And Scorpion had also disappeared, probably forever. One good thing: I wouldn't have to listen to Spaceside sing any more.

"Oliver, what about Wotan?"

"He bit it, in the same blast that got U-Shant Eye. They were destined to die together, I'm afraid. M'Bell, heh-heh, bit it too, but not before she took advantage of the confusion and escaped to bite off the fingers of her father's left hand. Her atoms were blown all over the vicinity, thus proving that even the undead can die in ways other than those prescribed by religious superstition."

"Oh, forget the fucking vampires," I said with sudden impatience. "Who cares about the past anyway? It's the future where I've got to spend the rest of my life. But what if I don't want to spend it as a cyborg?"

"You've no choice, really. The robomeds have their programming to adhere to, after all. They're going to make you a fully functional being whether you want to be or not. In fact, they're tooling up outside the door right now."

I glanced at the nondescript swinging doors. My room was very plain, the white walls devoid of so much as a mass-produced hologram, and the window faced only the windows of another hospital wing. The plastic flower vase on the stand beside my bed was empty. A holovision hung from the stucco ceiling, but the remote-control device was nowhere to be found. I wondered how long I was going to be cooped up here. I'd never become a cyborg before.

I settled back to accept my fate. I was thankful for Oliver's presence; I needed a friend. I was disappointed in 00π, though, for giving up so easily. Sure, he'd lost a daughter, thanks to the efforts of some murderous, far-future heathens, but he had nonetheless promised to help me find Floyd.

Poor Floyd. And here I'd thought the Farce had dealt me such a straight hand. I'd foolishly believed that all I had to do was follow the path that came to me, and Floyd, or at least the solution to the mystery of his passing, would be at the end of it. What a naive jerk I'd been.

Of course, I guess that's why they call it the Farce.

I tried to relax, to let my future rain down and flow through me.

"Boss, there's something else I have to tell you," said Oliver gingerly.

"What could possibly be worse?" I asked, instantly regretting it. Of course—anything could be worse. "Be gentle."

"Well, I was going to come straight out and tell you, but I suppose a little bit of euphemism is in order. I don't like using euphemisms, just like I prefer not to put things off. But in this case, I don't mind making an exception. I've seen how seriously you organics take these things, and—"

"Tell me, tell me!" I shouted, leaning over to grab him by the shoulders. I stopped in midmotion, because I had this sinking feeling that I already knew what he was trying to say.

"Well, Boss, let me put it this way: your legs weren't your only extremities damaged beyond repair by the blast." He produced a little transparent bag filled with dust from a compartment and held it before my eyes. "The reconstructors found the cells of your missing organs, but they're not going to do you much good in their current chemical state."

At last I found the desperate courage to find my groin. Something was missing, all right. And furthermore, the area was perfectly smooth, sheathed with cold metal. "I've already been prepped!" I exclaimed.

That's when I fainted. When I came to my senses a few minutes later, Oliver still stood at my bedside. Suddenly the presence of my faithful robot companion became anathema to me. What was left of my body ached for the soul-drenching comfort of warm, feminine friendship. As personal a kind of friendship as possible, under the circumstances. And there was this faithful, cold mockery of life—the only friend I had at the moment, the only kind of friend I was likely ever to have again—!

It is a difficult thing, to feel life's possibilities slip away, one by one, even when you hadn't taken those possibilities seriously beforehand. How I hated Blather at that moment. He still had a snowball's chance in Hell of making love with Reina or Coryban. More than you could say for me.

I realized with a cold shock how low I'd sunk! For the first time in my life, I actually envied one of Blather's parts. I could have chosen any other red-blooded humanoid male in the entire galaxy to envy, and I'd picked Blather. The annoyed indifference I'd always felt toward him turned into sheer hatred, thanks to my altered state of being.

"Oh Seldon, what if the vampire bit it off?" I exclaimed, hopelessly adrift in spiritual agony.

"Oh, don't worry!" said Oliver impatiently. *"That* wouldn't make you a homosexual!"

"It doesn't matter what I am now! Great Falwell! The last time I got laid was by that fat jailkeeper in Kemp City." I slapped my hand to my forehead. Two fingers were missing. *Terrific. Are the robomeds going to fix them too?* "There was nothing . . . nice about my tryst with the fat jailkeeper from Kemp City. How could there be? It was just pure, rotten, sensual animal lust, totally devoid of redeeming spiritual value! How am I possibly going to look back with nostalgia on such a subhuman moment?"

"Oh, that should be relatively simple," Oliver said.

I looked at him.

"When I was the Holy Spectre, women told me about such incidents all the time. They didn't seem to have any trouble being nostalgic."

"Women?" I asked.

Oliver held his palms before his chest. "Yes," he said, "as in 'women.'"

I thought about it. Perhaps my fat jailer in Kemp City indeed might one day feel nostalgic about our encounter, provided she'd survived the war. Perhaps I would too, provided I survived my oncoming fit of depression.

Get a grip on yourself, Hunter, I told myself. *Not that you've as much to grip as you used to have.* Desperately I sought not to permit myself so much as a glance at my crotch, but to no avail. I was going to miss it.

"It's okay, Boss, there's always the future," Oliver said kindly.

"Yes, but what sort of future? You know how straight I am. I don't know if I'm going to be able to change, or even if I want to. I don't know what I'm going to do, Oliver, I just don't know!"

Whereupon Oliver reached out and slapped me briskly, once on each cheek.

I dropped back on the pillows like a stone. "Thanks," I said coldly, my cheeks stinging. "But I seriously doubt I needed that."

"You were acting hysterical," he replied. "You just may not have noticed it. Trust me, I have experience in these things."

"Thanks to your days as the Holy Spectre?"

"You got it. I've made lots of women hysterical in my day, and I know from bittersweet experience that nothing keeps them in line better than a slap on the face or a slug from a forty-five. Besides, you should look on the bright side. You think you're the first straight biped to have this problem? You think you're the first to have his natural weenie blown off in an accident?"

"Forgive me, but I fail to see what that has to do with me personally."

"Science is a fine and terrific thing," Oliver said, sliding open a compartment on his chest to reveal a digitized lock. He began pressing buttons on the panel. "In fact, the minions of modern medical science have foreseen everything, not because they have any imagination, but mainly because they've already faced everything before. Under circumstances like that, how could they possibly face anything new?" He withdrew a thing from his compartment and held it forth proudly.

My gorge caught in my throat. The thing most greatly resembled a giant tubifex worm: limp, moist, and somewhat decayed. "What the hell is that?" I asked.

"Behold—your new penis!"

Suddenly I was too ill to be sick. My gorge settled as if it had been punctured. "They're going to put that . . . that *thing* on me—a dead man's dick?"

"No, no, it's made of epiplastic. Check it out! Feels almost like the real thing."

I waved the thing away. "I've never touched one besides mine in my life! And what's more, I never intend to!"

"Go on. You're going to have to anyway, sooner or later."

"You mean they're going to force it on me?"

"Here on Aurelian, it's not only *de rigueur* that men walk around with penises, it's the law!"

"Terrific." Rationalizing the situation with the observation that untold millions of doctors had touched untold billions of penises without having their sexual orientation skewed in unappreciated directions, I touched it. It did feel real, sort of. It just wasn't very warm. "You say this thing works?"

"Basically. It's totally mechanized, of course, with positronic, neuromancered, metaplastic digitizers being responsible mainly for the stretching of the muscled cells underneath. Certain fluids help make the skin tougher as well."

"What triggers these, ah, digitizers?"

"Ah, you're becoming interested despite yourself. Sensation. Response. The mind, mostly. Just like in real life. But you can also get it to work like this." And he stroked it.

It got bigger, and harder. I stared in amazement. "Amazing. It's started to glow."

"Wait till you see it in the dark! And it'll get lots hotter too."

"How hot?"

"Hotter than ninety-eight point six, that's for sure! That's when it turns white."

"White? That's an insult!"

"Maybe, but even an insult is about the best thing you've got to look forward to now, fella," Oliver said. "Besides, this model is an improvement over the real item in more ways than one. For one thing, this baby can be cranked up entirely by manual control, *like this*, thus relieving the man of any fears he might have about his ability to perform. Furthermore, the angle of the dangle is no longer strictly proportional to the hoot of the root. And you know what *that* means, don't you? Besides, look at it this way: Before, whenever you disliked your old penis, you couldn't exactly trade it in on a newer model! Now you can!"

"Great, it might have been outdated but at least it was attached."

"Not necessarily, nor was it designed to withstand a fifteen-megaton blast, like this one."

"All right," I said. "If wearing a penis is the law, it's the law."

"Good thinking." He produced a pen and a bulky consent form. He whistled nonchalantly as he flipped through the pages which smoked as if a case of spontaneous combustion was imminent. "Yep, everything looks in order!" he exclaimed cheerfully. A pen unscrewed itself from his forefinger and sped toward me like a heat-seeking missile, landing in my lap just as he thrust the final page into my face. "Just sign here."

I did so with but a glance at the contents above the line. Only one portion was in a language my translator could interpret; the rest was in binary—the code of the robomeds. The dirty deed done, I relaxed on the bed and listened to the whirr as Oliver's finger reinstated itself. I stared uncomfortably at the ceiling. Suddenly I realized something else was missing. "Say, what about . . . ?"

"Yeah, I almost forgot. You just press this slightly raised tab here and—*voilà!*"

Two steel balls in a transparent sac lined with empty blood vessels came out from a concealed fold in the epiplastic and flipped down into place so fast they quivered as if they'd just ricocheted off a tungsten post. "These babies automatically swell with mad desire," said Oliver. "At least, that's what it says in the instruction manual."

"This penis has a manual?"

"Apparently it's equipped with auxiliaries, not to mention some spare parts. Truth to tell, this model is the latest, most up to date available on the black market."

"You got this through illegal sources?" I exclaimed.

"If I'd waded through channels, we would have had a sixteen-thousand-chron wait, at least."

"What did you use for credit?"

Oliver shrugged. "Your first-born. I told you this model was up to date. There's nothing this machine can't do. It's a miracle, I tell you, a modern miracle of science. Boss? Boss? Are you okay?"

"Yeah, I'm fine," I said. "I just flashed on something unexpectedly. I started thinking of that pillbox man."

"So?"

"He died a grisly, horrible death that I wouldn't even wish on one of my own kin."

"Now *that's* a horrible death!"

"And just before he croaked, he said he'd arrived too early. He was from the future, perhaps from a future rivaling that of the entities who'd set the time bombs."

"Makes sense, but what's the point?"

"Well, he was a cyborg, and he was nevertheless somewhat dead, you know, like M'Bell. You think it's possible that in one of the potential time lines we're poised on top of, cyborgs and robots and other creatures of metal and plastic might form the basis of a civilization that will enable their kind to evolve into the race the pillbox man appears to have represented?"

Oliver moved an eyestalk toward the doors. "I have no idea. And frankly, neither do you. Now I've got to make myself scarce before these quacksaws get it into their microchips to give me an inspection up the oilpan."

The doors creaked open. Oliver chucked the leg and the penis on the bed and darted out before the robomed in the forefront of the team could fully register that an unauthorized being was in the room.

"Where's my other leg?" I asked, deliberately distracting the front med. "I ain't going to walk around with one leg."

"You'll get it. Now be quiet or we'll equip you with a set of wheels instead," droned the robomed lifelessly, as he injected me with about 600 c.c.s of glowing crimson thorazine.

"I still—want—my—ot—her—le—eg," I managed to mumble before slipping back into the sea of holes.

Only now I was engulfed in all the holes at once, and they bore down on me with all the exquisite weight only consummate nothingness can achieve.

Time passed. But there was no time. Time passed anyway, and I slept.

When I woke, I was in pain. I ached. Seldon, how I ached. I had become one huge ache, and all I could think of, through the blazing fire of my agony, was how I didn't even have a pecker of my very own to hold on to. The future sure looked bleak.

And bleak it remained during my slow, steady crawl to consciousness. Somehow I kept my eyes open throughout the entire process. The white light on the ceiling made the stucco protrude like the peaks of a desolate moon. The upper corners of the room sank just beyond my visual range, making it difficult to tell exactly what was rotating and making me so dizzy—me, the ceiling, or the whole damn island.

I realized that by now my legs must have been surgically attached. I tried to flex my muscles. Nothing happened. Evidently I hadn't been switched on yet. It was too bad my fingers felt so dead and heavy, and my arms like chains holding me down by the neck, otherwise I would have taken an immediate look see and tried to switch myself on. Too bad. The first time in my life I'd been able to turn myself on without having to worry about social condemnation if I happened to be found out, and I was too zonked to commit the tiniest exploration. At least now I wouldn't have to worry about going blind or my organs turning green. Because even if I did go blind, the robomeds would fix me. They can fix almost anything. They just couldn't make me back into the way I was.

My eyes rolled to the left like slots in a one-armed bandit. The sleek, barren, white wall appeared a thousand meters away. My eyes rolled to the right. It was the same there.

I was absolutely alone, but I couldn't shake the feeling that some other presence was with me. The very fact of its being triggered all manner of emotion and thought. What a bagatelle the gift of life was, and yet what worthiness and nobility the conspiring forces of the universe had conferred on me just by making possible my existence. Perhaps in some small way my existence had been foretold during the Big Bang. Foretold by an intellect cognizant in ways beyond my bipedal ken, mere moments after those fateful first ten seconds, when the tubular flow of filamentlike chains of matter, spanning millions of light-years, was quickly settled. These chains of matter formed the mere components of this intellect and possessed a kind of life we mortal beings can never hope to understand: as such it was beyond traditional definitions of life and death.

But this being knew who it was. It had a purpose, a reason for being. And it went about its business, ruminating upon the implications of its unfathomable reasonings. The passing of time, of billions of years, was nothing to this intellect. All time meant was change, as the composition of the intellect altered with collapse of stars and the explosions of novas.

But as the composition of the universe changed, so did the emotional nature and lofty ambitions of the intellect; its personality broke down into mere fragments of what had once been a vast network of completeness. By the time of the Third Empire, all that remained were vague inklings that had managed to hold themselves together like the lingering vapors that might escape from a petrified corpse, caught by chance in the slight curvatures of space created by the masses of stars and worlds and satellites.

Worlds and satellites where creatures of intellectual pretensions lived, such as the Avidya System.

What's that smell? I asked myself in sudden panic. A mere moment earlier, the hospital had possessed the odor of antiseptic nothingness; now the air was fetid and salty, as if it had become mixed with shit and perspiration. And the odor had changed within the time it had taken me to look from one direction to another.

I looked back to my left. The wall had changed somewhat—it was no longer white. Instead, it glistened and bled with organic matter, of a kind. The crimson liquid was like blood, only thicker. It seeped through pores as if gravity was squeezing the wall like a sponge. Soundlessly the liquid dripped onto the floor and formed a pool that ebbed toward my bed with deliberate purpose.

I rolled my eyes to the right. There the wall bled a greasy black liquid—crude, unrefined, like midnight oil. Its odor permeated the room and seeped into my skull, making me even dizzier. The feel of steam manifested itself, though the actual humidity had increased not a whit. It sapped even my strength to breathe: it stiffened my joints and rusted my hinges.

More lubricants dripped from the ceiling; they appeared to be mixed with different organic plasmas, some of which probably came from nonhumanoid species. The drops that landed on the bed were absorbed into the sheets. I should have been drenched, but the lubricants didn't touch me; this I suspected of being the result of purpose, though the more sensible side of me explained it away as the mere repulsion of one kind of life for another.

The lubricants slithered down the sheets and onto the floor, mixed with the crimson blood and the midnight oil, and together they generated a new kind of electricity in the air. Bright flashes of yellow and white light ricocheted off the walls like jet-propelled ping-pong balls; they made the noises a meteor makes when it crashes and there's no one around to hear it, as if the universe had, somewhat preternaturally, decided to unfold the fabric of space before me and reveal its innermost layers.

Soon all the fluids had coagulated in the center of the room, leaving the walls and my sheets immaculate, but I could only sense it because the ping-pongs of light had become blinding. Summoning the strength of the fearful, I sat up and covered my eyes, but to no avail. Soon the light became so lustrous the outlines of my bones were silhouetted against skin and tissue that had become like scrim. Yet there was no pain; my eyes had dealt with the glare without apparent physical harm. It was like being in the middle of a fire and remaining somehow whole and unsinged.

Then a flash of nova-like proportions exploded throughout the room. I cowered like a knave, and instinctively pulled the covers over my eyes.

After the flash had died, I lowered the sheets. Only a few sparks danced around in the air twinkling here and there about a clay-like figure standing at the foot of my bed. For a moment its amorphous configuration reminded me of Dr. Proty, but Proty's surface, I realized, was smooth and rippled, like that of fine pudding, whereas this creature was thick and lumpy. Indentations on its surface appeared and disappeared, with an effect not unlike that of watching the rippling skin of a claymation monster on the holovision, where the touch of the special-effects master has left his fingerprints behind; only in this case the creature was a real thing, solid and pulsing with its own kind of blood, writhing with the agony of its birth.

It tried to make arms and reach for the ceiling, but the creature's amorphous shape restricted their movements. Their clumsy efforts did perhaps help the creature shape a globe roughly resembling a head. It managed to speak, though it had as yet no mouth. **I hurt, therefore I must be,** it said.

"Floyd?" I asked.

I am . . . not Floyd. I hurt. I am . . . something else. That much was for certain. The ping-ponging lights had returned, this time muted and ricocheting within the very body of the shape. Evidently a series of internal explosions were transpiring, heating the metal bits and pieces inside into malleability.

"Who are you?" I asked.

Someone who hurts. Someone you love.

"I hate to disillusion you, but at the moment I'm not *in love* with anyone. So unless you happen to be the ghost of my dear, sainted mother, you'd best make yourself scarce."

I am not saintly, said the shape haughtily, as if it had been grievously insulted. **I who hurt also confer sainthood, but am under no obligation to live in such a state.**

"Are you saying that sainthood is a state intended to honor you?"

Yes, but not to bind me. On its chest, wires of gold and silver alloy wove together in complex patterns that, as they rotated inside and out like the jigsaw pieces of a computerized image, gradually became mechanical auricles and ventricles lined with flexible plastiglas sacs to protect the circuits and coils from the plasma that slithered in filaments between the fibers of musculature only beginning to separate themselves from the contorting, amorphous mass. The mass had finally succeeded in creating a heart of hi-tech mechanics based on the principles of low-tech bioengineering.

AAAAWWWWWRRRRRGGGGHHHHH, the thing screamed. **Is this what it means to be real?**

"I assure you, I'm the last person you should ask." I watched, fascinated, as the heart disappeared inside the mass, as concentric vane mechanisms bloomed roughly in the positions humanoid joints would take and then also disappeared beneath folds of metatissue; as rough-hewn arteries and veins chiseled themselves like scars on the changing surface; and as raw, generic plasma mutated into different colors and textures analogous to, perhaps, amino acids, fats, and layers of tissue—all this and more drenched with oil and other lubricants. Sharp-edged incisors, broad molars, and canines, reflecting distorted images of the world outside, arranged themselves around a hole evidently intended to become the oral cavity. Initially the oral cavity was situated to the left of the heart, but when two lidless, white eyeballs, with their putty-like *vitreous humors* completely exposed, came into being one on each shoulder, the mouth inched its way up past the neck. The eyes followed. The mouth soon decided its proper place on the face. The eyes then found their proper location, though they did keep exchanging places for some time.

I an not dead! the mouth cried when it was fixed. **I'm alive I'm alive I'm alive!** With quickness and surety of purpose, two defiant fists, their fingers gnarled and bent, their metal oxidized by the agony of the creature's internal heat, rose like frozen lava from the undulating metal mass, clenching and unclenching with unfettered determination. Occasionally the mass erupted in all directions at once, always snapping back into a slightly more defined shape at the last possible nanosecond before dissolution. It was like watching a cartoon trying to figure out how it should make itself more presentable for the future frames of life.

Soon I was able to define the identity taking shape as feminine in nature. The clenching and unclenching fists gradually became smaller, somewhat elongated, and the movement of the fingers resembled the hypnotic snakes on a medusa head.

The thing in my room soon reached the point where she could regard herself clinically. Oh how so carefully she examined her arms, like a newborn babe somehow endowed with the gifts of maturity and intelligence.

"Good space-time to you," I said nervously, figuring this was as good a time as any to break the ice. "Welcome to my presence. I'm not much, but at the moment I'm all I've got. Which, come to think of it, is about half of what I'm normally used to having."

She said nothing. She just kept looking at her arms, getting used to the idea that the closer she held them toward her newborn hips and legs, the easier time she had trying to stand.

"This, ah, isn't your first time at being alive, is it?" I asked, hoarsely.

It might as well be, she groaned. **Each time it is always this difficult. Each time I hurt. Each time it is always the first.** The voice was on the verge of working perfectly, as contrasted to the fact that elsewhere on her transmuting body, cogs and gears still meshed imperfectly, regulator clips leaked, piston rods bent, wires smoked, transistors fizzled, circuits snapped, and swivels became stuck. Even so, it was possible to discern the general parameters of the goal the mass had in mind. And it was impossible for me, as someone who had once been a man, not to approve profoundly at the goal's overall sense of aesthetics, and not to feel an equally profound sense of resentment at life, the universe, and everything.

Meanwhile, my balls hummed. They quivered like twin engines. Evidently the circuits inside were programmed to signal their own approval, independent of my emotions, of the way things were shaping up. *Contents be damned!* they seemed to be saying. *You can't let a little thing like an artificial penis dampen your sex life!* Even so, I had prided myself on never letting my head be ruled by my balls (well, hardly ever), and I wasn't about to let these upstarts sneak up on my common sense. "Well, listen, if being born is such a pain," I said, "why don't we just take a rain check on this appointment? At least until a time when I'm in better running condition, should things come down to that."

You might very well wish to run, said the creature, without malice or even a sense of irony, **but our properly appointed time has arrived.**

"How do you know it's—properly appointed?"

Trust me on that. This one has a hurt that tells her she knows.

She groaned and nearly fell over. At the last moment she grabbed the sheet at the foot of the bed, and leaned on the mattress for support. Her narrow torso seemed to be primarily responsible for the humming of my balls. Its general outline had evidently meshed with images from my brain. I realized that from now on, my susceptibility to arousal, whether or not I wanted to do anything about it, would be wholly involuntary.

And wholly intoxicating. This would not do. Not when my survival might depend on it.

I searched my memory for a clue to the torso's familiarity. I discovered that not so long ago, while actively visualizing the essence of my basest impulses, I'd wondered lustfully, like an armchair satyr, how a certain youngish, boyish torso, equally naked, with golden, silken skin, would feel held against my own. *Maybe when she's older,* I had consoled myself as I permitted the thought to drift away. In the wake of recent developments, however, I hadn't expected ever to experience a quiver of desire toward such a torso again, but, contrary to the laws of logic and life and death, I most definitely was.

"Uh, have we met before?" I asked suspiciously.

It is a part of the truth to say we have, after a fashion; but it is equally true to say we have not.

"Well, my name's Homer B. Hunter, and I might as well confess I'm not ready to run away yet. I have to learn how to make my new legs work first."

This one has not come here to learn how your legs work, the creature said impatiently. Something about her smart-aleck tone was familiar too, not quite jiving with her dominant essence. As her pain lessened and her posture improved, becoming gangly and moving toward the merely awkward, I realized with a sudden flash of insight that her body language and, to some extent, her tone of voice were completely the result of the physical body that had aroused my programmed response, and had nothing to do with the personality in command of it. In that personality I could read all the inklings of a cosmic maturity, struggling to overwhelm the younger soul.

"I've had enough of this! Just who are you anyway? Let's start with the part I haven't met yet."

You know. You just have not admitted you know.

"You're making ten or twelve assumptions."

This one hurts. This one hurts with the pangs of birth, and you cannot say you are unmoved.

"It has nothing to do with you."

Au contraire, it has everything to do with me. And I have everything to do with it. This shape was fated from the dawn of time to be the one this one would ride onto the mortal continuum. This soul was the one that was fated to be mine, for a time.

"Your soul is Yangtze's?" I blurted out.

Yes.

"And what, exactly, is a soul?"

That would be telling.

"Then why should I believe you, when you say you have Yangtze's soul?"

Just trust me, and you will believe. The night, after all, is young.

I couldn't help, I am certain, reacting to that one, for the creature inside my room had uttered those words in exactly the same manner Yangtze might have said them. "How do you know it's night out?"

Trust me, she said with a smile. She had begun to take on color, a metallic color to be sure, but it still resembled a bronze shade of skin. That meant the interaction between her inert and organic matter had reached new levels. It worked for me. I couldn't stop staring at the subtle textures highlighted in the reflections of her skin; already her presence drew me like a magnet, and the promise of her charms hypnotized me like a rat frozen before the most beautiful cobra imaginable.

"I'd like to, but I need to know more about the part of you that isn't Yangtze first."

This one thought you might say that. You heathens are so predictable.

"As predictable as a dead soul?"

In a different way. In a more secular-humanist fashion.

"It wasn't just fate?"

Knowing the whims and wisdoms of Fate enables one to know so much more, but in the main, all one must do to understand mortals is to observe them from a distance for a few millennia. They are almost always the same, everywhere.

"Who are you? I warn you, I'm getting tired of asking that."

And I am getting tired of hearing it. I am part Yangtze, true, but in the main I am the

goddess Marie. **This one is pleased to make your acquaintance.**

"And where do you normally live, Marie?"

This one has bent the curves of space to be at your side at the appointed time, regardless of where destiny may take both of us. Are you prepared to waste precious chrons asking impertinent questions?

"Yes. Are you prepared to go on evading the answers?"

This one will refrain from doing so in the interest of achieving her ultimate goal, which, judging from the emotions in the well of your soul, could be easily accomplished without earning your trust.

"Just think of how much more fun we'll have if I do trust you a little."

A little is all that will be necessary. You will be happy to know that you were right when you were unconscious. At the dawn of time this one was part of a much greater thought, in a much greater soul. But as time passed and space curved and matter changed, the whole degenerated into its component parts. All that is left are vapors, wisps of mental energy capable of becoming reality for brief periods of time, provided they are nurtured by the dreams and passions of mortals who have named them and who worship them.

"So that's who the gods are—the remnants of a greater intelligence who existed at the dawn of time as we know it today?"

You ask too many questions. Permit this one the opportunity to learn if you can answer the one I have come here to ask. Gently she felt her breasts and found pleasure in their size and shape and texture. She ran a forefinger around one nipple that rose at her touch like a blooming flower. She smiled at the results. So did I. Gracefully but with great purpose, she walked over to the bed and slowly pulled the sheet off me. The smile on her round face grew progressively bolder. **Hmmm! Nice craftsmanship.**

I couldn't help but notice the segments of my cybernetic member had extended into a proudly erect posture.

She leaned down and kissed my belly button—an innie. Her mischievous grin indicated my innie stirred her up inside. (I couldn't help but notice she was devoid of a belly button herself.) Tenderly her tongue explored my stomach, and her cold, hard mane of hair grazed my skin. At first every touch of her ice cold body, though immensely pleasurable, made my teeth chatter but as she moved against me, her body gradually warmed and most of my goosebumps disappeared. She buried her face in my neck for a protracted period, and I stared lightheadedly at the ceiling, not really seeing anything. After that, the two of us warmed up remarkably fast, and I even felt a glow in my legs and feet considerably like the organic glows I'd had with my real legs and feet. The power expenditure here was going to be considerable. But well worth it.

Meanwhile, my penis glowed like a Meridian Power Eel.

She pressed her chest against mine. Her nipples were as hard and erect as sharp-edged razors. The edges of the tiny flecks of tungsten metaplastic made tiny slices in my skin, corrugating me in two series of tiny intersecting circles. **Feed me,** she whispered, as she absorbed tiny amounts of blood from my chest into her system. This made her epiplastic skin surface heat up even more, and some of the blood on my chest hissed as it evaporated. **Feed me, Homer B.**

Hunter. Feed me and taste me. Do not hold back, for this is the last respite of mortal passion the soul of your friend Yangtze will ever know. This will be her last chance to touch the night with one she might have loved. And then I was inside her. My body worked perfectly, responding all at once, instead of piecemeal, as I'd feared. The interaction between my artificial and biological selves was complete. The sensations of the two sections felt different from each other, true, but the shiver running down my spine and to the tips of my toes as she expertly sailed me along the waters of ecstasy was as continuous and wavelike as any I'd ever experienced. It stirred my legs into action, and from that point on, things got damn hot in the hemisphere of love. I did my best to steer us through the rapids. I did not conceive of her as Marie but rather as the Yangtze I would never know, and this incident as the opportunity to realize an experience that had been stolen away. Whoever she was, she delightedly permitted herself to become an instrument beneath my tutelage as we did our best to deliberately waste the other via sheer mental fatigue. When I finally ran out of ideas, she came up with a few of her own.

Thus we whiled away the chrons in perfect lovemaking until my organic half simply became too exhausted, my breathing too labored, for us to continue. I was incredibly disappointed in myself. Her metallic body showed no sign of tiring (or of perspiring, for that matter), nor had my own metallic half; my mind and all my programming urged me to continue and continue, the consequences to future health and happiness be damned. Perhaps she sensed my dissatisfaction, for she spoke the first words either of us had said for chrons when, with a sly smile, she whispered in my ear, **The dawn has come and gone. The sun Avidya is high in the Aurelian sky.**

"How do you know this?" I asked, knowing in my heart she was right.

This one knows what this one needs to know. One thing this one knows is time.

"And what, may I ask, is time?"

Something you mortals erringly believe proceeds solely in a single direction.

"Is that how you knew the time had come to visit me?"

In a manner of speaking, yes. I have known everything that was going to happen. But so did you, after a certain point.

"But you knew long before me, and you've probably got some idea of what's going to happen next."

You're *so* predictable. As the warmth went out of her eyes her body became icy cold again, but the moment was quickly over and she smiled, admittedly with an effort, and some of the heat returned to her body. I relaxed with a sigh, belatedly realizing how quickly and unknowingly I'd tensed up. **Even so, recent memory informs me that in comparison with other mortals who ask no questions at all, your curiosity is refreshing.**

"Ah, has your recent memory just noticed that?"

Yes. Generally it pays for a god to concentrate on long-term aspects of the identity fortress, and not ponder recent memory unless it has some bearing on current events.

"Goddess," I corrected.

Whatever, she said, shrugging, even as she reached beneath the sheets to tweak my manufactured member.

"Say, I'm trying to be serious here! I don't like this! Why was it so important that Yangtze had to die before you would come to me?"

Someone had to die. How else was I to make the connection? Would you have had another die?

"Frankly, yes, especially someone I hadn't met yet, if you must know."

She sat up and haughtily folded her arms beneath her breasts, arching her shoulders and shaking her mane of metal hair exactly the way Yangtze had when Spaceside's band had ignored her.

"Why was it important that you come to me in the first place? It doesn't matter that it had been foretold; you wouldn't have blown off all the agony of getting born if it hadn't been important."

A *goddess* has needs. After all, I have been weathering a feminine turn of the wheel since before the dawn of the First Empire.

"But why Yangtze? Why did anyone have to die for you to get what you want?"

That this one does not know. Because it is the way it is, I suspect.

"Did the intelligence who encompassed the universe know this was going to happen as it dissipated after the Big Bang?"

The one who was all might have known it, but this one seriously doubts anything could have been done about it, even if the one who was all had wanted to.

"That's no reason! Don't you understand? I have to know why? Why did Yangtze have to die?"

Why does anything happen? You might as well ask why hydrogen and oxygen in the proper configuration make water, and why water has certain properties that under certain pressures create certain conditions. You might as well ask why most life-forms are carbon-based, or why fish swim instead of fly, or why life in general exists as you know it instead of some other way.

"If you're trying to tell me that I should ask why

effect should follow cause, then I fail to see why the death of Yangtze should cause us to make love."

It is not for this one to know. It is for this one to do. It is for you to answer why.

Looking into her eyes, the colors of which swirled and mixed the way clouds move in the night, I actually imagined a faint inkling of the great intelligence of which she was but a vapor—and I knew, through a leap of faith that was as logical as it was surreal, that the mysterious machinations of the unfathomable cosmic intelligence were somehow tied up in the reasons why. And that those reasons were all tied up, somehow, with my search for Floyd.

Was it possible that even though I had come to the right solar system, I was still on the wrong plane of existence to find my little buddy? I had been struck by what the goddess had said about most mortals erring when they assumed that time only ran in one direction. Maybe it was possible that—

Unfortunately, that was exactly how far I came to formulating my conclusions, when suddenly all time and space broke loose.

Chapter Twelve
The Roar of the Demigod, The Smell of the Hero

OH NO! NOT NOW!
exclaimed Marie when the flying glove—the jet-propelled, rocket-powered, radar-equipped, supersonic nasty Thing I'd seen tumble into nothingness in the sea of holes—reached out from the wall, grabbed her by the head, and yanked her off the bed.

For an extended moment I stared helplessly, not knowing what to do except lie there.

The glove attempted to crush her, but the strain was too great for it; its fingers made an eerie sound, like a building whose foundations are being twisted out of shape by a massive earthquake. **Curse you to the ultimate!** snarled Marie as she took advantage of the glove's weakness and attempted to pry the fingers open. She had gotten as far as freeing her arms when the glove unpredictably scissored her neck between the tips of two fingers and tried to snap her the way you might kill a flea in your hand. Her neck buckled and tore, and electrical sparks flew from the openings. For the first time, I perceived something akin to humanoid emotion in her eyes as she said pleadingly, **Help me, you big galoot.**

265

"You mean me?" I asked stupidly, wondering what I could possibly do against that glove. "How?"

She managed to point to her bottom, but she meant for me to look at mine own, as it were. At some point during our intimacies, she had surreptitiously left behind an item that could conceivably tip the balance of the battle taking place in my hospital room. So unused was I to my metal behind that I hadn't even noticed the alien mass embedded there. It was one of her fingers. I wondered, naturally, how she had known in advance where to put it, but I could only assume that she had done so with the same foresight that had enabled her to realize that this had been the time and the place to ride the form of Yangtze.

Unfortunately, I had no idea what she intended me to do with the finger. So I continued to watch helplessly as, with the grace of an acrobat, she attempted to swing her legs above her head to relieve the pressure the glove was inflicting on her. It was clear she was not going to be able to instruct me herself on the workings of the finger in my hand in the near future.

But when steam started hissing from the holes in her neck, my mind began racing, and frantically I began studying the finger. It looked just like your average metal finger, no more, no less. It hadn't even come from her own hand; all her fingers were on her hands, digging themselves into the glove and tearing out fragments, but accomplishing little in the way of saving her.

Then something clicked in the back electrodes of my translator. She was whispering to me, attempting to hide her words from whatever intelligence was notivating the glove. **Twist it,** she hissed. **Shoot the finger.**

I'd never heard the phrase used in quite that

context before, but at least it was an action I could understand. I pointed the finger at her and twisted it. Nothing happened, so I tried to twist it at a lower knuckle.

It moved! I twisted it some more, but nothing happened.

Marie waved at me frantically; evidently I was doing something wrong, something that was so obvious to her it must have made her sufferings all the more painful.

Then I realized I'd felt a slight tingling in my spine. The finger was pointed in the wrong direction, and must have been inundating me with invisible rays. I turned it around so that the other end pointed at Marie and the glove.

And then I twisted it again.

Sure enough, the rays were still invisible, but this time they had a definite effect.

A shower of purple sparks erupted from the joints of the glove. It released Marie and she slumped prone against the floor, wheezing for breath and actually getting some once she clamped her own fingers over the tears in her neck. The glove extended its fingers stiffly, crookedly, as if rigor mortis was setting in. It dropped through the floor, as if it had fallen through an invisible hole. As a result, the person attached to the glove was unwillingly pulled through a sudden rupture in the time-space wall.

Marie covered her eyes; evidently she was being blinded by lights on a wavelength I could not perceive. The hole disappeared as soon as the person had passed through; it had fulfilled its purpose.

The person was another version of Marie. She too had come to my room buck naked. Her hair and skin appeared more natural and were of a lighter hue, but she too was basically made of metal, and her components appeared to be at least one technological generation ahead of those of the Marie I had bedded. It was immediately apparent that there was little of Yangtze in this one. The body was taller and the shoulders broader; the hips were wide and she had cloven feet. Her long arms were lean and muscular, her thighs rippled like knotted cables. In addition, she had a balcony you could do Shakespeare from.

Most significant, however, was the fact that on one hand was written the word *Love* and on the other *Hate*. This was the Marie that Yangtze had described to me. This was Marie undiluted by Yangtze. This woman, if you could call her that, was the genuine item, as opposed to the watered-down version who had made love to me.

Yangtze/Marie was the first to speak. **You! You are this one!**

"How wonderful! You remember," said the newcomer from the side of her mouth. Her voice was nasal and grating. There was nothing divine about it. She was chewing gum. She lorded it over Yangtze/Marie for a few moments, then suddenly appeared quite confused. "Or do I remember? I've been shuffled up and down this continuum so much lately, I can hardly remember where I'm supposed to be, much less what I'm supposed to doing and *when!*"

You are who this one once was—who this one will become!

"That's what I'm here to make sure of, anyway."

"And how do you propose to do that?" I asked.

The newcomer smiled and popped her chewing gum. "Funny you should ask." She slammed the fist labeled *Hate* into the hand labeled *Love*.

"Sounds promising," I said. I pointed the finger at the new Marie.

"No! Don't!" the newcomer said, a nanosecond before Yangtze/Marie took advantage of the distraction to roll on the floor and deliver a terrific kick to her other self's crotch. The resulting clang sounded like two anvils hurling themselves at one another, but the effect on the newcomer was more one of surprise than of pain. The newcomer staggered back against the wall and stared wide-eyed at her other self. "You treacherous vixen," she exclaimed. Then she smiled. "I didn't know I had it in me back then."

"Or in the future!" I said. "Don't forget."

"Yeah, I guess maybe I did, that is, if maybe I didn't. It doesn't matter. I always lose control of myself whenever I ride the soul of a mortal, and I guess maybe I always will."

This one supposes she should do her best to erase you from both her future and her past, said Yangtze/Marie, just before she made a lunge for her alter ego.

Within instants they were writhing about like two battling tiger worms on the floor, kicking, choking, scratching and biting, but mostly gouging and punching. Bits of metal were knocked or chipped from their bodies, and precious bodily fluids of many types and colors soon spotted the entire area. Not all the strange sounds they made were growls or groans—I had the distinct feeling that levers, gears and pistons were getting stuck or crunched.

"Get back, Marie," I said. "I'm going to use the finger."

Yangtze/Marie indeed tried to break free, but her other, less divine self held her fast, using her as a shield. The newcomer looked over Yangtze/Marie's shoulder with wide, fearful, pleading eyes. "Don't do it, you mortal scumbag!" the newcomer said. "If you keep using that kind of unholy scientific power, the very universe itself will rise up in anger against you!"

"What are you talking about?" I said, taking aim. "I don't even know what this frigging thing is!"

"We'll be traced!" said the newcomer.

"So what?" I said. "Who's doing the tracing?" I twisted the finger. I'd twisted it only a few centimeters when I was distracted by the suddenly rising bulge in the center of the floor.

A hoodoo! exclaimed Yangtze/Marie, taking advantage of the chaos to deck her less divine self. She leapt over the bulge and crouched down like a cat beside me. **A great wizard must be concerned with the proceedings here, for it requires great power, devotion, and sacrifice to tap into the hidden spiritual world of inert matter.**

"Now you tell me," I said, my eyes bulging in fear.

Perhaps he was impressed by the energies we released here today, she said, giving me a quick kiss on the ear. Her tongue was cold.

I didn't much care for these *hoodoos*, I thought, remembering the Lump, who had seemed to be promoting a hidden political agenda when he had tried to crush me in his brick-and-mortar fingers. This particular *hoodoo* was manifesting itself on this floor. In lieu of becoming a body, it was simply becoming a giant face that stretched from wall to wall, with a long, toothsome mouth in the center, framed in a perpetual smile that ran under the bed. A thick black tongue composed of filaments like a paintbrush licked the shiny lips, and I had the feeling the tongue was long and dexterous enough to grab me and pull me down into the slippery abyss of its other-worldly esophagus. The ears were barbed wads of cartilage bunched up against the walls, and the nose was sufficiently broad and strong to tip the bed into one of the bloodshot pink eyes. **Yo-yo, fo-do, vo-de-oh-do!** said the *hoodoo*. **I smell the blood of a bipedal pig dog.**

"Speak for yourself, you . . . you . . ."

Don't call me a you-you, and get this fucking bed off my eye. I can't see a damn thing.

The tongue reached up to grab hold of the light fixture. The *hoodoo* breathed an almost subliminal sigh of relief once it succeeded, as if now it had somehow saved itself from sinking into the nether dimensions below the plane.

"I suppose you're after me too," I said.

Either that, or I suppose I'm after the same image of the same dead one you're after, said the *hoodoo* cryptically.

This one will be decked out in the halls of folly! exclaimed Yangtze/Marie, her words evidently being an oath of some sort which I did not understand. **You will find no dead image here! Why interrupt this one, just when she was winning?**

"Just think of it as kismet," I said, "and try to figure some way out of here before we all get crushed in the stateroom scene of life!"

Yangtze/Marie cocked her head like a puzzled bull terrier; something significant chose that moment to come to her mind. **Why? This one begins to suspect it is your kismet to be swallowed today.**

I inched away from the treacherous little bitch.

From the other side of the mouth, the not-so-divine Marie recovered her consciousness and said, "Come on, little sister. Let's work together and push him in."

Yes, that would be nice, said the face on the floor. **I am feeling a tad voracious. And then, after I've satiated my culinary desires, then maybe somebody can remove this fucking bed from my eye?**

It is agreed, said Yangtze/Marie. **But mark my words, other self, this one is your big sister.**

Okay! said the *hoodoo*. **It's chow time!**

"See? It's unanimous!" squeaked the Marie with the chewing gum, advancing around the *hoodoo* lips toward me. In a few moments I'd be sandwiched between two Maries. Not so long ago such a fate would have seemed like a blessing. Now it was definitely the end.

Luckily for me, fate had selected that very moment for a puff of sulphurous yellow smoke to suddenly go *poof!* in my hospital room, and—who should appear but an obese gentleman with a bulbous proboscis, wearing baggy trousers and big flat shoes. He was perched with the delicate grace of a five hundred pound canary on a bicycle. The Anti-Curly had arrived! He'd save me!

Unluckily for me, however, he just happened to materialize directly over the *hoodoo's* mouth. The *hoodoo* grinned and the Anti-Curly, bicycle and all, dropped like a meteor into the abyss. Vainly the Anti-Curly tried to grab hold of the tongue, but it was too greasy for him to get a good grip on, and he disappeared an instant after his bicycle dropped down that awaiting esophagus.

Hee-hee-hee, the *hoodoo* said.

A dim shout echoed from below: "You haven't seen the last of me, you vicious *hoodoo!*"

Ah, but it was definitely the last time I would see the Anti-Curly in my life story, I observed grimly as I took advantage of the distraction to edge toward the door.

And even then, I was already too late. The Yangtze/Marie looked at me. The not-so-divine Marie from the past or the future also looked at me. And so did the grinning *hoodoo*, its mirthful eyes rolling in my direction like Brobdingnagian watermelons turning on a stick over a blazing fire.

The Maries smiled. **Hi.** "Hi."

The thrill that shot through me as my fingers grasped the door knob almost made an artificial heart the next necessary addition to my body parts.

The Maries stepped toward me; something in their

manner indicated they were restraining the impulse to pounce on me like a helpless rabbit. "You know, I'm beginning to remember why I used to admire my soul-riding self so much." **Be sure to tell this one when you find out for certain.**

"Listen, you're making a big mistake, ladies . . . uh, Maries," I protested. "You don't have to go to any extremes. Just tell me what it is you don't like about me and I'll do my best to change it. And you"—I directed my statement toward Yangtze/Marie—"you should be more resistant to peer pressure."

Why? She is myself.

"All right, but that doesn't mean you have to start giving in now. Wait. Savor the sensation of change. Besides, how do you know that gum-chewing version of yourself isn't manipulating you into being something you don't really want to be?"

Yangtze/Marie stopped and glared suspiciously at her other self.

"Sure, she may be cool, a real swinging goddess," I continued, "and I grant you, you maybe want to be as evil and as—how shall I say this?—as animalistic as her someday. But how do you know she's the kind of beast you want to be? Maybe she represents a substandard divinity that's contrary to your elevated principles."

Don't listen to him! the *hoodoo* implored. **He's jerking you off!**

"You're just jealous because nobody can do the same to you!" I said. And then, to Yangtze/Marie: "And besides, how do you know this goddess is operating under the principle of free will? She could be under someone else's control!"

"I am not!" said the not-so-divine Marie indignantly, shaking her fist at me. "Don't listen to him!"

Yes! Don't you see that he's trying to turn you against yourself? the *hoodoo* said.

Yangtze/Marie looked her other self in the eye. **And with good reason. This one should know better than anyone never to trust myself with a man.** She lunged at her other self, grabbed her by the neck, pushed her down without letting go, falling on top of her. The not-so-divine Marie's neck buckled violently and a geyser of oil spurted toward the ceiling.

Sticking the finger for safe keeping in a compartment (which had been a secret from me until I needed it), I twisted the doorknob and pushed open the door. I did not, however, watch where I was going because I was afraid to turn away from the fighting, which was very brutal but somewhat entertaining in its own right.

Consequently, I was completely unprepared for the pair of cold hands that grabbed my waist. I shouted and whirled, ready to take on any heinous brute who might be standing between me and freedom.

Fortunately, it was only Oliver, and so I didn't have to face the more realistic prospect of immediately losing my freedom to the first heinous brute who happened by.

"Boss! Boss! You were wonderful in there!"

"How do you know?" I asked.

"Easily!" he said with a shrug. "I watched you every minute!"

"*Every* minute?"

"Sure. You didn't think I'd let you face your first close encounter as a new man alone, did you? I thought I'd give you some moral support."

"Then why didn't you tell me you were watching?" Now I was discovering how a cyborg could feel embarrassed all over.

"Well, I didn't want to interrupt you, for obvious reasons. It's probably better that you didn't know, anyway. It would have hindered your performance and then you would have blamed yourself."

There was an explosion in the room behind me. I heard metal parts bounce from the walls, and a few bolts, springs, and screws fell from the crack of the open door.

"Let's get out of here!" I said.

We had just reached the dilating elevator doors when we heard a muffled voice from the other end of the hall. **No—no—not the face!** pleaded the *hoodoo*.

The building was shaking when Oliver and I fled through the lobby, which impressed me as being unusually crowded. Nobody seemed to mind that I was naked, perhaps because I was a cyborg who with the help of his faithful robot companion had figured out how to retract his private parts, and perhaps because there were many other naked people and bipeds in the lobby already, as well as many others in various states of undress.

Most of these people, I realized with my gorge rising, were burn victims. Many were in states of shock too great to be much concerned about the shaking building; others were panicked, but too sedated or bedridden to flee. Those who tried were stopped by the robomeds. The stench of scalded skin was sickening, and the victims' physical suffering created an almost tangible fluid in the air. They were all ages and sexes. Cyborg and one hundred percent organic alike were injured, and their wounds were all fresh. This misery was the result of a disaster more recent than the one I had endured.

So recent that in fact the robomeds were still bringing in the patients. Some cases were so urgent that the robomeds smoked and stalled due to conflicting mandates between their programming and the events—their charges desperately needed medical attention that was available only in the hospital that was dangerous to be in.

"Don't dawdle!" I ordered Oliver as he paused to ease the stress of one of the robomeds. "We're still on a mission from Floyd."

Oliver's eyes tipped toward the upper floors, where my room had been. "Uh-oh! You don't have to tell me twice, Boss!"

We had just turned away when a great flash erupted from the windows above, illuminating for an instant the buildings on the opposite side of the great landing area where the pneumatic choppers were coming in with their loads of the wounded. The light blinded a pilot—I cringed as he covered his eyes— and his chopper spun out of control. For a moment the chopper swayed in the air like a great stunned wasp, unable to decide in which direction it wanted to strike back. And then it crashed into another chopper. People screamed.

The choppers struck the ground as one and all erupted into flames.

So terrified was I at the sight of a biped completely engulfed in flame emerging from the wreckage that I was unaware that the glass in the upper stories had shattered, which I realized only after the ground around Oliver and me was covered with tiny crystallized pieces. A sliver of glass pierced my neck and grated against my poor sensitive tissue as I looked up to see that all the hospital windows were gone, and great columns of green and purple smoke stretched like undulating snakes from the frames.

Meanwhile robomeds were already attending to those unfortunates involved in the crash. The burning biped's fire was being put out with foam—but there didn't seem to be enough of him left to salvage; even his brain, which would normally have been put into a new body, had literally been fried. A few others had been sufficiently lucky not to have caught fire, but they were nonetheless terribly wounded, with bones protruding from their limbs and, in a few cases, the limbs dangling from torn muscle and skin. They were all potential cases for deliberate memory erasure as far as I was concerned.

"Come on!" I told Oliver, moving in a wide circle around the site of the crash.

"But, Boss, we've got to get you some clothes!"

"Later son, for Seldon's sake, later!"

We passed many robomeds standing still and shaking like electrocuted leaves, turning uselessly in this direction and that, wondering who they should help first—the burn victims being brought in, or those who'd crashed on the way.

The circuitry of one robomed was so overpowered by his dilemma that the top of his head flew right off. I had to drag Oliver away. "Let me help him! Let me help him!" he pleaded.

"Help me instead and tell me what's happened here!"

"I don't know! I just heard it was another disaster —the fourth one this week."

"What kinds of disasters? Terrorism? Natural causes?"

"The first was definitely of the religious-outlaw variety. That was the explosion in the fetal banks."

"Hmmm. Sounds like a few destinies have been altered."

"Now, Boss, just because we've been involved in a few events orchestrated by beings from the future doesn't mean all events are."

"Just go on . . ." and he did as we passed a deserted security booth and went out the gate to find the space island transformed. Where once there had been tall, gleaming buildings, there were now only deserted hulks, the rubble from their upper stories still lying in the streets; a few still had aircraft protruding from their sides. If anyone was concerned for the public safety, they clearly had problems more pressing than the possibility that some precariously dangling aircraft might tilt off-balance and fall on an unsuspecting pedestrian below.

I stumbled wearily through the debris-strewn streets as Oliver told me of disaster after disaster that had struck Aurelian. Such a tale of woe I'd never heard, outside of myths; and in myths disasters were usually spaced out over long periods. Here they had happened during the course of one week, a week I happened to have spent sound asleep. One disaster was an unexpected meteor shower that shattered vast portions of the island's protective shell; a few populated buildings, along with a great deal of air, were sucked out of the holes before they were repaired by the automatic defenses; now the oxygen was thinner than normal, and since the buildings just happened to be the recycling kind, the water was beginning to have an astringent aftertaste. People were starting to get sick.

Another disaster occurred when a parade got caught in the crossfire of two battling mercenary factions that no one had ever heard of before; half the provisional government of the island had shuffled off this mortal coil in that incident, which had naturally resulted in celebrations in some quarters. But an entire high-school class of youths from all over the solar system also happened to have been caught in the crossfire, so a lot of grief and worry put a damper on some of the high spirits.

All the mercenaries left behind of their own factions were two stacks of bodies which disintegrated upon examination.

Still another disaster had occurred when some damn fool thought it would be an amusing idea if the

Brain Police spent a day scurrying about after false alarms that were, in reality, caused by a bunch of hidden dog whistles. But the prankster had miscalculated the effects of the high-pitched whistles on the B.P.'s sensitive minds. Even now, half the force was on burnout detention, and about half of *those* were so far-gone that the only time they showed interest in the outside world was when someone shoved a vegematic into their faces, causing their lives to pass before their eyes.

And as if all that wasn't bad enough, Oliver kept remembering disasters as we went along. A flood, according to unofficial sources, had appeared out of nowhere and washed a ritzy residential district into the Aurelian River, i.e., an open chemical treatment facility. A neighboring space island would have crashed into Aurelian if someone hadn't blown it up first, scoring a diplomatic low point for the Aurelian Corps. The very next day a nuclear meltdown contaminated the chocolate factory, thus putting the kibosh on Aurelian's single biggest cash export. The day after that, the foundations of some underground facilities buckled—some said it was due to metal fatigue, others blamed it on trolls and demons—causing untold casualties and screwing up the island's centralized air-conditioning system besides. Naturally, while the authorities were preoccupied with these problems, religious factions unleashed an uncoordinated series of attacks on their rivals; many times, according to robomed exchanges of information Oliver had tapped into, a band about to launch an attack on an opponent stumbled onto a team representing a third faction, resulting in bloody free-for-alls that all factions lost.

"You can stop now," I advised Oliver when it appeared the conclusion to his litany of disasters was not soon forthcoming.

"Can I help it?" he asked. "It's been a busy week."

"Where's 00π? I have the feeling we won't get to the bottom of this without his help."

"You think this is all mixed up with what's happened to Floyd?"

"I hope so, otherwise I don't know how I'm going to explain myself to Admiral Boink."

"Don't worry about that. Just explain the facts."

"Just worry about helping me find 00π."

"We're already well on our way," said Oliver, guiding me down a crumbling stairwell leading into black depths. "Watch your step."

I tried, but it was too dark. I feared I would fall onto my face at any moment. But my replacement parts evidently were radar equipped, so I navigated the steep and winding way much more easily than I could have imagined.

We came to the uppermost of a series of open residential levels, which extended downward for as far as I could see, like a gigantic prison lined with apartments instead of cells. The lighting was sporadic at best—evidently the electrical system had been damaged as a result of one disaster or another, and the authorities thus far lacked the resources to have it repaired.

Either that or else the electrical system was always in a state of disrepair. Even so, it was still somewhat easier to see now, and we made quicker progress down the stairwell. Gradually it dawned on me just how dingy the walls were, how fragile the metal platforms were, and how pathetic were the drunken, stoned, or otherwise-medicated power junkies stumbling in and out of their rooms, usually with their arms or tentacles wrapped around the waist of some prospective john, mary, or inhuman party. I didn't have to ask Oliver if this was some kind of bowery; that was obvious, almost as obvious as the fact that he seemed to know his way around the maze of platforms pretty well.

Oliver took me to where 00π, stewed in oblivion, sat in an easy chair on a makeshift front porch before the open door of a dingy apartment; a quick peek inside revealed a living room strewn with wasted bodies. Cyborgs and power junkies were plugged into an illegal circuit bank. Some of them were being worked on by johns and marys or inhumans, in a lurid display of abilities that would have stilled the heart of the most cynical gritologist, while the others were just being worked on by the electrical juices. An alien resembling a walking butterscotch-and-blueberry confection defecated on the floor.

"00π, there's someone to see you," said Oliver in his singsong mode to my drunken hero.

00π responded with a groan I feared would be the prelude to a messier response. A stack of empty plastic liquor bottles lay beside his easy chair; a puddle of piss lay beside the empty bottles, adding its own distinctive contribution to the symphony of odors. On the other side of 00π was a stack of full plastic liquor bottles and a barrel half full of salted soy nuts—a bland concoction famous throughout the galaxy as the snack of choice for people too far-gone to care what their snacks tasted like. I could hardly believe my hero had sunk that low.

But I had to admit, he did look like shit. The old age that was once a cloak of honor now hung on him like a shroud of impending doom. His shoulders were slumped, his eyes baggy, and his skin pallid. He smelled as if he'd been kissed by a Rigilian hinnyskunk, and he had misplaced his teeth. His sense of fashion had likewise deteriorated—he wore a torn lumberjack shirt and sequined blue jeans, a designer-casual outfit pathetically out of place on him, as if he'd decided to relive the rock-and-roll youth he'd never had, the kind of youth that Yangtze had in fact enjoyed.

"Hi there," I said, taking his current bottle away from him.

Finally seeming to notice me, he stared at a point beyond me as soulfully as a dying bird. "Hello, Homer. I presume you've come to see me about Yangtze."

"Yes . . ."

"Well, you can't! Yangtze's dead—dead, and it's all my fault. I knew there might be danger, and still I permitted her to tag along."

"So did I. Furthermore, neither you nor I could have stopped her."

"I could have hit her over the head, tied her up, and put her in a closet."

"Maybe that would have worked on her mother," said Oliver, "but I daresay it would have been supremely ineffective with her."

"And considering what's been happening here lately, she could still have wound up dead," I said.

"Kismet," said Oliver. "We have it on good authority that serious kismet was heavily involved in her demise."

"Whose kismet?" 00π looked completely startled. "What's been happening?" He belched; it had the odor of sour succotash.

"You know, a curious thing happened to me while I was in the hospital," I said, and then I explained how the goddess Muile had ridden the soul of Yangtze to the corporeal plane.

"You screwed the ghost of my daughter?" snarled 00π indignantly when I was done. He tried to slap me, but I ducked and he missed and fell over. While struggling back into his easy chair, he said, "You scumbag. Couldn't even wait until her memory was cold?"

"It's not like I could get her pregnant or anything," I protested.

"I don't know," said 00π, "I've seen some pretty strange things in my day!"

"And done a few strange ones too, I'm given to understand!" I retorted. "Besides, Marie may have looked like Yangtze, but she was the one who was robbing the cradle, if you take my metaphor."

"I don't," snarled 00π, "so what's the point?"

"You'd better sober up, guy," said Oliver with uncharacteristic (or at least unprogrammed) anger. His arms extended and he grabbed 00π by the collar and shook him vigorously. Not knowing how else to snap Oliver back to his own senses, I slapped my little buddy on the back of the head. My hand really smarted, but Oliver did return 00π to his chair, with a deft toss.

00π landed with a *thump!* "Thank you," he mumbled gratefully. "I prefer to be shaken, not stirred."

"That's the way it usually is with sedentary drunks," I said with a hatred that surprised me even as I willingly gave in to it. "It's too bad you're too busy feeling sorry for yourself to realize the essence of what I'm trying to tell you. The shell of Yangtze had to exist somewhere, even if it was only a pattern for Marie to ride. Something of Yangtze—I don't know what or where—has survived the experience of death!"

"Just like the ghost of Floyd?" said Oliver.

"Or his voice," I said. And then it hit me. I don't know why it hit me, because I hadn't consciously been thinking about it in those terms, but you could have bowled me over with an ion once it had. "Stupid, stupid, stupid! I've been looking at this all wrong. I've been trying to make something metaphysical out of these gods and goddesses and disembodied robot voices and this . . . this shell of the spirit. It's a pattern—maybe even a common pattern. Of course

Yangtze's still alive—in an alternate universe where she didn't die at all! Reality is full of Yangtze Derringers everywhere, if we but know where to perceive."

"And these *alternatives* have been colliding!" exclaimed Oliver.

"Intersecting! Mingling!" said 00π. The glazed look was already receding from his eyes. It was apparent that he was forcing himself to become sober. He took one last drink, stood up uneasily, and then tossed the bottle on the pile of empties he'd chalked up during the past week. He looked toward the ceiling of the underground apartment complex as if it was a sky full of stars. "Wrathful—mysterious—ever-changing!" He whirled toward Oliver and me; his eyes were as cold and as steady as ever. "The universe is changing, and if we can figure out what's making it change, then we might be able to find Yangtze's soul, or even—"

"Let's not get our hopes up," I said, although mine secretly were, "before we have a better idea what's going on."

"Your friend Floyd must have something to do with all this too," said 00π.

"Remember, the subject of that forthcoming diplomatic conference is being kept under such tight wraps because of its historic significance," I observed. "The fate of races who haven't even evolved yet is supposed to depend on the outcome of the upcoming negotiations. *Our Lady's Hornblower* was on the way to the conference. Perhaps Oliver and I being ejected in that survival pod ties in too."

"Maybe," said Oliver, "though I'd sure feel a lot better about it if I had any idea who did it and why."

"Don't worry about that," said 00π, unzipping his pants and peeing through the grille at his feet. Somebody below screamed with indignation, but 00π appeared not to have heard. "You know something—" he said, then paused.

The pause stretched on. Oliver and I looked at one another. Oliver shrugged. I almost said something. Then he finished, abruptly:

"I've got a funny idea that I've been wrong about my mother all these years, that she didn't really leave my father."

"But you said—" Oliver started.

"Sshh!" I said, once again slapping my faithful robot companion.

"Yeah, it's all becoming clear to me now," said 00π with a smile. "She didn't leave my father because she was never with him. I distinctly recall Father in one of his less morose moods, telling me that she had her duty to attend to. I wonder if she's still alive, if there's some way I can ever meet her. It would mean so much to me. Perhaps she would want to know that for a time she was a grandmother. I don't have any concrete information to base that supposition on, I just feel it *here*, in my heart. Isn't that strange?"

"Considering everything that's been happening here lately?" I said. "No, I don't think it's strange. I am wondering, though, what you think our next step should be."

"Oh, that's easy," said 00π, zipping up. "I've always had this hankering to check out a Divinity School."

Chapter Thirteen
The Penultimate Truth

T RUTH TO TELL, I think 00π just had a hankering to see young nubile flesh. In any case, Baron Hardehar Cohen's Divinity School certainly wasn't the place we'd been anticipating it to be when we arrived there via a "borrowed" vehicle.

For one thing, the tidal waves of change had struck the grounds beneath the dome too—struck with a vengeance. All the buildings were heaps of rubble; an occasional wall still stood and a gazebo leaned against a tree. Entire rows of bushes and trees, which had once formed rigid mazes that only the most logically thinking mystic wanderer could easily traverse, had been uplifted and laid in piles, obviously intended to be pyres. Amidst the pyres were heaps of ashes with a few bones scattered inside. Evidently a great deal of social activism had transpired here recently, not always to the benefit of the individual.

"From the looks of things," said 00π, "whoever's left in authority here can be thankful the shell hasn't cracked and the life-support systems haven't broken down."

"How do you know someone's here?" Oliver asked.

"I can feel it," was the answer.

"How do you know they're in authority?" I asked.

00π shrugged.

Oliver didn't appear convinced, and for the moment I agreed. The Divinity School was on its own island, in a wide elliptical orbit around Aurelian, and consequently was usually off the beaten spaceway route. We saw only rubble everywhere. Not a sister or a student was in sight. The entire population of the island could have been wiped out by any significant epidemic or sufficiently murderous outbreak of mass hysteria, leaving all that fresh wood behind with no one to burn it, or burn in it. Add to that the consideration of all that had happened elsewhere, and there was no logical reason for us to expect to see anyone. After all, the docking bay hadn't opened automatically, nor had someone opened it for us. We'd been forced to override the program and had Oliver to thank for deciphering the password (somehow he'd known it was "swordfish"). No one had greeted us as we'd made our way to the residential grounds. There was no sound, anywhere. Not even the artificial currents of air conditioning stirred (and the air was becoming rather stale).

"Maybe only a few students are left," I ventured.

"Only a few would explain my feeling," said 00π, idly wandering through an area of debris near an ashen pyre. "Aha!" he suddenly exclaimed. He bent down to pick up something.

It was the skull of a shrunken head.

"I'd know that forehead anywhere!" Oliver ejaculated. "That's got to belong to Scorpion."

"Not necessarily," said 00π. "Scorpion may not have much of a head on his shoulders, but he's not about to lose it easily in a wasteland like this."

"How do we know he didn't lose it with difficulty?" I ventured.

"I assure you, if this is Scorpion's head, then he didn't lose it in this space-time continuum," said 00π. "Someone who expected us placed this head here, knowing the path from the dock to the dorms would make discovery of the skull inevitable. It's meant as a message of some sort. I think you can guess just what kind of sort." He tossed the head aside.

"Don't you want to keep it?" I asked, shocked.

"Why?" he asked with a shrug. Still, he didn't appear to be particularly concerned one way or the other when Oliver, at my nod, silently retrieved the head and stored it in a compartment.

We walked on for a spell, and then 00π broke the silence by saying, "Yes, I'm glad you kept that skull, Oliver. It might be some other Scorpion's head."

"From a parallel universe?" asked Oliver incredulously.

"Like the ghost of Floyd," he said with a nod in my direction, "only more substantial."

"But then how could we tell?" Oliver asked. "Would the atomic structure be different?"

"Maybe, maybe not. This Scorpion could be identical to ours in every respect, except for the dead part, of course. Besides, let's say our Scorpion was dead and we encountered another one just like him. Would you treat him any differently?"

"I can sum up my reaction to that premise in two words," Oliver said. "*Im*-possible!"

"I agree," I said. "You seem to be making a leap of logic here. When I saw there were some aspects of Yangtze still alive, or perhaps parallel Yangtzes, I meant just that. I was only extrapolating that any aspect or version of Yangtze we might come across would bear a great resemblance to your actual daughter."

"Humor me," said 00π with a smile, indicating that on one level he indeed agreed with me, but that on another level, perhaps the intuitive one that had kept him alive all these years, he agreed with the premise he was laying down.

"That would depend on the behavior of the Scorpion in question," I observed, "but I'd keep an open mind."

00π responded by motioning us forward. We made our way to the center of the island. The island's rotation was slow and gentle, but due to its kilometer-long diameter, the stars had the illusion of spinning around like the lights inside a turning picture-box. I got dizzy just looking at them.

"So don't look at them," 00π suggested when I pointed it out. "Besides, it won't be the stars that will get you."

"Yeah," said Oliver, his orbs protruding from their stalks like the eyes of a fly. "It'll be something here."

I glared at him. Normally that would have been one of his typical misfired jokes, but he was serious this time. He was also intent upon examining something. I had no idea what. One orb turned around on its axis, drinking in everything in its sweep, while the other was pointed to the ground, meticulously examining the surface of the rubble surrounding his tiny feet.

"Fascinkanayting!" he kept saying. "Fascinkanayting!"

"Xanth! What is it now?" I demanded. I reached out with fingers itching to create a metal throat to choke, but 00π put a restraining hand on my shoulder. At first I could not abide its message either, but somehow 00π managed to convince me. A few moments later, as my circulation returned and I'd recovered sufficiently from his nerve pinch to get up off the ground, I calmly inquired why the fuck he'd done that.

"Sorry, I didn't mean to get so carried away!" 00π said, helping me stand. "It's just that old instincts die hard, and in my line of work there's only one way to stop a guy without killing him—and that's paralyzing him. It's a good thing you're half metal now or you'd have been bedridden for a week."

"So what do you see, Oliver?" I asked.

"For some reason the ripples of change are accelerating here—things are happening so fast that we're completely unaware of them," said Oliver. "Unless of course you've got a pair of eyes that can automatically see in time-lapse mode. A few moments ago I slowed my perceptions down enough to notice that the percentage of iron in this glorified asteroid had altered, almost as if—and I confess, folks, this is a serious leap in logic—as if one of the circumstances resulting in the very creation of this island, when civilization was just being built in the Avidya System, had changed. I could actually see the ripples of change."

"Have you been taking anything that we should know about?" I asked.

"Take him seriously, son," said 00π, "and I think you'll understand the implications of what he's saying. Evidently one of the major decisions regarding the construction of this island has changed within living memory, if you can grasp that."

"How can you say that? This island is supposed to be thousands of years old!" I exclaimed.

"Exactly," said 00π with a knowing nod.

I looked at those rows of decimated blue cacti in the mud, the broken pillars, the overturned portable outhouses, and the yellow brick road: were these not pieces of the decor typical to Divinity Schools? Did not such schools throughout the galaxy boast these and many other similarly tacky attributes? And yet, was it possible these attributes had not been here a few moments before? Was it possible they might have changed, leaving 00π, Oliver, and myself reasonably intact, changed in the past without our knowledge? Was it possible that our very memories were transforming, so that what we believed true and permanent about reality was, in actuality, only true for the moment—until the next change came?

"Is this what it means to be . . . loony tunes?" I asked.

"It's close," said 00π in hushed, awestruck tones.

"Say," said Oliver, "did you folks notice those cracked onion domes over there on the ground being formed? Boy, this is something. A few chrons ago they did not exist, and now they've been tragically broken artifacts from the distant past for weeks."

"Yeah, I think I did notice something along those lines . . ." I said, not really knowing if I did or not.

At least the pentagrams spray-painted on the few walls still standing tended to remain the same, I noticed, though the colors often changed.

Finally I noted, vaguely, the lights in the sky changing too. Some changed sizes and others changed colors, while in some sectors of the sky they became either more solid or more translucent. It occurred to me that although the universe was altering in ways unknowable with a vengeance, my friends and I were remaining stable—as far as I could tell. There was simply no way of guessing, even subjectively, just how many tricks my memory might be playing on me. All I could hope was that my comrades and I would finish our fact-finding tour without changing into tap-dancing slugs or singing moles who could hear only on the police band frequency.

Or worse.

Of course, maybe we had already changed. I noted a bird overhead—part of a flock the baron had seeded here to give the girls the illusion of a pastoral place of study—change into a green-winged gecko that left trails of blue sparkles behind in its path. The gecko, which evidently couldn't see all that well, crashed into a wall, and by the time it landed it was already something else, something green, with a hard shell over its powerful wings.

"Wait! Did you hear that?" 00π asked.

"Hear what?" Oliver asked.

"We're being watched," 00π said.

"You can hear that?" Oliver exclaimed.

"Well, don't fall all over yourselves looking for me," the voice said.

I whirled to see—no one! The voice sounded as if it had originated in thin air.

"It's the cybernetic vampire," I said. "I'm certain of it."

A whirlwind—displaced energy coming together— began to spin between Oliver, 00π, and me. The resulting breeze should have struck us in the face, but instead it ruffled the hair on the back of my neck. Or maybe that was just the result of fear.

Unnoticed by all, I picked up a moss-covered wooden board and held it with both hands so as to facilitate any bashing that might be forthcoming.

It came as no surprise to me that the whirlwind quickly began to take on the outline of a biped in a codpiece. I couldn't help but notice the blurry outline of the mouth, with its unholy grimace and its long, sharp canine teeth. That was reason enough, I assumed, to swing at the sumbitch before he could say another word.

Which I did, but he lifted his entire arm and caught the board in his blurry hand before it could reach his skull.

Too bad, I thought as I noted the end of the board coming right back at me. Stupefied me! I was still holding it, limply, when it caught me on the chin. My legs sparked against concrete boulders as I fell, bruising my elbows on the ground. *Fuck!*

"Stand back!" the cybernetic vampire in the codpiece commanded the instant he materialized in full.

He stood over me as nonchalantly as a tyrant might stand over a defeated enemy private. His red eyes stared wide at 00π, and he held his upraised palm in Oliver's direction. "You will not touch me!" the vampire said in hypnotic tones.

"I will not touch you!" 00π declared, instantly hypnotized.

"But I might pinch your ass!" Oliver blurted out, lunging for the beast.

But the vampire glided upwards in the air with the grace of a spectral hummingbird, and Oliver crashed into me just as I was getting up, knocking me down for the second time. The spinning of the island accelerated, it seemed, as I struggled to my hands and knees. Oliver lay on his back, kicking and thrashing wildy, uttering expletives, as the vampire, supremely confident despite being surrounded by foes, merely looked down on us and smiled. He snapped his fingers at 00π, who promptly sat. Oliver rolled over onto his side, but stayed on the ground. We too realized we had reached our assigned positions for whatever would happen to us next.

The cybernetic vampire floated to the ground. I had the distinct feeling that behind him the arms of the ruined statues were changing from traditional limbs to boneless tentacles, and the transparent dome above was becoming as black as coal, creating the illusion that the stars were going out. However, I had eyes only for the cybernetic vampire's gray and lifeless flesh, a fit home for maggots.

The undead cyborg raised an eyebrow at me. Flecks of skin dropped onto his cheek. "Remember that ancient curse, my friends?" he asked casually, as if we were lifelong friends. Again the picture of my first sight of him flashed in my mind's eye, but this time I could *feel* the blood pouring out of my amputated leg.

"All right, I'll bite. What curse?" Oliver inquired.

"An interesting choice of words, little one. The curse I was speaking of is the one that says, 'He who is truly cursed lives in interesting times.' "

"Interesting times?" asked Oliver. "What the hell kind of curse is that?"

"Th-that's al-all r-right," said the hypnotized 00π, speaking independently through sheer force of will. "I-I understand."

"Good, good. So you understand, then, that you three are infinitely more cursed, because you're living in so many interesting times at once."

Overcome with hatred, I renewed my grip on the board and lunged toward the vampire. So forceful was my thrust, and so soft was his decomposed flesh, that the board's dull edge penetrated easily into the chest.

The vampire looked down at himself with surprise. I stepped away, leaving the board protruding like a malformed toothpick stuck in a potato. "I'm impressed," he said.

00π shook his head and stood. "I'm myself again!" he exclaimed. "Homer, you're a genius!"

The vampire shook his head. "Homer, you're a failure!" And with that, he pulled the board from his body. I noted with horror that it was coated with dry and rotting tissue. The vampire took advantage of that horror to *bap!* me briskly upside the head. I fell down like an ion being flattened in a dwarf star.

When I got my wits together, mere moments later, I saw 00π and Oliver chasing the vampire in the rubble. The vampire disappeared behind a building, and my friends were right behind him. "Hey! Wait for me!" I said, staggering to a standing position.

"No, don't go that way!" someone said.

I whirled to see a hole in the middle of the air. In the middle of the hole was an old man with long white hair, a power pack connected to his temple, and a familiar glazed look in his eyes. However, I didn't truly recognize him until he grinned, thus resembling a man about to sit down and consume his favorite flavor of merde.

"Spaceside Hodgson!" I exclaimed.

He waved. "And still front man for the Ashton Gluons, I'm proud to say—older but not necessarily any higher, if you know what I mean!"

"But where have you come from?"

"The future, of course. Wow, I never thought I'd be glad to see your homely face again, Homer. It's been decades."

"How many?"

"That would be telling. But you're going to find out soon enough, anyway."

"What makes you say that?"

He reached out. A hand that moments ago had appeared somewhat two-dimensional was now solid and whole. "Because you're coming with me to the future, that's why!"

"But I can't! Oliver and 00π are chasing the most heinous fiend I've ever encountered. I can't desert them now!"

Spaceside's grin grew wider. "Yes, you can."

"What makes you so sure?"

"You want to find Floyd, don't you?"

"Yes."

He gestured impatiently. "Then come with me, sucker!"

I did. I stepped into the hole, and out of my native space-time continuum, perhaps forever.

Chapter Fourteen
Strange Epilogue

DMIRAL BOINK sat in his office, idly playing with the set of tiddly-winks strewn out over his desk.

He jumped up in his chair, startled, as the Mother Superior barged in. "Admiral—sorry to bother you this way, but a shuttle's arrived next to our hyper-route. The pilot is asking for docking privileges."

Boink rubbed his hands in delight. "At last! Coryban's returned with Hunter!"

The Mother Superior took her unlit cigar from her mouth and waved it helplessly in the air. "I'm afraid not, Sir! Apparently it's someone from the Avidya System."

"The no-man's system?"

"The one." The Mother Superior rubbed her chin. "He claims to be a bigwig there, a Baron Hardehar Cohon."

"Well . . .'" said Boink disappointedly.

"Maybe he has news," said the Mother Superior helpfully.

"Maybe." The Admiral raised an eyebrow. He blinked. "News of what?"

"Well, I'm hoping he has news of my son. I've

never really known him, but I've been keeping track of him down through the years."

"Really? What's his name?"

"That I don't know. He does have a code name, though—one he uses because, as they say, the tales of his exploits stretch into infinity . . ."

to be continued in
FUTUREFALL

The son of an American doctor, ARTHUR BYRON COVER was born in the upper tundra of Siberia on January 14, 1950. He attended a Clarion Science Fiction Writers' Workshop in 1971, where he made his first professional sale, to Harlan Ellison's *Last Dangerous Visions*. Cover migrated to Los Angeles in 1972. He has published a slew of short stories in *Infinity Five, The Alien Condition, Heavy Metal, Weird Tales, Year's Best Horror Stories*, and elsewhere, plus several SF books, including *Autumn Angels, The Platypus of Doom, The Sound of Winter*, and *An East Wind Coming*. He has also written scripts for issues of the comics *Daredevil* and *Firestorm*, as well as the graphic novel *Space Clusters*. He has been an instructor at Clarion West and was managing editor of *Amazing Heroes* for a time. Arthur Byron Cover is a co-editor of the anthology *The Best of the New Wave* and the author of three Time Machine books as well as Book 4 of *Isaac Asimov's Robot City* for Byron Preiss Visual Publications.